CAPTIVA HEARTS

CAPTIVA ISLAND SERIES
BOOK SIX

ANNIE CABOT

CABOT PUBLISHING GROUP

ISBN ebook, 979-8-9874624-5-4

ISBN paperback, 979-8-9874624-6-1

PROLOGUE

The month of June on Captiva Island, Florida, was hotter than the rest of the year, but that didn't keep tourists from traveling to the island.

School closings and vacation time from work meant families crowded the island's beaches and restaurants daily. The Key Lime Garden Inn was busier than ever, and Maggie had to hire two new employees.

The island's businesses thrived during their busy season. Even Powell Water Sports had a steady stream of customers lined up on the sidewalk waiting to get inside.

"Did you see the line going out the door of Crawford's place?" Chelsea asked.

Maggie nodded.

"I sure did. Good thing Crawford's got three sons working with him. Ciara volunteered to help. I think she's working a couple of days a week."

"That's a bad idea."

Maggie made a face at her friend.

"What's wrong with her helping out now and then?"

Chelsea rolled her eyes.

"Are you kidding me? It's never a good idea to mix business with personal relationships. I don't care how in love you think you are. Besides, Ciara is already spread so thin; I think she's nuts to add more work."

"Well, I wouldn't worry about that. Ciara's only volunteering for a bit. It's not like she's working there full-time."

Maggie noticed her friend seemed edgy and distracted.

"Are you going to tell me what's on your mind, or do I have to guess?"

Chelsea shrugged.

"How can you ask me that? You know perfectly well what day it is."

Maggie did indeed know. Today, Sebastian Barlowe returned to his home on Captiva Island, bringing his new wife with him. Chelsea hadn't said a word about it since she announced the news back in March. As much as Chelsea pretended not to care about Sebastian, Maggie knew her friend had lingering, albeit ambivalent, feelings for him. It wasn't love. She was sure that Chelsea wasn't in love with Sebastian. Maggie knew the truth. Chelsea considered his flaunting Isabella around Captiva a territorial betrayal.

"I know what day it is, and I also know that there is no way Sebastian won't come looking for you when he gets here. Didn't he say he wanted you and Isabella to become friends?"

Chelsea let out a heavy sigh.

"Don't remind me," she responded.

"All I'm saying is that you best get used to the idea. I know you love this island, but you don't own it. Sebastian has a home here and the right to share it and his friends with his new wife. It will be her home after all."

"I know you're right. I'm just not sure I'm as mature as you are about this. Don't I have the right to pout? He did date this woman behind my back," she complained.

"You're not certain of that. You need to find out the details

2

about the two of them. Why not give Sebastian a chance to explain himself?"

Chelsea nodded.

"I'll see what I can do. In the meantime, I'd love a nice tall glass of iced tea. I'm going to see if there's any left in the refrigerator. Would you like a glass?"

Maggie's cell phone buzzed as she was about to join Chelsea in the kitchen.

"It's Brea," Maggie said.

"Hey, there. How's my favorite daughter-in-law?"

"Maggie, I'm so sorry. I've been calling everyone but I just go to voicemail. I've left messages for Chris, Beth, and Lauren to call me back. I didn't know what else to do."

Brea's voice cracked, and Maggie could tell something terrible had happened.

"Brea, what's wrong? Are the children all right?"

A brief moment of quiet on the line had Maggie reaching for her throat.

"It's Michael. Maggie, he's been shot."

Maggie's legs went weak, and she dropped onto the porch chair. Chelsea quickly reached for her friend as Maggie asked the question no mother should have to ask.

"Is he...?" she whispered.

Brea started to cry.

"No. He's still alive, but they don't know if he'll make it. He's in surgery. He was shot at least twice, which I know about. Once in the arm and another in his chest near his shoulder, but I think a third hit him. I don't know more than that. I'm scared. I'm just so scared."

Maggie wasn't sure where her calm came from, but some-where deep inside, she didn't believe her son would die. She didn't know why she was so confident, but at that moment, she felt it was important that Brea believe it too.

"He's going to make it, Brea. My son is not going to die. That's all there is to it. You have to believe me. Tell me you believe me, Brea. I want to hear you say it."

"I believe you," Brea answered.

Brea's voice was so weak and unconvincing that Maggie knew what she had to do.

"I'm coming to Boston. I'm going to pack my overnight bag and I'll be there tonight. You tell Michael that I'm on my way. When he gets out of surgery, you tell him. Do you hear me?"

"I'll tell him, Maggie. Hurry," she said.

She hung up the phone and looked at Chelsea. Maggie wouldn't cry because if she did, it meant that there was no hope, and Maggie had already been through too much in her life not to believe in miracles.

She looked up at the sky and clenched her fist. The universe owed her just one more.

CHAPTER 1

*M*aggie Wheeler watched the slow drip of the fluid flow through the IV tube and into her son's arm. Having spent the last several months getting chemotherapy infusions, she was familiar with tubes and the sound of machines keeping track of blood pressure and heartbeat.

But her medical issues meant nothing as she sat beside her son, who was struggling to stay alive. Unconscious after getting shot several times when he answered a domestic violence call, Michael's fate was out of Maggie's control.

She hated seeing Michael look so helpless and frail. She'd gladly switch places with him if she could but since that wasn't an option she vowed to never leave his side.

"Michael. I know you can hear me. The doctor said it's good for your family to talk to you. So, that's what I'm going to do. Can you hear me, sweet boy? It's Mom. I'm sitting right beside you, and I won't leave you. I promise."

Maggie played with the wet tissue in her hands and then dabbed the corners of her eyes. She could feel her daughter-in-law, Brea's eyes on Michael, waiting for a sign that he'd heard her, but there was nothing.

"What if he doesn't come out of this?" Brea asked her.

"Don't even think such a thing," Maggie whispered, unable to control her outrage. It was the first time she'd lost patience with Brea, and Maggie didn't care how she sounded. She was angry. None of this was Brea's fault, but her daughter-in-law was the only one in the room, and Maggie needed to vent.

There were many others to be angry with. I there was any justice, Maggie vowed that whoever shot Michael would pay dearly for their actions. She wouldn't rest until they did.

The rage inside her body was something she'd never felt before. She didn't take even one moment to evaluate her feelings. She'd live in this rage until it was no longer helpful to do so. Until then, she didn't care what she had to do or say to bring her son back to her and his family.

Still, she realized Michael would be upset if she fought with his wife.

"I'm sorry, Brea. I didn't mean to be so curt."

Brea didn't respond except to shake her head and wipe the tears from her cheeks, and Maggie knew that was the best she'd get from the woman and understood that Brea was as broken as she was.

Maggie's husband, Paolo, stood helplessly in the doorway. He'd been pacing in and out of the room and seemed lost for something to do.

"Hey, Lauren," Paolo said as his stepdaughter entered the room.

Maggie didn't turn to look at Lauren but instead kept her eyes focused on Michael.

Lauren bent down and hugged her mother.

"Mom. It's time that you and Paolo head back to the house. You haven't slept since you got here."

Maggie brushed Lauren away.

"No. I'm staying here."

Lauren persisted.

"You're not going to help Michael if you get sick yourself. I just dropped Grandma back at the house. She's making you and Paolo a nice lunch. I got a call from Christopher. He'll be here shortly. Becca is working in the hospital today, so she'll look in on Michael too. He'll have plenty of people watching over him. Take a few hours of rest, and then you can come back. I promise you if anything happens, I'll call you. Please, Mom."

Maggie sighed and turned to face Lauren. She grabbed her daughter's hand.

"You promise to call me the minute anything changes?"

"I promise," Lauren said.

Maggie didn't want to admit she was exhausted, but Lauren was right. She'd be no use to Michael if she got sick. All she could do was nod her head and look at Paolo.

He walked to her and took her in his arms.

"Everything will work out, my love. You'll see. Let's get you home."

Before they left Maggie returned to Michael's bed. Bending over his body, she kissed his cheek.

"I'll be back in a little bit, sweetie. So you rest and I'll come back soon."

She wanted to say that she'd be here when he woke up, but she couldn't promise that. Her body was giving in to the stress and tension, and she was afraid that her legs would give out from under her if she didn't rest.

She went to Brea, and the two women wrapped arms around each other.

"Maybe you need to take the same advice, young lady. We don't want you getting sick either."

Brea nodded as she smiled at her mother-in-law.

Maggie leaned on Paolo as they walked out of the room and down the hall leading to the elevators. She looked at her watch and thought about the next few hours. Having a bite to eat and then a nap would keep everyone from fussing. She'd pray until her eyes closed, and with any luck, there'd be a call from Lauren that Michael was awake and alert. It was the only acceptable scenario.

"Well, that was a first," Lauren said to Brea.

"I'm sorry?" Brea answered.

"The first time my mother listened to me and did what I told her to do."

They laughed as Lauren pulled a chair next to Brea, who had taken Maggie's place next to her husband.

"I'm not surprised. Your mother isn't one to take advice from anyone."

Lauren could tell there was more to Brea's comment than she let on and wondered if she might put out the beginning of conflict between her mother and Brea.

"Mom means well, Brea. You know how much she loves all her children, including you."

Brea smiled. "I know, and I feel guilty for resenting her, but…."

"But?"

"Michael is my husband. I should be the one to talk to the doctor and make decisions for his care."

"And my mother is taking control of the situation?"

Brea nodded. Lauren could tell her sister-in-law didn't want to say one word against her mother, but she was right to feel the way she did.

"I'll talk to Mom," Lauren said.

"No. I don't want to make a big deal about this. Maggie loves her son and wants the best for him. I understand that. I just need her to lighten up a bit."

Lauren chuckled. "Maggie Garrison Wheeler Moretti doesn't know the meaning of the phrase 'lighten up.' We'll need to be more direct with her. I promise I won't make a big deal, but I'll ensure she understands what she's doing is wrong. It will come from me, not you. Don't worry."

"Thanks, Lauren. I appreciate it."

"No problem. By the way. We're going to have more family here soon. You know how it goes. There has yet to be a family crisis where my siblings don't come together, and this time is no different."

"All of them? What about Beth? I thought she was in California visiting Gabriel's family?"

"She was, but she's on her way home now. When she heard about Michael, she booked her flight. I'd be surprised if her plane hasn't already landed."

"What about Sarah? There's no way she and Trevor can make it. It wasn't that long since she had the baby."

"I know, but she's going to come anyway. She's bringing little Maggie with her. Noah and Sophia are staying home in Florida with Trevor. She said that she and the baby have a surprise for Michael."

"A surprise?"

"Yup, she wouldn't tell me any details."

Lauren had an idea what the surprise was but kept her thoughts to herself. She didn't want to spoil the news. Besides, if it helped Michael to wake from the coma, she was all for it.

"I'm glad everyone will be here," Brea said. "I envy how you all get your strength from each other."

Lauren nodded. Brea was right. There had never been a trauma or significant event in the Wheeler family where her siblings didn't gather to support one another. Never before did their love for each other have more importance. If that love, strength, and closeness helped Michael recover, Lauren couldn't wait for the five of them to be together again.

Maggie's mother, Sarah, met them at the door.

"Hi, Mom."

"My goodness Maggie, you look awful."

"Gee, thanks. You always know the right thing to say."

"Hello, Sarah," Paolo said. "Nice to see you again."

"Hi, Paolo." She hugged him and then turned her attention to Maggie. "Any change?"

Maggie shook her head. "No."

"I'm so sorry, honey. It's just awful. I guess the man who shot Michael is dead."

Maggie stiffened. "What?"

"It just came over the news. I thought you knew."

Maggie shook her head. "No. I didn't know. Did they say who it was that shot him?"

"Not specifically. The news reporter said that the police returned fire and that the shooter was dead. Do you think that it was Michael who shot him?"

Maggie sat on the sofa and put her head in her hands. She couldn't imagine her son shooting anyone. Michael had been a police officer for so many years, she long ago put those fears aside and tried not to think of such things. He was doing what he loved, and that was enough for her.

She sat back against the cushion.

"I don't know, Mom. Right now, all I can think about is getting Michael well. But I'm sure everything will come out in time."

Her mother hurried about, reminding Maggie of when she was a child home sick from school.

"Why don't you and Paolo come into the kitchen and have something to eat? I've made a nice chicken with broccoli and ziti. You two need to get some food into you and maybe a nice nap followed by a warm bath."

Maggie's agitation brewed again; she didn't want to be

pampered or fussed over. Her son was lying in the hospital, possibly dying. The last thing she needed was a spa treatment.

Regardless of her mood, she chose a polite response.

"Thanks, Mom. I'd rather take a nap. I'll eat something when I wake up. I promise."

The concern on her mother's face was more than she could stand. She needed to get behind closed doors and grieve in private.

Looking at Paolo, she could see the hurt on his face, but her pain was impossible to explain to anyone, even him. Slowly walking to the spare bedroom, Maggie entered and closed the door behind her.

"What are you going to do about this?" Sarah asked Paolo.

Confused, he shrugged and looked at Sarah. "What do you mean?"

"I mean that my daughter is pushing you away. I understand she's worried about Michael, but can't you see there's more to this than she's letting on?"

Paolo had been through enough trauma and family drama over the past three years to know something beneath the surface always needed attention. However, as hard as he tried, he couldn't understand Sarah's insinuation.

"Like what?" he asked her.

"Like that, she'd rather stay in Massachusetts with her son than return to Captiva Island and get on with her life. Including the crucial task of undergoing radiation for her cancer."

"Sarah, Maggie has already been through surgery and chemotherapy, which she tolerated well. So why would she not want to return to Captiva and have the radiation to kill this disease once and for all?"

Sarah took Paolo's hand and led him to the sofa.

"Because, dear Paolo, she's questioning whether her move to Captiva was the right idea."

"You're wrong. Maggie loves living on Captiva and running the inn. She always says that she's been living her dream. I think you might be wrong this time."

Sarah lightly punched Paolo in the arm. "You men have no idea what it means to be a mother, and you certainly can't understand what it feels like to think you might never see your children again."

"Huh?"

"I know my daughter, Paolo. Of course she's terrified that Michael won't make it. I can tell that she's struggling with not being here when he got shot. It's silly of course. Even if she were here, Maggie wouldn't have been able to stop this from happening. Maggie's devoted her life to this family and her children; when it finally came time to be selfish and to think of herself, this family got hit with one disaster after another—Christopher's leg, Lauren and Jeff's marriage troubles, and now this. You mark my words. It's only a matter of time before Maggie says she wants to sell the inn and move back home. I'd put money on it."

Paolo didn't know what to think. His stomach turned at the thought. Surely Sarah was wrong about Maggie's feelings. Nonetheless, he needed to prepare for this eventuality.

Years earlier he'd had traveled to the United States to be with his sister Ciara and to start a new life. He had a thriving business on Sanibel Island and was part owner of the Key Lime Garden Inn. He couldn't imagine giving all that up and moving to Massachusetts.

He loved Maggie and would follow her wherever she wanted to live, but he couldn't shake the one thing that bothered him more than any other. That his wife would once again put everyone before her needs and throw away her dream. He'd do whatever he could to keep that from happening.

CHAPTER 2

*T*he airplane cabin buzzed with the muffled hum of conversation and the occasional chime signaling the beginning or end of an announcement. Beth Wheeler and her boyfriend, Gabriel Walker, settled into their seats, their faces etched with weariness and worry. The journey back to Boston, Massachusetts, carried a heavy weight on their hearts.

As the plane taxied down the runway, Beth stared out the window, her gaze lost in the vast California skyline. Gabriel watched her, his hand gently finding hers, intertwining their fingers in a gesture of support. Beth had felt his eyes on her for the last hour.

"How do I look?" she asked.

"Like you've been crying. Is that the look you were going for?" he teased.

Beth knew he was trying to lighten the mood but she also knew how lucky she was to have someone who loved her so dearly. Gabriel knew the weight of her fears, for they mirrored his own.

"I'm glad I got to meet your mother. She's such an amazingly strong woman, and I know how hard it's been to accept her illness. Do you ever feel like we're in this vortex of traumatic events? Just when I think our lives are on an even keel, we get hit with another wave of drama."

He looked into her eyes and squeezed her hand.

"Beth," Gabriel said softly, his voice barely audible above the aircraft's engines. "I know what you mean, but listen, we'll get through whatever comes. As far as Michael is concerned, he's strong. I know he's going to pull through but no matter what happens with all this trauma as you call it, our families will be right by our side. Isn't that what you always say? That we're stronger when we're all together?"

Beth turned to face him, her eyes glistening with unshed tears. "I know, Gabriel," she whispered, her voice trembling with emotion. "But it's just... seeing him lying there, motionless, in that hospital bed... it's tearing me apart. I'm scared to see him like that, and I'm terrified he won't wake up, that he won't make it."

Gabriel leaned closer, his gaze filled with compassion.

"I understand, fear is natural in times like these. But we have to hold on to hope. Michael is a fighter, and he has a whole community rallying behind him, praying for his recovery."

Beth nodded, a mixture of gratitude and sadness etched on her face.

"I'm grateful for the support, for all the prayers and well-wishes. But there's this nagging feeling in the pit of my stomach, that tells me things might not turn out okay."

Her voice faltered as Gabriel squeezed her hand tighter.

"Don't think like that. We can't let fear consume us. We have to stay strong for Michael and for each other. That's what I'm doing for my mother. I can't fall apart around her because it won't do her or any of us any good. Together, we'll weather this storm. Remember, miracles happen, even in the darkest moments."

Beth's tearful eyes met Gabriel's steady gaze, finding solace in his faith.

"You're right," she whispered, her voice gaining a hint of determination. "I won't give up hope. I'll be there for Michael every step of the way, even if it scares me to my core."

Gabriel smiled gently, his warmth radiating through the touch of his hand.

Beth thought back to her childhood and how much she looked up to Michael. He was smart and funny and made her feel like she could do anything. He'd given her confidence to reach for the stars. That was the kind of brother he was for all of them.

Even if her brother's support did nothing more than help her climb a tree, the experience helped her years later. Beth smiled realizing that she'd been climbing virtual trees ever since.

For however much she loved her brother, her sister Sarah's feelings for him were magnified by a thousand. Michael and Sarah were very close and as Beth looked out the window at the land below she wondered how Sarah was dealing with the shooting. She'd already spoken with Lauren and now, she made a mental note to contact Sarah as soon as they landed.

As the airplane soared through the clouds, Beth clung to Gabriel's words. Together, they vowed to weather the storm that awaited them, as they journeyed home to face the unknown. If Gabriel believed that Michael would recover, then she'd believe too.

She took comfort in knowing that when her family came together in love, they could accomplish anything. Until then, she'd pray for a miracle and the strength to accept it if one didn't come.

Chelsea Marsden was never good at waiting. So if phone calls, emails, or dates were late, she'd take matters into her hands and light a fire wherever necessary to move things along.

This time, however, she didn't know what to do. A call to her best friend, Maggie, to find out how Maggie's son Michael was doing seemed intrusive.

Hospitals rarely let people talk on their cell phones anyway.

As much as she wanted to know what was happening with the Wheeler clan in Massachusetts, Chelsea didn't think she could handle bad news. The chance that Michael might die was very real and to think otherwise was wishful thinking.

Usually a glass-half-full kind of woman, Chelsea couldn't shake the feeling that her best friend was about to be emotionally destroyed, and there wasn't a thing Chelsea could do about it.

Once Maggie decided to fly to Boston, Chelsea, and Emma Thurston, the young woman who only recently had been hired to clean the rooms at the Key Lime Garden Inn, immediately stepped in to run the place while Maggie was away.

Maggie's sister-in-law, Ciara Moretti, did the bookkeeping and helped in the garden whenever possible. However, with all the work at the Outreach Center and assisting at Powell Water Sports, Ciara had so much on her plate she appeared overwhelmed most days.

Inside the bustling kitchen of the Key Lime Garden Inn, the clattering of pots and the aroma of culinary delights filled the air.

Chelsea poured herself a cup of coffee and watched the two chefs, Riley and Iris, clean up after the guests finished breakfast.

With a hint of weariness, Chelsea sat perched on a stool at the kitchen island. The challenges of running the inn had become apparent, and she sought solace and advice from her trusted colleagues.

"You look beat. Are you okay?" asked Riley.

"I'm glad to know that I look exactly how I feel. Who knew that running an inn was so much work?"

As they discussed the intricacies of managing the inn, Maggie's daughter, Sarah and her husband, Trevor came into the room.

"Sarah, honey, I didn't know you were coming over this morning. Good morning, Trevor."

Sarah and Trevor hugged Chelsea and sat at the kitchen table.

Chelsea could tell by the mixture of determination and concern on Sarah's face that she had news.

"Any news on Michael?" Chelsea asked.

"I talked to Lauren earlier and Beth called me. She just landed at Logan. She and Gabriel are headed to the hospital now. She'll call me later to update me."

Sarah took a deep breath, steadying herself for the conversation ahead.

"I wanted to check on you and see if there's anything you need before I leave. You've been holding down the fort here, and I can't thank you enough."

"Of course, sweetie. You know I'd do anything for you and your family. Did I hear you say, 'before you leave?' I'm assuming you're headed to Boston?"

Sarah nodded. Her eyes welled with tears. She reached out, grasping Chelsea's hand.

"I have to go. I just have to. Trevor and I have decided that it's crucial for me to be there for Michael and our family."

Trevor, standing by Sarah's side, nodded in agreement. "We believe that Sarah's being there with little Maggie, might be the light that helps Michael find his way back to us," he said.

Chelsea squeezed Sarah's hand in reassurance, her voice filled with encouragement.

"I have no doubt, Sarah, that your presence and the love you carry for Michael and your family will make a difference. Like I told your mother, we'll handle things here at the inn. Don't worry about a thing. You focus on being there for Michael. You're doing the right thing."

Sarah's face softened, and she took a deep breath, her voice trembling slightly as she continued.

"Chelsea, there's something else I need to tell you. The man who shot Michael, he... he's dead. The news is saying that Michael is the one who shot and killed him."

Silence fell over the kitchen, the weight of the revelation sinking in. Chelsea's eyes widened with shock, her heart aching for Michael. She reached out, gently touching Sarah's arm, offering comfort and understanding.

"Oh, Sarah," Chelsea whispered, her voice filled with compassion. "This is an unimaginable burden for all of you to bear. But remember, we know Michael, we know his heart. We can't let the judgments and speculations of others define who he is. We'll stand by him, supporting him through this ordeal. Together, we'll find the truth and ensure that justice prevails."

Sarah nodded, her gratitude evident in her teary eyes. "Thank you, Chelsea. Your belief in Michael gives me strength. We'll face this storm, and we'll do it together as a family. After all, that's how we roll, right?"

Chelsea smiled and nodded but her heart broke for everyone involved. Nothing about this situation held any promise of a happy ending. Ignoring the lump in her throat, she asked, "Is there anything else you need me to do while you're gone?"

Sarah shook her head.

"No, we're fine. Trevor is going to stay here to take care of Noah and Sophia. I think we've thought of everything. We just wanted to come by and let you know that if you need anything at all, you call Trevor. I know you've got your hands full around here."

Trevor nodded.

"Yes, please, Chelsea. Give me a call if you need anything. Our nanny, Debbie, is helping out too, so don't worry about me leaving the kids to come here. If you need me, you call. Okay?'

Chelsea nodded.

"You got it and thank you."

They were about to leave when Sarah made a request.

"There is one more thing you can do for me." She looked at Riley and Iris. "Please pray."

Chelsea got up from the stool and hugged Sarah and then Trevor. She couldn't imagine how difficult all this was for them. Watching over the inn and its guests was the least she could do for her best friend and the entire Wheeler family.

"You got it," Chelsea answered.

Sending prayers to Massachusetts was bound to help and she'd sneak a few prayers in for herself that she'd get through running the inn without incident.

The dimly lit living room of Christopher Wheeler's childhood home in Andover cast a comforting embrace as he entered, his prosthetic leg making a soft thud with each step.

Becca Powell, his fiancée and a dedicated medical student at Tufts, looked up from the sofa where she had been deep in thought, her face etched with worry.

Christopher settled beside her, his strong presence a source of comfort amidst the heaviness that hung in the air. Their shared concern for Michael tethered them together, their love serving as an anchor in the storm of uncertainty.

Becca's eyes, weary from sleepless nights spent at the hospital, met Christopher's gaze.

"How are you doing, Chris?" she asked softly, her voice laced with emotion.

Christopher's hand found hers, his touch gentle yet firm.

"Seeing Michael in that hospital bed, fighting for his life... It's all so overwhelming. When you stand there looking at him, you feel helpless. It's impossible for me to see my big brother so vulnerable. He's always been this towering tough guy. When I was a kid I wanted to be just like him. He can't die. It's just not possible to accept that."

"I know what you mean. It's hard to see him like that."

Feeling Christopher's pain, tears welled in Becca's eyes.

"I can't help but think of all the dreams Michael had, the life he wanted to build. It feels so unjust, so cruel that it might be taken away from him," Christopher said.

Becca's grip tightened, her voice steady and resolute.

"I get it but we have to find strength in the present moment, in the love and support we can offer Michael and one another. We can do that without expecting for the worst to happen. I'm not in denial here, I'm practical. Your brother is strong and I'm certain that he's going to make it."

Christopher smiled at her and she could tell that he was starting to feel a bit better.

"I've been at the hospital through the night, talking to him, hoping that my presence can somehow reach him, bring him back to us." Becca said.

Christopher pulled her close, his embrace a shield against the storm of uncertainty.

"That's my Becca. Your empathy is what will make you a great doctor."

"I hope so. When I feel helpless to do anything, like I feel right now, I wonder if I'll be able to handle it when a patient's fate is out of my hands."

"You'll do whatever you have to. It's what we'll all have to do. I'm not sure if you've noticed but us Wheelers aren't particularly good at giving up control."

Becca smiled and Christopher felt grateful that he'd found something to make the love of his life smile.

"Yes, I'm aware."

He pulled her tight against him and cradled her in his arms. In the embrace of their love, they found solace amidst the uncertainty. Their hearts were heavy with the weight of the situation, but their support for one another and their commitment to Michael's well-being would carry them through no matter what.

CHAPTER 3

The gentle breeze caressed the shores of Captiva Island, its salty whispers carrying a sense of tranquility. Inside the small beach cottage, Emma Thurston stood by the window, her gaze lost in the ebb and flow of the turquoise waves.

In just ten days, her time on the island would come to an end. She had sought refuge on Captiva, seeking solace and clarity amidst the turmoil of her thoughts.

Her heart was torn between her adventurous life as a National Geographic photographer, capturing the essence of humanity's triumphs and tribulations, and a newfound calling that had been quietly tugging at her soul.

With exposure to several convents and retreats throughout Europe, Emma had spent the last several months gaining insight and understanding on the difference between a calling to become a nun and a need to shut out the world and all its pain and suffering.

She'd seen much devastation, hate, war, pain and misery around the world. As much as she loved her job, her experiences had changed her.

No longer the innocent and naïve young woman from Naples,

Florida, Emma now carried a profound sense of purpose and a desire to make a difference in the world. The tranquility of the convents and retreats had provided her with solace and contemplation, allowing her to reflect on her own path and the calling that moved her deeply.

Coming to Captiva Island, Emma stayed close to friends but not family. She knew that her parents would never support her decision to become a nun. At every opportunity, they'd remind Emma that a wedding and children were in her future, and as soon as she was done fulfilling her dream of travel and adventure, she'd come around to their way of thinking.

Months earlier, in the quiet chapel of the medieval convent where she'd spent time in quiet reflection, Emma had knelt before the flickering candlelight, her hands clasped in prayer. The gentle aroma of incense filled the air, mingling with the soft chants of the nuns echoing through the stone walls. She closed her eyes, allowing her thoughts to drift and merge with the serenity of the sacred space.

Her mind wandered back to her hometown in Naples, where she'd grown up surrounded by the pristine beaches and the warm embrace of a loving family. She'd been shielded from much of the world's pain and suffering until she stepped beyond its boundaries.

As she traveled through Europe, witnessing the scars of conflict and the resilience of those affected, her perspective shifted.

Emma's heart swelled with a yearning to alleviate suffering, to bring hope to those who had lost it, and to share the love she'd been blessed with.

The quietude of the convent had allowed her to nurture this newfound purpose within her soul, guiding her toward the path that felt right. But she still grappled with the question that lingered within her: Was she truly meant to dedicate her life to the cloistered walls, or was there another way to fulfill her calling?

As the sunlight filtered through the windows of her small cottage on the beach, she sipped her tea and thought about her time on the island.

She'd spent hours talking with her college roommate and best friend, Sarah Hutchins as well as Sarah's mother, Maggie Moretti. As much as they tried to help, Emma understood that ultimately, only she could make this decision.

Meeting her new friend and author, Gareth Graham, had some influence on her perspective although not in the way everyone around her wanted. Sarah insisted that the handsome writer had fallen in love with Emma and Emma was fighting her feelings for the man.

The enigmatic author had come to the island seeking solace of his own. The weight of guilt burdened his spirit, a tragedy forever etched in his heart. Despite their different paths and circumstances, a connection had blossomed between them during their time together on Captiva—a delicate bond that held the promise of something more.

Gareth left the island a month earlier, leaving Emma to grapple with her conflicting emotions in his absence. Their encounters had stirred something within her, awakening feelings and desires she hadn't anticipated but she wouldn't allow those feelings to cloud her judgment.

Besides, with her impending departure and the uncertainty of Gareth's own journey, she couldn't help but question the timing and feasibility of any potential connection.

Emma's thoughts were interrupted by the distant sound of seagulls and the gentle creaking of the cottage's front door.

"Hello?" she called out. "Who is it?"

A suitcase entered the room before the person. Emma's sister Jillian stood at the open door. Her wide-brimmed hat and beach coverup signaled that she'd come for a holiday.

"Jillian!" Emma screamed. She ran to her sister who'd dropped her luggage on the living room floor.

They hugged in a tight embrace and Emma rocked her baby sister back and forth.

Giggling, Jillian tried to pull away but Emma wouldn't let go.

"I have missed you so much," Emma said as she stepped back to get a better look at her baby sister. "I can't believe it's really you. What in the world made you decide to come out here?" Emma asked.

Jillian pulled her hat off her head and tossed it to onto the sofa.

"My dear sister, nothing about our last phone call seemed normal. Mom and Dad are worried sick, and you weren't very forthcoming when I talked to you."

Taking a deep breath, Jillian flopped down on a chair and put her feet up on the ottoman.

"I figured if you won't come home I'd better come to you."

Not wanting to confess anything, Emma sat across the room in another chair and twirled the rings on her hand.

"Come on, Emma. This is me now. I didn't come all the way out here for you to avoid talking to me."

"Don't push, Jilly," Emma warned.

"Push? You won't budge. I can get more out of my patients than I can from you, and most of them have four legs and can't speak English."

Emma laughed. "Not the birds. They talk and don't have four legs."

Jillian's face turned serious. "It's not funny, Em."

"I know that. But you can still get me caught up with your life. How is my favorite veterinarian anyway? Any new boyfriends I need to know about?"

Jillian rolled her eyes. "Don't get me started.

Emma crossed her arms over her chest and smiled.

"I'll make a deal with you. We've got plenty of time. Now that you're here you might as well tell me everything. If you do, I'll do the same, but you have to go first. Deal?"

These were the kind of exchanges Emma had with her little sister over the years. They cut deals and negotiated about the littlest thing. It was a game to both of them, but now, Emma had an important decision to make and there wasn't any room for game playing.

"I'm done with men," Jillian announced.

Emma laughed. "That's hardly telling me anything. So what? You've been done with men before. What happened this time?"

"Do you remember Jonathan Quinby?" Jillian asked.

"Was he the guy you said talked with his mouth full?"

"What? Seriously, Emma? That was two guys ago."

"Pardon me for not keeping up. So, what was wrong with Jonathan?"

Jillian shrugged. "Nothing actually and it was really annoying."

Confused, Emma made a face. "Huh? I don't get it. If there wasn't anything wrong with him, why break up?"

By now, Jillian was playing with her hair, which she always did when she was nervous.

"Do you have any idea how frustrating it is to be with someone who everyone thinks is so perfect? I mean, honestly, I couldn't find a flaw anywhere except for the fact that there weren't any."

Emma rolled her eyes. "I swear, Jilly. This is a stretch, even for you."

"What does that mean?"

Emma got up from the sofa and went to the refrigerator.

"Do you want a bottle of water?"

"Yes, please," Jillian answered.

Emma threw a bottle to Jillian and then grabbing a bottle for herself, popped off the top and gulped the liquid down until half the bottle was gone. When she finished, she put the top back on and put the bottle back in the refrigerator.

"What I mean is that Mom was right when she told me that you'll never get married."

"Mom said that?"

Emma nodded, grabbed a pillow and placed it under her head as she sprawled out on the sofa.

"She did."

"Why in the world would Mom say that to you?"

"Because we were talking about your love life and she said that you always fall in love right away but then find something wrong with the guy. She said that weeks one through three were usually spent blissfully happy but that by week four the guy was gone."

"Gone? You mean they'd run away?"

Emma screamed at her sister.

"No, dummy. She said you got rid of them. I'll never forget the guy you dated who had a habit of opening doors and paying for everything the two of you did. He had the audacity to want to take care of you."

"Not true. Not true at all."

Laughing, Emma continued.

"I'll never forget the time you guys went out to dinner and he ran to your side of the car to open the door. He carried an umbrella over your head so you wouldn't get wet. You saw it as an affront to your strength and independence as a woman. You said that you couldn't believe that he saw you as some weak and delicate thing who would melt if the rain hit you."

By now, Emma was laughing so hard she had to hold her sides to prevent breaking a rib. Jillian, however, wasn't laughing at all.

Shaking her head, she sighed. "I can't believe Mom and you were making fun of me about that."

"Oh, Jilly, come on. You have to see the humor in it. I thought by now you'd have lightened up about these things. It sounds to me like you've given poor Jonathan the heave-ho for another of your ridiculous reasons."

Emma sat up realizing that Jillian seemed genuinely confused.

"Honey, do you think maybe it's nothing more than that you haven't found the right guy yet? I really think that when you do, you'll overlook lots of things. When you finally meet 'the one' I predict you'll think the guy walks on water."

Jillian leaned back in her chair and shrugged. "I don't know. I suppose it's possible. Maybe Mom was right. Maybe I'll never fall in love or get married. Not everyone does you know."

Emma shook her head. "Oh, about marriage, I couldn't say, but love? You'll fall in love one of these days and when you do, you'll fall hard and I promise it will change your life forever."

"Speaking from experience?" Jillian asked. "I know how much you loved Timothy."

Sadness always followed discussions of Emma's former boyfriend who had died during a gun battle in Afghanistan. She'd worked hard to think of the good times and not grieve so much, but it was still difficult whenever his name came up.

Emma nodded. "I did. I was very lucky to have met Timothy and to have had him in my life."

She didn't want to say more and hoped a change of subject and scenery might help.

"Hey, how about you and I get outside and enjoy this gorgeous day? Get your swimsuit on and I'll race you to the water."

"Just like the old days?" Jillian asked.

"You bet."

Jillian got up from her chair and pulled Emma off the sofa and into a bear hug. Emma squeezed her sister and buried her face in the crook of her shoulder. She didn't know why but she felt like crying. Maybe it was sadness thinking of Timothy, or maybe joy to be with her sister again. Whatever it was, Emma couldn't let go of Jillian.

After a few minutes Jillian pulled back and looked her sister in the eye.

"I held up my end of the bargain. Don't think because I'm about to beat you in a race you'll get out of telling me why you're hiding out on Captiva Island."

Emma smiled and picked up Jillian's luggage. Walking to the guest bedroom, she said, "I'm well aware little sister. I'm well aware."

CHAPTER 4

"*H*e's in a coma for a very good reason, Everyone comes out of this in their own time. However, he should be out of it by now. Don't worry Mrs. Wheeler. Your husband will come around soon."

The doctor's furrowed brow did little to reassure Brea. She repeated the words in her head several times after Dr. Rodriquez left. *He should be out of it by now.*

Although concerned, there was much to be thankful for. Michael was alive and the doctors felt he would recover but how long that recovery would take, they couldn't say.

Maggie and Paolo had spent most of the day by Michael's side and just left when Becca came into the room.

Hugging Brea, Becca asked, "Hey, how's he doing?"

"Better, I think. I mean it's impossible to tell. I'll believe everything is going to be fine when he wakes up."

Becca was a tremendous help to Brea explaining things in simple, non-medical terms. Brea didn't question the doctor's competency but talking circles around her didn't help.

Michael had lost more than twenty percent of his blood volume. When that happened his body went into hypovolemic

29

shock. Blood vessels constricted, his blood pressure dropped dangerously low and he eventually lost consciousness.

It wasn't until they quickly took him for surgery that Brea understood the seriousness of his condition. His spleen was removed and he had a blood transfusion. Becca explained that they had to stabilize Michael by restoring blood volume, administering fluids.

"He's going to recover, Brea. I'm certain of that."

"I just don't understand why he's still in a coma," Brea said.

"Because he's the most stubborn brother in the world," a voice from the hall announced.

Becca and Brea turned to find Beth and Gabriel standing in the doorway. Behind them, Lauren and Jeff waved.

"Sarah is on her way," Lauren said.

Becca laughed as she looked at Brea.

"I forgot to tell you, Chris is coming after work. He should be here any minute."

"Really? Do you think they'll let all of us in here at the same time?" Brea asked.

"No worries. I spoke with his doctors. I explained the situation and they understand. The truth is that it probably will do Michael some good to hear your voices," Becca said.

"Oh, I just had a great idea," Beth said. "Why don't we plan a party?"

Confused, Lauren shook her head. "Seriously, Beth. Is there ever a situation where you don't think a party is the answer? Did you notice our brother is in a coma? That's hardly conducive to celebration."

Beth rolled her eyes.

"Honestly, Lauren, you're such a wet blanket. A party is exactly what Michael needs."

Lauren punched Beth's arm.

"Wet blanket? Nice name calling there, Beth."

Jeff, who had been observing their exchange with a mix of

amusement and exasperation, stepped in, hoping to diffuse the tension. "Would the two of you stop arguing?"

"Who's arguing?" Christopher joined them and gave Becca a kiss. "Hi, hon. Who's arguing?"

"Beth and Lauren," Becca answered.

Beth sighed, "Oh for heaven's sake. No one is arguing. I was just saying that we're all going to be here tonight, why not make it festive? We can tell stories and remind Michael of exactly why he needs to get out of that coma and join us."

"Sounds like a good idea to me, but I didn't bring any beer," Christopher said trying to contain his laughter.

"You guys have permission to gather, not have a frat party in the ICU," Becca reminded them.

"Hey, everyone," Sarah whispered. "Wow, I didn't know you all would be here. Did I just hear that there's a party in the ICU?"

Beth gave Sarah a hug. "Yup. We are, right here in Michael's room. What do you think of that?"

"I think it's a wonderful idea. I'm only sorry I didn't bring little Maggie with me," she answered.

Sarah smiled at Brea. "But no matter. What I want to say to my big brother might give him reason to get out of that bed sooner rather than later."

Brea couldn't imagine what Sarah had to say to Michael, but she was grateful for her sister-in-law and the bond her husband had with his little sister.

Brea held on to the possibility that it would be Sarah who might reach through and pull Michael out from wherever he was. If this party and the bond between his siblings was the precise power Michael needed, then this night would be the miracle Brea had been praying for.

Beth stood next to the bed and turned to face her family.

"Let's get this party started!" she shouted in as controlled a whisper as she could manage.

"Well, I'd love to stay for this little get-together, but I have to get back to work," Becca said. "I'll come by later to see how everyone is getting on. Try not to get kicked out of here."

Brea grabbed Becca's arm and walked her out of the room. "Thank you for everything, Becca."

Becca tapped Brea's hand. "Not to worry. That's what family is for. I'll check in with you later."

Brea watched Becca stop at the nurses' station before getting on the elevator. Becca's words carried tremendous weight. As a medical school student she didn't have to be at the hospital all hours of the night. Becca's presence was strictly to support Michael and his family.

Christopher was a lucky man to be engaged to Becca. They were a perfect couple and Brea couldn't wait for the day when Becca would officially become a member of the Wheeler family.

Brea rejoined the group as Jeff and Gabriel enlisted several nurses to corral as many chairs as they could find without sacrificing the needs of other visitors.

"I know it's not alcohol, but Gabriel and I are going downstairs to get coffee. How about I get some for everyone?" Jeff asked.

"Thanks, honey. We can save the alcohol for when we celebrate Michael's return home," Lauren said.

"Okay, we'll be back in a bit."

"Maybe I should leave you guys to reminisce," Brea said. It was more of a question than a statement.

"Are you kidding?" Christopher asked. "You've been in this family long enough that you've got a bunch of stories to share just like the rest of us. Take a seat next to your husband."

Brea smiled and found a chair next to Michael. "Thanks, guys. I'd hoped you'd say that."

Sarah's mouth dropped open and her eyes went wide as she looked at Beth's hand.

Beth caught her sister's eye and quickly dropped her left hand to her side.

"Oh no you don't," Sarah said.

Lauren looked at Sarah and then at Beth.

"What?"

Confused, Christopher looked at Lauren. "What's going on?"

Looking at Christopher, Beth shrugged and shook her head, but Sarah wouldn't let it go.

"Do you have something you'd like to share with us, Beth?"

Brea had no idea what was going on but looked at Beth who now was smiling. Beth lifted her left hand and held it up for everyone to see. "Gabriel and I got engaged in California."

Lauren squealed and Sarah jumped out of her chair and ran to Beth. Christopher looked at his sister who was grinning from ear to ear.

"Seriously? Like, for real?" he asked Beth.

"Yup, for real."

Brea joined the women, who now were circling Beth and admiring the ring. For the next ten minutes the talk was all about the proposal and whether they'd set a date yet.

Brea hugged Beth. "I'm so happy for you guys. This is wonderful news. I can't wait for Michael to see this ring."

Sarah agreed. "It's gorgeous, Beth. Gabriel has good taste."

Christopher got up from his chair and went to Beth. The two of them had not only been close since childhood but competitive as well.

"Is this because I beat you running the Marathon?" he teased. "I mean seriously, I get engaged in April and now you get engaged in June. I knew you were competitive but this is ridiculous."

"I'll tell you what's ridiculous. You beating me in the race. I ran side-by-side with you just to keep you company and you decide that you'd beat me? I knew you'd say that you won. That's why I made it a point to step over the finish line one foot before you got that prosthetic leg of yours over," she teased him right back.

Laughing, the two of them fell into each other's arms.

"Seriously, I'm so happy for you, Beth. Gabriel is a great guy, and he's getting an incredible woman."

"Did I hear my name?" Gabriel said as he and Jeff entered the room with several cups of coffee.

"Hey, here's the groom-to-be right now," Christopher said.

Everyone hugged and laughed and not one of them noticed when Michael opened his eyes. It wasn't until they heard his voice. "Can't a guy get some rest? How can anyone sleep with all this noise?"

Quiet fell over the room as the group realized what was happening.

Brea turned to look at Michael, who was looking at his family at the foot of his bed.

"Can you guys keep it down? People are trying to sleep," he teased.

"Michael," Brea whispered his name and then ran to his bedside. "Michael."

She leaned over him and placed her hand on his face.

"Hi, honey. How long have you been here?" Michael asked.

Lauren ran out of the room and to the nurses' station. Within seconds two nurses and a doctor came into the room.

Looking at the group, the doctor asked, "Can everyone please leave?"

Brea wanted to stay but instead, did as the doctor asked. Everyone quickly moved into the hall and Lauren wrapped her arms around Brea. They all had tears in their eyes and hugged each other.

"I've got to call Mom," Sarah said. "If I know her, she's going to want to get over here right away."

Moving away from the noise, Sarah walked down the hall to place the call. When she rejoined the rest of the family she was laughing.

"What did Mom say?" Lauren asked.

"Well, it's as I expected. No, actually, it's more than I expected. She and Paolo are coming of course, but they're bringing Grandma and little Maggie too."

"They are definitely going to throw us out of here," Brea said.

"You know Mom, Brea. There's no stopping her when she sets her mind to something. Besides, I'm glad they're bringing little Maggie. It's important that Michael see the baby. I've been thinking of…"

Just then, the doctor came out of the room and searched for Brea.

"Looks like your prayers have been answered, Mrs. Wheeler. Michael has a long road to recovery ahead of him, but now that he's out of the coma is a very good sign. You all can visit for a bit longer, but he's going to need his rest."

"I understand, Doctor. Thank you so much," Brea said.

As the doctor walked toward the nurses' station, he stopped and turned to look at everyone.

"As a doctor I've seen what the love of family can do for healing. I think that Michael is a very lucky man to be surrounded by so much love."

For the first time in days, Brea felt like she could breathe. She didn't realize how tense she'd been. So much so, that a physical release of stress, worry and fear left her body at the doctor's words.

Becca ran down the hall toward the group and hugged Brea. "I had the nurse text me if Michael woke. This is wonderful news. Did anyone call Maggie?"

Brea nodded. "Yes, Sarah did. They're on their way."

Brea and Becca joined everyone surrounding Michael's bed.

"Your mother and Paolo should be here soon. How are you feeling?" Brea asked.

"Sore and a little tired, which sounds crazy considering I understand I've been sleeping for a bit."

Christopher slipped his arm around Becca's waist.

"So, big brother, the plan was that we all were going to stay here for a few hours and have a party with you. I think after mom gets here the doctor wants us to let you rest. We'll party with you as soon as you're up to it," Christopher said.

Michael lifted his hand and Christopher took it in his. Brea watched the two men as her heart grew seeing the tears in their eyes.

"Come over here and let me look at that rock Gabriel got you," he said, looking at Beth.

Beth dangled her hand in front of Michael.

Looking at Gabriel, Michael teased, "That's a serious diamond. That's what happens when you get engaged to a high maintenance woman."

Beth pulled her hand back and stuck out her tongue at her brother.

"Nice, Michael. Awake for only a few minutes and you're already giving me attitude."

As expected, it didn't take long for Maggie, Paolo, Grandma Sarah and little Maggie to arrive.

Maggie pushed through her family to get to Michael.

"Hey, Mom," Michael said.

Maggie couldn't control her tears. "Michael. Oh, Michael," she said as she bent down and put her arm around her son.

Sarah took little Maggie in her arms and moved beside her mother. When Maggie stood back, she let Sarah and the baby get closer to Michael.

"Hey, little one. You are so beautiful," Michael said.

Sarah leaned over and let her baby get close enough for Michael to kiss her cheek.

"Michael, I've been waiting to talk to you about this. Trevor and I want you and Brea to be little Maggie's Godparents."

Although Sarah had mentioned there was something she wanted to ask Michael, the gesture was a surprise to Brea. She walked to Sarah and took the baby in her arms. Looking at her husband and then at Sarah, she said, "We'd be honored."

Michael reached for Sarah's hand. "Thank you, sis. Thank you so much."

CHAPTER 5

Finn Powell sat on a weathered beach chair, his gaze fixated on the row of jet skis standing beside him. Joshua, his younger brother, appeared by his side, wearing an impish grin that never failed to lighten the mood.

"Let me guess, you've fallen in love for the second time this week," Finn teased.

"Why do you always assume that if I'm smiling there must be a woman involved?"

"Because there always is. So, who is it this time?"

Joshua leaned against the rental booth and ran his hand through his wet hair. Finn's hair was slightly lighter. His hazel eyes came from his father's side of the family, and Joshua's were ocean blue just like their mother's.

Laughing, Joshua said, "I didn't get her name, but I think she's staying at the Captiva Island Inn with a friend."

Finn shook his head. "For your sake, I hope it isn't her boyfriend. It wasn't that long ago that you almost got your teeth knocked out of your head over the woman from Michigan."

"I learned my lesson that time. Never flirt until you're sure there isn't a significant other. As long as I stay clear of that, I'm golden. I have to say, I do love my job."

Shaking his head, Finn didn't respond. Instead, he did what he'd done countless times before while sitting in this very spot. He thought about learning to fly. Finn struggled to find the words to tell his father that he was done working at the family business and wanted to leave Powell Water Sports and Captiva Island just as soon as possible.

Joshua thrived working the beach. He flirted with every woman who crossed his path, and no matter the outcome, there was always tomorrow and a new woman to charm. Yet, Finn and his brother Luke had dreams beyond the sea, and their father seemed unaware of that fact.

With their mother gone almost eight years, their sister Becca in medical school in Boston, and their father beginning a new relationship with Ciara Moretti, the Powell brothers shouldered the responsibilities of the day-to-day operations of the business.

Each of them started working in the shop when they were boys. Although their father began the business before they were born, Finn and his brothers were the lifeblood of the store, and an integral part of its fabric since their teenage years. It seemed an impossible situation and Finn's frustration only grew with each passing day.

There was no use in sharing his feelings with Joshua, since his brother showed little empathy for Finn's worries in the past. As he watched Joshua help bring a jet ski in, Finn decided that he would talk to Luke to get his opinion on how best to approach their father.

The sky started its nightly theater with hues of pink and orange, creating a dance upon the ocean's gentle waves.

Finn smiled and waved to beachgoers who were closing their umbrellas and beach chairs, and bidding a farewell to the sandy haven, preparing to embark on an evening of live music, dancing and walks along the shoreline.

Several groups sat at the picnic tables in front of The Mucky Duck, enjoying a cocktail while watching the sunset.

"Are you coming up?" Joshua asked.

"No. I think I'll stay here for a bit and enjoy the sunset."

"Suit yourself. I'm eating out tonight. I got a phone number and a possible date."

Finn laughed. "Of course you do."

He watched Joshua walk the path to the street and marveled at how carefree his brother's life seemed. Finn admired the simplicity of it all. Perpetually living on island time, his brother embodied the essence of "hang loose."

As most of the people left the beach, there were a few newcomers carrying bottles of wine and beach chairs. Watching the sunset in front of The Mucky Duck was a nightly ritual that Finn attended alone. It was the perfect time to be alone with his thoughts. Occasionally, someone would approach the rental booth and ask for a flyer or request information about the jet skis.

Tonight, no one bothered him and so he closed his eyes before the sun set and listened to the waves crash against the shore.

Something tickled his toes and when he looked down at his feet, a small dog with light brown curly fur looked up at him.

"Hey, there. Where did you come from?"

Finn looked around to see if anyone was looking for the dog, but he saw no one. Worried that the little pup was lost, Finn picked him up to search for a name tag.

"Well, hello Cooper. Nice to meet you."

The dog licked Finn's face. "Thanks for the kisses, but I think we'd better find your human."

In addition to the dog's name there was a phone number on the tag. Just as Finn reached for his phone, he could see a man and a woman running toward him.

"Cooper! Come on boy!"

Cooper jumped out of Finn's arms and ran toward their voices.

"There you are. Get over here," the man yelled.

Cooper ran fast and leapt into the man's arms.

Looking at Finn, the man shrugged. "I know I'm supposed to have him on a leash but I took it off only for a minute. It got tangled and I was trying to untangle it when he took off. Fortunately, this woman...I'm sorry, I didn't get your name."

"Jillian," she answered.

"Jillian helped me look for him."

Finn looked at the woman who was about his height. Her long, thick, light brown hair was braided and she wore a wide-brimmed hat. Wearing a swimsuit under a tropical coverup that looked more like a dress, Finn was suddenly glad that Joshua left earlier. A woman as pretty as Jillian would surely catch his brother's attention.

Jillian petted Cooper and let him lick her face. Laughing she looked at the man. "I was happy to help. I'm just glad we found him."

"Well, thanks again to both of you. I've got to get back to my wife and kids. They're frantically looking for him in the opposite direction. Have a nice night."

The man placed the leash on Cooper's harness and the two of them ran toward Andy Rosse Lane leaving Finn and Jillian standing next to each other with nothing to say. After a few awkward minutes, Jillian spoke first.

"Looks like we missed the sunset."

Finn looked at the horizon and laughed. "So we did."

"Well, I guess I should get back to my sister's place. Have a nice rest of your night."

She took only a few steps before Finn stopped her.

"Are you doing anything tonight? I mean, would you like to get something to eat or drink or, I don't know, maybe look for more stray dogs?"

Jillian laughed at Finn's attempt at charming her, but he could tell she was only being polite.

Shaking her head, she looked directly into his eyes. "No. I don't think so."

She quickly walked away before he could say anything more. Placing his hand over his mouth he blew into it, checking for bad breath. When he didn't smell anything offensive, he looked in her direction and wondered what it was that made her say no.

For the first time in his life he thought something he'd never considered before.

Maybe I could learn a thing or two from Joshua.

As she walked toward Emma's cottage, Jillian didn't look back in the direction of the handsome guy at the rental booth.

That was stupid. At least you could have asked him his name.

A mixture of regret and curiosity tugged at Jillian's thoughts. For so long she'd convinced herself that she was better off alone, shielding her heart from the potential pain of another failed relationship.

But now, a flicker of doubt crept into her mind. Was she being too cautious? Could the handsome stranger change her perspective?

She replayed their brief interaction in her mind. His warm smile, the kindness in his eyes, and the genuine concern he'd shown for the puppy attractive to her.

A guy who likes puppies can't be all bad.

He seemed like a genuinely good person, the kind she had longed to meet. Secretly, she accepted the fact that her sister was right. No matter how wonderful the man, in time he'd show his true colors and he'd have to go. She was better off alone than getting her heart broken once more.

When she reached the cottage, Emma was sitting on the porch, reading a book.

"Hey, how was your walk?"

"My walk turned into chasing a dog."

"What?"

"Yeah, some guy lost his little mini poodle and I helped chase down his pup. What a cutie. His name is Cooper. Anyway, I missed watching the sunset completely, and some guy asked me out on a date."

"Wow. That was some productive stroll on the beach. Who's the guy?"

"No idea. He was sitting down near a bunch of jet skis watching the sunset all alone. Somehow the dog found his way to him. When the owner and I got close and called Cooper's name, he jumped out of this guy's arms."

"How did you manage to get a date out of all that?"

Jillian shook her head. "I said no. I'm not here on Captiva Island to find a guy, Em. I'm here for you. Maybe you didn't get my point yesterday when we were on the beach. As much as I need a vacation, this visit isn't about chilling on the beach. It's time you tell me everything."

Emma stalled every time the subject came up, but Jillian could tell the walls were coming down and Emma was ready to talk.

"Let's go inside. It's getting chilly out here."

Once settled on the sofa, Emma explained everything that she'd gone through in the last year, starting with her relationship with Timothy and her subsequent hike of the Camino de Santiago in Spain after his death.

Although she had what felt like a million questions, Jillian did her best not to interrupt her sister. She could see how emotional Emma was while sharing the events of the past year and it pained Jillian to see her sister struggle to find the right words.

"I was so confused after Timothy died. I thought I could just go back to work and things would settle in place like they were before he died, but I was wrong. Nothing was the same and my life felt like it was spinning out of control."

Jillian reached for Emma's hand and squeezed it.

"Of course you were confused, anyone would be."

Emma continued, "This constant pull toward something more has had a hold on me, Jilly. Ever since I spent all that time visiting convents, and monasteries, that pull brought me here, to Captiva Island."

Jillian's empathy for what her sister was going through magnified, and she wanted to do something to help Emma, but, what?

"You should have called me, Em. I might have helped you," Jillian insisted.

"Jilly, trying to decide if you want to be a nun is not exactly the kind of thing someone else can help you with."

"I know, but we could have talked about other things that might help you decide."

Emma smiled, tapped her sister's hand and got up from the sofa. "I'm going to open a bottle of wine. Let me get a couple of glasses."

Jillian needed to get her reason for coming to Captiva front and center. Emma still hadn't addressed the problem of their parents and the lack of communication that had them worried sick.

When Emma came back into the living room, she handed Jillian a glass.

"Cheers."

They each took a sip of their wine, and then Emma returned to the sofa.

"It's all in the past now anyway, Jilly. I've made up my mind about what I plan to do."

Jillian's eyes widened. "You have? Well, don't leave me hanging. What are you going to do?"

Emma sat back against the cushions. "I'm going back to work

for National Geographic. As a matter of fact I called my old boss while you were out on your walk. This rental is up in ten days, but I need to get a few things done before I go back to work. I'm headed to Sardinia next."

"Oh, wow, Em, that's amazing. What made you finally decide?"

"I love being a photographer. For as long as I can remember, I've wanted nothing more than to travel the world and capture moments that represent the human condition. Oh, I know there is much that is in turmoil and as an empath, the suffering I witness can sometimes feel overwhelming. But that's the point isn't it? I need others to see the world through the eyes of my images. To bring attention to these things is a huge responsibility that I take seriously."

"You're an amazing photographer, Emma. You've even won awards for your work so I know you're well respected, but I've always known you were talented. So does Mom and Dad by the way."

Emma nodded. "I know. I'm going to go see them before I head to Sardinia."

"I'm glad, Em. They've been so worried."

"I get that, but I needed to do this, Jilly. I needed this time alone. I've got to get to the Key Lime Garden Inn and talk to Chelsea. I'd love to call Maggie in Boston, but she's got so much on her plate right now with her son being in the hospital."

"So, what's in Sardinia?" Jillian asked.

"My friend, Gareth Graham."

"The mystery author?"

Emma's mischievous smile hinted at a deeper bond with Mr. Graham, implying they were more than just friends.

Emma filled their wine glasses and sighed.

"I guess I better tell you about him."

CHAPTER 6

*M*aggie sat up in bed and looked at Paolo. Deciding to stare at him for a few minutes before speaking, she waited for him to feel her gaze.

"Why do I think this isn't a good thing?" he asked without opening his eyes.

"I can't sleep. Besides, I need to talk to you," she answered.

"Am I going to like what you are about to tell me?" he asked.

"Oh, for heaven's sake, sit up already. What's the point of drilling me with these questions when I have more important things to go over with you?"

She could tell he wasn't pleased that she chose this hour to have a conversation, but the urgency felt real and that's what mattered.

"Okay, I'm sitting," he said as he put on his glasses. "What's so important that you have to talk to me at two o'clock in the morning?"

"I'm going to sell the inn," she said.

She waited for him to look shocked, and when there was no discernable change in his expression, she said it again.

"Did you not hear me? I'm going to sell the Key Lime Garden

Inn."

"I heard you. How about we go to sleep and talk about this tomorrow?" he answered.

Hitting his arm, she frowned. "No, I don't want to talk about it in the morning. I want to talk about it now. Don't you want to know why I want to sell the inn?"

"If I had to guess, it's because you feel guilty for not being up here when there was a crisis with one of your children. Although Michael doesn't quite qualify as a child. Do you really think that your kids want you to sell the inn and move back to Massachusetts?"

Losing her patience, Maggie felt hurt that Paolo was taking this in stride. She'd struggled for days with this monumental decision. The least he could do was pretend to be surprised.

"Probably not, but that's because they love me and think that staying in Florida will make me happy."

"Won't it?"

Maggie shook her head. "Not if I'm thousands of miles away from my kids when something bad happens. And don't tell me they're not children. I know that, but they're *my* children and they always will be. You've never had kids of your own, so you haven't got a clue how I feel."

Not once in all the time they'd been together had Paolo been angry with her, but Maggie could see that she'd struck a nerve.

Paolo got out of bed and changed out of his pajamas and into a pair of jeans and t-shirt. Slipping his feet into his loafers, he turned to Maggie.

"Maggie, I love you. I've never denied you anything, nor have I ever found fault with anything you've ever said or done. I've been careful not to hurt your feelings. I've stuck by you through the cancer and at every turn, I've been a loyal and supportive husband. Maybe it's because of that you think you can say and do whatever you want without pushback from me. But you're wrong. Right now, I don't like you. I thought you should know."

With that, he stormed out of the bedroom and closed the door behind him, leaving Maggie sitting in the bed, stunned at his words.

"He doesn't like me?" she said out loud. "What is that supposed to mean?"

She leaned back against the headboard and crossed her arms over her chest. To say that she was pouting seemed childish so she justified their conversation as a mature discussion that somehow went off the rails because her husband didn't understand her feelings.

Several minutes of quiet introspection passed before she realized that Paolo was right after all. They didn't need to agree about selling the inn, but that was no reason for her to be unkind to him. That he had no children of his own had no bearing on his ability to empathize with her situation, and she knew it.

Maggie got out of bed and covered her nightgown with a long sweater. She gingerly walked down the stairs so she wouldn't wake the rest of the family. She looked everywhere in the house for Paolo until she saw him sitting outside on the patio.

He didn't look at her when she approached him, but rather stared off into the garden. She wiggled herself onto the outdoor loveseat where he sat, so that she could be as close to him as possible.

"Hi," she said.

"Hello," he answered.

"You really don't like me?"

Paolo turned to face her and smiled. "Not right now. No."

"Will you like me again if I apologize? I'm really sorry. I never should have said anything about you not understanding or being supportive. You've been great. I think I'm just so upset and you're the only one I can yell at."

"Lucky me," he said.

She nudged him with her body. "You know what I mean. It's nothing more than venting."

Maggie put her arms around Paolo and leaned her head on his shoulders.

"What can I do to make you like me again?"

He faced her and pulled her close. "I'll take a kiss for starters. After that, I think we should hold off on any talk of selling the inn, at least until we've had some time to think about this more. Not to mention, I have no doubt that the rest of the family will want to weigh in."

Maggie kissed him and then arm-in-arm they walked back to their bedroom. She'd been so focused on Michael and her certainty that she needed to come back to Massachusetts that she hadn't considered anything or anyone else.

If Paolo was right, she'd need more time to consider selling the Key Lime Garden Inn. She knew of five people who might think she was crazy, six, if she counted her mother.

Chelsea threw the invitation into the trash barrel and placed the RSVP in her outgoing mail box. Pleased with her ability to avoid Sebastian and his new wife, Isabella, Chelsea declined yet another invitation to a party at their home. Citing conflicts due to running the Key Lime Garden Inn, she silently thanked Maggie for giving her a perfect excuse.

Nonetheless, she was sick with worry about her friend and the entire Wheeler family. No one had called her yet and she went back and forth, reasoning that no news was good news, but no news could also be devastating news.

Ciara sat at Maggie's desk updating the bookkeeping software.

"How's it going?" she asked Ciara.

"I'm always surprised when I see the numbers. The inn is doing well and it looks like profits are up this year."

"I'm not surprised. Every room is booked from the beginning

of the season to the end of the summer. I think we have a few in the fall, but then it looks like Christmas will be crazy all over again. Have you heard anything from Maggie?"

Ciara shook her head. "No. Becca called Crawford two days ago, and nothing had changed. She hasn't called since so…"

Chelsea banged her hand on the desk. "I can't stand this. If business wasn't so booming, I would have gone up to Boston with Maggie and Paolo. I'm glad to help out here but the waiting is killing me."

"I know what you mean. Powell Water Sports is crazy busy too. Thank goodness Crawford has Finn, Luke and Joshua. Those boys keep that place afloat."

"I hear you've been helping out too," Chelsea asked, trying to get more information about Ciara and Crawford's relationship."

"I have. Although mostly I've taken over the books. I can do that from home or if I have down time at the Outreach Center. A few times I've run the register at the front of the store."

"So, things are progressing nicely with Crawford?" Chelsea asked.

Ciara laughed. "Why don't you come right out and ask me for all the romantic details? You've been dying to know what's going on with us."

"Oh Ciara, you know me. No one could ever accuse me of being subtle."

Ciara was about to share when Chelsea let out a scream at seeing Jacqui Hutchins come through the front door.

"Jacqui! I can't believe you're here."

Chelsea's bear hug and subsequent rocking back and forth made Jacqui giggle.

"Does this mean you really missed me?" Jacqui asked.

"You were a pain in my…well, you know, but I missed you the minute you left. How's college?"

"Fantastic. I'm learning so much."

Chelsea turned and looked at Ciara. "I'm sorry for being so

rude. Ciara, this is Trevor's sister, Jacqui. Do you remember her?"

Ciara got up from behind the desk. "Of course I remember Jacqui. She was taking painting lessons with you last year, right?"

"I think we spent more time talking than painting, but it was worth it. Chelsea has limitless wisdom. I've thought back to several of our conversations. I did learn a thing or two about painting as well."

The three women laughed. "Oh, I don't know about wisdom, but I shared some common sense stuff with her. Hopefully, I didn't come off as a nag."

Ciara gathered her briefcase and closed the laptop. "I've got to get over to the store. Finn said they need some help tonight. Not sure what's going on but I think he and Luke aren't going to be around. I said I'd help out. Jacqui, how long will you be on Captiva?"

"Oh, I'm staying at my parents' place for the summer. They live in Cape Coral. I thought I'd drive over and visit Chelsea for a bit."

The front door opened and Finn Powell walked into the front foyer.

"Speak of the devil," Ciara said. "Hey Finn. Is everything all right?"

"Oh, sorry to interrupt you all. Ciara, Dad wanted me to see how much longer you'd be. Hello, Ms. Marsden," Finn answered.

"Hey, Finn. This is Jacqui Hutchins. She's Trevor's sister. I'm not sure if you know Trevor or not."

"Nice to meet you, Jacqui. Yes, I know Trevor. He's Sarah's husband, right?"

Chelsea nodded. "That's right."

"As it happens, I am leaving right now. I'll walk back with you," Ciara said. She hugged Chelsea and then turned to Jacqui.

"It was nice to see you again, Jacqui. Don't be a stranger. I hope we'll see more of you this summer."

Finn and Ciara headed out onto the porch, leaving Jacqui and

Chelsea at the desk.

"Looks like I might have to visit more often," Jacqui said.

Chelsea wasn't surprised at Jacqui's interest in Finn Powell. Most young women were the minute they saw him.

"I guess this means you're not seeing anyone at school?" Chelsea asked.

Jacqui shook her head. "They're all so immature. There was this one guy, but things weren't working out. We broke up at the end of the term."

"Oh, I'm sorry," Chelsea said. "Although you don't look too broken up about it."

Jacqui shrugged. "You know me, Chelsea. I don't let the grass grow under my feet for long."

Chelsea's cell phone buzzed.

"Excuse me, Jacqui. It's Maggie." Chelsea ran into the den and answered the call.

"Maggie? What's the latest news?"

"He's going to be fine, Chelsea. Michael is out of the coma. He's got a long road ahead of him, but I think he's going to be okay."

Chelsea let out a breath. "Oh thank heavens. I've been beside myself with worry. How is everyone up there? The kids? Paolo? Your mother?"

There was a pause on Maggie's end. "Everyone's fine. Everyone but me that is."

Chelsea's heart beat fast in her chest. Maggie's stress level had to be through the roof, and that wouldn't help her recover from the cancer.

"Are you feeling all right?" Chelsea asked.

"Oh, I'm fine. I've been resting and trying to get a bit of fresh air every day. You know how much I loved my garden when I lived up here. It's in full bloom right now so I sit out on the patio and admire the flowers. It's very meditative."

"Maggie. This is your best friend talking. Stop giving me

everything but the weather forecast for Boston. I need details. Tell me what's wrong."

"I think I want to sell the inn," Maggie said.

Chelsea clearly heard the words, but the shock meant that she needed to hear them again.

"What did you say?"

"I said, I think I'm going to sell the Key Lime Garden Inn and come back to Massachusetts."

"Are you out of your mind?" Chelsea asked, her voice raising. "You love this place. You went through so much to reach your dream and now you're going to throw it all away? Why?"

"If I thought you were going to yell at me, I wouldn't have called," Maggie said.

"You're lucky you're fifteen hundred miles away because I'd do more than yell."

"Chelsea, please calm down. I can't talk to you when you're like this. Maybe go make yourself a Key Lime-tini."

"I'll make one and then you and I are going to talk but not on the phone. I'm coming to Boston."

This time it was Maggie who yelled into the phone.

"You will do no such thing. I need you there."

Chelsea tried to calm down. She took a few more breaths and then sat at the desk. "Ok, listen to me, Maggie. I can't do this right now. I have company. I'll make myself a drink and so will you and then we're going to calmly get on video and talk this through. How about in a couple of hours?"

She looked at the clock. "How about nine o'clock? You and me and Zoom?"

Another pause and then Maggie agreed. "Fine. Don't forget the Key Lime-tini."

"I won't," Chelsea said.

They ended the call and Chelsea went back to Jacqui.

"Trouble?" Jacqui asked.

Chelsea nodded. "Big trouble," she answered.

CHAPTER 7

Finn found a table in the corner at The Grouper Shack and waved to his brother Luke when he came in.

"Want a beer?" Luke asked.

"Yeah, great, thanks."

Of the three brothers, Luke was the most sensitive and probably the most ambitious. Finn counted on both brother's personalities to find a solution to his dilemma.

Returning with two bottles, Luke smiled at Finn and shrugged. "So, this is a first," he said.

"What?"

"When was the last time you and I got together for dinner and a beer?"

"I guess it has been a while. That's what happens when you work twelve hour days."

Luke took a sip of his beer and nodded. "That's how you make the big bucks, bro."

"Yeah, well, money isn't everything."

"It isn't?" Luke joked.

"Not for me, it isn't. I want to be happy too. I think you can do both. Don't you?"

"Why do I feel like there's more to this conversation than you're letting on?" Luke leaned forward, his voice laced with concern, "Something's been bothering you for weeks. What's on your mind?"

"I've been doing a lot of soul-searching lately, and I've come to a decision about something. I wanted to run it by you before I talked to Dad. I want to go to school to become a commercial airline pilot."

Luke's eyes widened, a mix of confusion and surprise on his face. "Whoa. What? That came out of nowhere."

Finn shook his head. "No, not really. I've wanted this for a very long time. Just because I haven't talked to anyone in the family about it doesn't make it a whim."

"I didn't mean that. Look, this is a huge change from what we've always known. Are you sure about this? How exactly do you plan on telling Dad?"

"That's what I wanted to talk to you about. I need a strategy, but more important than that, I need support. I was hoping for yours."

Luke's brow furrowed, his voice tinged with concern for his brother. "You know how Dad is. He's poured his heart and soul into this business. He might not take it well. Have you thought about the consequences? The impact on all of us?"

"When you say all of us? Do you mean you?" Finn asked.

Luke squirmed in his chair. Finn always felt that Luke was just like their father, ambitious and driven. But their father had one thing that Luke didn't, a softness and empathy that made talking to him easy on the one hand, and complicated on the other. No one ever wanted to disappoint Crawford Powell. Not because he was an ogre or a demanding father, but because he was so loved that no one dared hurt him.

"I thought maybe I'd have your support when I talk to Dad. I can see that I was wrong to ask you."

"Listen, I didn't want to say anything before, but I've got plans too. I want to expand the business to e-commerce and maybe even open more stores. I'm tired of the small Mom and Pop business plan. That worked for Dad but it's not going to do much in the future. He's content for things to stay the same, but I want to grow," Luke explained.

"You mean get rich," Finn asked.

"What's wrong with that?"

"You're selling Dad short. He's always been ambitious. He's the one who opened the store on Captiva. Grandpa would have been perfectly happy to stay in Fort Myers. It was Dad who saw the potential on the island."

"Yeah, Finn, but that's still in the past. I've talked to Dad about partnering up with other retail sports companies. He's always balked at the idea."

"What does this have to do with me becoming a commercial pilot?" Finn asked.

"I need you, bro. I thought the two of us would build this thing together."

Finn's mind raced, searching for a solution that could salvage their dreams and keep the family united.

"Luke, what if we bring Joshua into this? He's part of the business too, and although he may not take it as seriously as we'd like, maybe he can help with your expansion plans. Joshua has a knack for connecting with people, and maybe he could leverage his charm to bring in new partnerships."

Luke scoffed, his frustration deepening.

"Joshua? Are you serious? The only thing he uses that charm of his for is getting women to go out with him. He has zero interest or capability to do anything other than have fun."

"Our business *is* about having fun, Luke. Think about it. Please. For my sake, let's see if we can both get what we want,"

Finn pleaded. "I know Joshua isn't the ideal partner, but he's still our brother. Maybe if we talk to him, make him understand the significance of this opportunity, he might surprise us. We need each other now more than ever. Besides, I think it's what Mom would have wanted."

Luke sat back and looked Finn in the eye.

"Don't do that."

"What?"

"Don't use Mom to make your point."

"You know it's true. Before she died she made us each promise to care for one another. If Becca were here she'd remind you of what Mom said at the end. We can't break up this family. You can't keep Joshua out of this. No way. We have to at least try."

When Luke's face softened, Finn knew he'd convinced his brother to see things his way. They'd first have to talk to Joshua before Finn spoke with their father. Although he'd convinced his brother that including Joshua was a great idea, Finn wasn't quite sure he believed it himself.

———

"Before you start in on me, why don't you tell me what's been going on down there? Any complaints I need to know about?"

"Maggie, I told you, if I have any issues to report I promise you'll be the first person I call. The guests are happy, the employees are fine. Ciara was here yesterday to update the computer bookkeeping system. We did get a last minute cancellation, but other than that, things are going along swimmingly."

Seemingly relieved, Maggie took a sip of her drink. Chelsea was surprised to see something other than a glass of white wine in her best friend's hand.

"What are you drinking?"

"I scrounged around and found all the ingredients I needed to make your Key Lime-tini. I thought it would be fun to bring a bit of Florida to Massachusetts."

"A Captiva Key Lime-tini is not the same when you drink it in Massachusetts. See what I mean? You can't move back to Boston when your home is Captiva Island. Your home is here, Maggie."

"But, my children are here, Chelsea."

"You have Sarah and your grandchildren here," Chelsea replied.

"And several more children and grandchildren up here."

"This isn't a tennis match. Stop meeting everything I say with a lob back in my direction."

Maggie half smiled and took another sip, trying to look innocent.

"Maggie, you knew all these things three years ago when you made the move to Florida. Your kids insisted you live your dream. You've sacrificed your entire life for others and after Daniel died, your children thought it was a wonderful idea for you to finally do something for yourself."

Maggie didn't respond, but since they were on video, Chelsea could see the worry on her friend's face.

"This is about Michael getting shot, isn't it?"

When Maggie didn't say anything to that, Chelsea pressed on.

"There was nothing you could have done to stop that from happening. It doesn't matter whether you were up north or down here. You listen to me, Maggie Moretti, your son is a police officer and has been for years. He was doing what he loves. That he could get injured on the job has always been a real possibility, and finally, it happened."

"Chelsea, you don't understand. I know there is nothing I could have done to stop it. That's not the point. It's more that when it happened, I couldn't get to him before…"

Chelsea knew exactly what Maggie was going to say.

"Before he died?"

Maggie nodded.

"But he didn't die, Maggie, and even if he did, God forbid, you still might not have gotten to him in time. Maggie, don't you see? You're thinking about sacrificing your life for everyone else. Do you honestly believe that Michael or any one of your kids would want that?"

"I hear what you're saying. I do. I need time to think more about this. So much has happened and I feel torn in so many directions," Maggie answered.

"Whatever happened to that woman who against all odds decided to listen to her heart? No one denies that you love your children. They know this more than anyone else. But, Maggie, self-love is just as important, and we're not getting any younger. If not now, then when?"

There was little more that Chelsea could say. The decision was Maggie's to make, but Chelsea was terrified that her best friend might soon leave Captiva, and the bond they'd formed these last years might go with her.

"Hey, let's talk about something else. Have you heard that Diana is getting a divorce?" Maggie asked.

"No way. I thought that marriage was solid," Chelsea said.

"I thought so too, but I guess not as solid as we thought."

"Do you think her husband is having an affair?" Chelsea asked.

"That much I don't know."

"How did you find out, anyway?"

"Jane called me to see how Michael was getting on."

Chelsea laughed at that. "Of course she did. Jane can't keep news like that to herself if her life depended on it. I bet the minute she found out she started making phone calls. I've got a bit of gossip myself."

"Oh?" Maggie said, her face closer to her cell phone screen.

"Jacqui Hutchins is back home for the summer and stopped in to see me yesterday. I guess she went to my house and when she couldn't find me there she came over to the inn, figuring I'd be with you."

"Oh, that's lovely. I'll have to tell Sarah. I'm sure she probably already knows. Trevor's been calling every day."

"Finn Powell stopped by yesterday to get Ciara and Jacqui was quite taken with him. I'm not sure the feeling was mutual, but you know Jacqui. Her middle name is 'I don't take no for an answer.'"

Maggie laughed. "Hey, how is Emma doing? I haven't heard anything about her and Gareth. I know he left Captiva, but I was certain the two of them would be a thing by the end of May. Has she said anything to you?"

"No, except she sent me a text this morning asking if when she came to clean the rooms tomorrow, we could have a talk. I didn't want to say anything but it might be that she's preparing to leave Captiva. I wouldn't blame her. That woman is incredibly talented. I never thought she'd be here much longer cleaning rooms when she could be traveling the globe, taking photos for the National Geographic. I mean, come on, how many people get that kind of opportunity?"

"I agree, but she's struggled with deeper issues than her career. I'm not sure what's been driving her decisions, but for her to think about becoming a nun, she must have considerable conflicting emotions. She's questioned everything about her life. Maybe since she plans to talk to you tomorrow, she's finally decided."

"That's what I'm hoping. I'll let you know what's up with her later tonight if you'd like."

"That would be great. I should get going. It's late and I plan to visit with Michael tomorrow. I think they've got him out of bed and walking around finally."

"Oh, Maggie, that's wonderful news. He's truly on the mend."

"Between you and I, Michael might have more than his physical condition to deal with," Maggie's whispered.

"You mean his career? There's nothing wrong with having a desk job going forward."

Maggie shook her head. "No. Not that, although that is an important issue. It was Michael who pulled the trigger and killed the shooter. He understands that he had no choice, but it's the first time he's ever killed anyone and it weighs on his mind."

Chelsea nodded. "Sounds not too dissimilar to what Christopher went through in Iraq."

"You're right, and I think Chris needs to talk with Michael and help him deal with the emotional pain of that day."

"I have no doubt that Chris and the rest of the family will help him get through this. In the meantime, someone I know has a date with radiation therapy. Please, Maggie, consider everything we talked about today. You need to come home…to your real home on Captiva Island," Chelsea pleaded.

"I'll think about it. I promise. I'll stay in touch."

They said their goodbyes and then Chelsea turned off her computer and sat back against her kitchen chair. It was almost ten o'clock and her eyes wouldn't stay open.

She thought about Maggie and her situation and hoped their conversation might influence her decision about moving back to Andover.

She'd give it a couple of days and if Maggie was still determined to do this thing, Chelsea would have no choice but to get on the first plane to Massachusetts and kidnap her best friend.

CHAPTER 8

The laughter from the living room made Maggie sit up in her bed. She reached for Paolo but he wasn't there. She got out of bed and put on a bathrobe. Checking that she didn't have bed head, she rubbed her eyes and ran a wet cloth over her face. She didn't bother to brush her teeth, instead deciding to do that after coffee.

She peered out from her bedroom and saw Beth, Becca and Gabriel sitting on the sofa while Christopher, sporting a way-too-tight apron, attempted to expertly flip pancakes while balancing on his prosthetic leg.

"You think I can't do it? I've done harder things than this. Might I remind you all that a person doesn't need two legs to flip pancakes," he said staring at Beth.

"Fine, doesn't matter to me. You fall on your face, Becca will have to pick you up because I'll be laughing so hard I won't be able to help," she said.

"What's all this?" Maggie said.

"Christopher is making breakfast," Paolo answered.

"Correction, Christopher is helping to make breakfast," Grandma Sarah clarified.

Lauren was sitting at the kitchen island being an audience for her brother's antics while little Maggie was screaming. Sarah tried to calm the baby by bouncing her and walking from the kitchen to living room and back again.

"Give her to me," Lauren said as Sarah willingly obliged.

"She's been like this for the last twenty-four hours. I swear she misses her brothers and sisters. They hover and doat on her more than Trevor and I do."

"I'm sure they miss her too. When do you think you'll fly back to Florida, Sarah?" Maggie asked.

"I'm taking the earliest flight I can get tomorrow morning. I want to see Michael one last time so I'm headed to the hospital in a bit. But before I go, I thought maybe we all should have a little talk."

Lauren's bouncing the baby did the trick. Little Maggie not only stopped crying, but she was smiling.

"About?" Maggie asked.

"About your plans to sell the Key Lime Garden Inn," Sarah answered looking at her mother.

Silence fell over the room and Christopher's last flipped pancake barely made it back into the pan.

Staring at Maggie, Beth asked, "What is she talking about?"

Maggie walked to the kitchen and poured herself a cup of coffee.

"Mom? What's going on?" asked Lauren.

Maggie sighed. "It's something I've been thinking about."

"Since when?" Sarah asked.

"I'm not sure…a while."

"You mean more like a week ago when Michael was shot and you flew up here to be with him and us?" Beth asked, already knowing the answer.

Frustrated by what she'd expected but tried to avoid, Maggie looked at Sarah.

"How did you hear anything about this? I haven't told anyone in the family."

"Chelsea told me yesterday," Sarah responded.

"Ah, of course. Good old Chelsea, always there when you need her and even when you don't."

"Mom," Christopher yelled out. "That's not fair."

Maggie was angry. She turned and looked at Christopher.

"You're right. It's not. None of this is fair. Michael getting shot isn't fair. You losing your leg isn't fair. Gabriel's mother getting Alzheimer's disease isn't fair. Your father dying too soon wasn't fair. My getting cancer isn't fair. Life isn't fair. You don't have to remind me. I get it."

No one said a word. The quiet in the room was palpable. Looking at her family, Maggie began to cry.

Sarah quickly ran to her mother and rubbed her back. "Oh, Mom. We're all struggling with what happened to Michael."

Maggie looked at Sarah, smiled and patted her hand. Then, she turned to continue speaking to everyone in the room.

"Each and every one of you is so precious to me. I hope you all know that. I don't think I could live if I didn't have you all in my life. I'm who I am because of you."

She looked at her mother and smiled. "You too, Mom."

Maggie's mother walked to her side and hugged her.

Christopher and the others joined them and formed a closed protective grouping around Maggie.

"It's true that I considered selling the inn and coming back to Massachusetts. But I'm a lucky woman to not only have so many friends and family who love me, but I'm also blessed to have two wonderful people in my life who have a lot of wisdom."

She looked at Paolo and extended her hand to him. He took it and Maggie pulled him close to her.

"Paolo helped me see how my fear of losing Michael influenced my thinking to such an extent that I lost a bit of perspective on what I want my life to look like. Then last night, I got a dressing down from Chelsea on Zoom. She made a point of reminding me that even though I've devoted my life to you all, it was time to shift some of that devotion to myself. So, no. I'm not selling, and to answer your question, Sarah, Paolo and I will probably leave the day after tomorrow. We've got a lot to do on Captiva and I've got several radiation treatments to deal with."

When everyone was done hugging each other, Christopher said, "All right. Who's eating pancakes?"

Solving a major problem before breakfast gave the newly engaged couples motivation to work on another when they finished eating.

"Come on, guys, we've got to figure this out. My first instinct when Gabriel proposed was to wait until after Chris and Becca were married, but Gabriel didn't want to wait," Beth said.

"I know it's stupid to imagine that my mother might make it to my wedding, and I realize there are no guarantees, but I thought we should move quickly just in case the disease progresses," Gabriel explained.

Trying to make him feel better, Maggie said, "Oh, Gabriel, we understand. Of course, that makes perfect sense."

"Why don't we tackle the first issue?" Lauren said. "Have either of you set a date?"

All four shook their heads.

Slowly moving the baby's bouncer, Sarah added, "Well that's something we better resolve right now."

"There is no way that I can get time off from school and work until Christmas. It's just not possible. That would be the soonest I could even plan a wedding," Becca said.

"I've always wanted a winter wedding myself. If it was near Christmas, even better," Beth said.

"Well, that sounds promising," Maggie said, "How about we shoot for a Saturday in December?"

Everyone seemed pleased with Maggie's suggestion.

Beth looked at Becca. "Don't worry, we'll make it work."

Looking at the calendar, Grandma Sarah yelled out, "How about, Saturday, December 14th. I like the sound of that."

Lauren nodded. "That seems like a perfect day. The kids are out of school for a month just the day before. I'd like to check with Brea though. I think her kids are out the same day, but I'm not sure. We could always take them out a little early, but they love doing Christmas stuff in the classroom on the last day."

Beth looked at Gabriel. "Honey, is that date too far away?"

He shook his head. "Let's face it, unless we elope to California, my mother probably won't make our wedding. There isn't anything we can do about that."

Beth smiled. "Not so, my sweet man. Not so. We can have a mock wedding at their home just as soon as you'd like. We can fly there and when your mother has a good day, we'll get dressed up and have a beautiful wedding just for her."

Maggie loved the way her daughter quickly stepped up to keep her future husband from feeling sad about his mother's illness.

Alzheimer's disease wasn't an easy illness to navigate for loved ones, but Beth and Gabriel were a strong, united and loving couple. As she watched the two of them hold each other in a sweet intimate embrace, her heart was content. Maggie believed there was nothing they couldn't accomplish together.

Jacqui stretched her arms up in the air and yawned.

"Thanks for letting me sleep over, Chelsea. I didn't think it was a good idea to drive back to Cape Coral after those Key

Lime-tinis. You certainly have perfected that drink since I was here last time."

Chelsea lifted her head off the lanai table and realized that she'd fallen asleep with her false eyelashes on.

"What's wrong with your eye?" Jacqui asked.

"Which one?"

Jacqui pointed to Chelsea's left eye which had the one remaining false eyelash half stuck on her eyelid.

Chelsea sat up and pulled the hairlike fibers and adhesive off her eyelid. Looking around the floor of the lanai, she searched for her other eyelash.

"I think this is it." Jacqui held up the eyelash and handed it to Chelsea. "I saw it earlier but I thought it was a bug. You don't look so good."

"I can tell you with complete confidence that I feel exactly as I look. Do me a favor will you? After I finish a pot of coffee in the morning, I always…"

Giggling, Jacqui finished Chelsea's thought.

"I know, I know. You always make another pot. I've been here before, remember? I'll go get us another cup. You just sit there and rest."

It wasn't like Chelsea to over-consume her alcohol. She could count on one hand the number of times she'd been hung-over. It wasn't a pretty look and so, she did her best to avoid it.

She sat back against the chair and massaged her temples. When the doorbell rang, she cursed under her breath.

"Who the heck can that be?"

"I'll get it," Jacqui yelled from the kitchen.

Chelsea could hear Jacqui questioning a woman and then returned to Chelsea. "There's a woman here to see you. She says her name is Isabella Barlowe. Isn't that Sebastian's…"

Chelsea put her hand up to stop Jacqui from talking. Panic over the timing of the visit made any thought of her hangover disappear.

Sweeping her hair behind her ears and pulling her bathrobe tighter, Chelsea whispered, "Look at me. I'm a mess. See if she can come back another time."

"You look beautiful," Isabella said from the doorway.

Chelsea got up from her chair and tried to arrange her appearance. "I wasn't expecting anyone this morning. We were up very late last night."

"Honey, I've had a few nights I can't remember, and several mornings after, that I'd like to forget. Please, sit down. You don't need to fuss over me. I will take a cup of coffee though. It smells delicious."

Chelsea returned to her chair and Isabella, not waiting for an invite, swiftly moved to the chair across from Chelsea.

"Of course. This is my friend, Jacqui Hutchins."

Isabella nodded and Jacqui smiled at her. "Nice to meet you."

"Jacqui, would you please get Mrs. Barlowe a cup."

"Please, call me Isabella, or Izzy as my friends do."

Chelsea didn't want to argue with the woman, assuming they were already friends seemed presumptuous.

Jacqui returned with two cups.

"Chelsea, I really should be going. I want to visit with my brother and the kids before I head back to Cape Coral. I'll catch up with you later."

She bent down and gave Chelsea a kiss on the cheek. Turning to Isabella, she said, "It was very nice meeting you."

"And you too, dear," Isabella responded.

The sound of the front door closing gave Chelsea's new guest freedom to speak her mind.

"I know you're not fond of me," Isabella said.

"I don't know you," Chelsea answered, her voice steady but resolute.

Isabella took a sip of her coffee, and then appeared to search for the right response.

"I'd like to change that, Chelsea. I'm not sure how much you know about me."

"That's the point, Isabella. I don't know anything about you. One minute, I'm in what I thought was a serious relationship with a man and the next thing I know he's marrying someone else."

"Is that what you think that Sebastian cheated on you?"

"As I said, I don't know what to think. It's water under the bridge at this point anyway. I don't understand what it is that you want from me."

Chelsea realized that she was coming across as a scorned woman which was the farthest thing from the truth.

"My understanding is that you and Sebastian had parted ways when he and I got together. He told me that you returned to the United States with a feeling that you either didn't feel you belonged or didn't want to be a part of Sebastian's world."

Chelsea hated when her own words were used against her, but Isabella had hit the proverbial nail on the head. Months ago, upon her return from Paris, Chelsea made it clear to Sebastian that they were two different people whose worlds collided but didn't need to remain entwined. She loved her life and was content to have Sebastian as a friend.

"I really don't want to rehash my relationship with Sebastian. It did seem to me, at the time, that your marriage came rather quickly after I returned from Paris. It was a shock, but I'm over it."

Deep inside, Chelsea realized how silly she sounded. If things were really over between her and Sebastian, why was she being so cold and difficult?

"I've known Sebastian since we were children. Our families were very close. We were extremely poor and Sebastian's family had much more than we did. I think we were like brother and sister for many years, but then when I was sixteen, that friendship grew into something more. We moved away and there was nothing I could do but say goodbye to him."

Chelsea knew how powerful the memories of a first love were. She listened with a softer demeanor as Isabella continued.

"For many years, Sebastian and I wrote to one another. He travelled all over the world and made much money, but he never came to find me again. I think that's what happens when you go out into the world. I think Sebastian had some guilt for never looking for me. He was more interested in making money and becoming successful. Anyway we both married, but years later, our paths crossed again. My husband and I became good friends with Sebastian and his wife. We took trips together and celebrated our children together."

"How many children do you have?" Chelsea asked.

"I have four, two girls and two boys. They all live in France, of course. When my husband was sick with cancer, it was Sebastian who travelled to France to support us. He paid for all of Phillipe's medical bills. Our children were still young. Sebastian created trusts for them so they could go to school. He was my angel, and my children's biggest supporter. I think we fell in love a little with each other all over again during that time."

Although Chelsea already knew what a generous man Sebastian was, her opinion of him grew as Isabella continued her story.

"We didn't act on our feelings of course, but when Sebastian's wife died, we began seeing each other. Not in a romantic way, but as very close friends. He came to France much more often then. His children however, kept a tight grip on him and I think made him feel guilty any time he wanted to do something for himself."

Chelsea was all too familiar with Sebastian's children, and their controlling ways, having dealt with them herself.

"I don't know what happened after that. I believe he met you and fell in love but during that time we would continue to stay in touch. I was happy for him but he shared his confusion about you and your relationship. He said you had one foot outside the door, so to speak."

"Well, it was true that I was often conflicted. I loved my husband, Carl, very much. It was difficult after he died. I never wanted to get involved with anyone. Sebastian was a surprise."

"When you and he talked about your doubts and then you decided to come back to America, Sebastian cried to me about it. In the end, I believe that we found that our love for each other was right in front of us all along. I never had one doubt about him and I think he felt the same about me. I'm so sorry if our marriage has upset you, but both Sebastian and I would very much like to be friends. Especially me. I don't know anyone here but I know this. If Sebastian was in love with you, then you must be a lovely woman."

Chelsea's heart softened. She had every intention of hating this woman and avoiding her completely. Coupled with the fact that Chelsea felt foolish for harboring any bitterness toward Sebastian, she now saw how ridiculous it was to do the same to Isabella.

Impressed with Isabella's courage to deal with such an awkward situation head on, Chelsea's admiration grew.

"I'd like that, Isabella. Thank you for explaining everything to me."

"I'm glad. Sebastian called me a very brave woman. He said not many people would confront you face-to-face. I don't know what he was talking about. You don't seem difficult at all."

Chelsea laughed at Isabella's words.

"Well, you've just met me. Give it time."

CHAPTER 9

*E*mma pulled the sheets from the bed and bunched them into a ball. There was no sign of the previous inhabitants except for a twenty-dollar bill left on the table. The guests checked out early but within hours the room would have new guests asking a million questions about where to go and what to see on the island.

Although no expert on the islands of Captiva and Sanibel, Emma did her best to advise visitors. Cleaning was boring. Meeting new people was everything to Emma. She couldn't wait to get back to work visiting new places and learning new cultures.

She was sorry to leave the Key Lime Garden Inn because she didn't like burdening Chelsea with one more employee problem, but with Maggie away she didn't have much choice.

Paolo had instructed the manager from his nursery to maintain the inn's garden. Robert (Bob) Moreau worked with Paolo for years and was the most senior employee at Sanibellia, having joined the garden center when it opened its doors years earlier.

At eleven thirty, with no sign of Chelsea, Emma sat on the

back porch swing and waited. Waving to Bob as he mowed the lawn, Emma tried to calm the butterflies in her stomach.

She didn't know why she felt so nervous. Everyone, including Maggie, understood that Emma planned to work at the inn for a couple of months, and could hardly get upset with her.

Still, it was the turmoil in the Wheeler and Moretti homes that made Emma feel guilty leaving the inn at such an inconvenient time.

It was noon when Chelsea finally showed up at the inn and by then Emma had talked herself into such a state she wondered if she should wait for another day to deliver the bad news.

"Hey, Emma. What are you doing sitting out here? Is everything all right?" Chelsea asked.

"Hi, Chelsea. I wanted to talk with you before heading home. I…well, you see…um..when I took this job. What I mean is…"

Emma couldn't form her words in any cohesive way, and Chelsea seemed amused by her situation.

"You're leaving," Chelsea stated casually as she carried items from the trunk of her car.

"Let me help you with that," Emma offered.

She ran to catch a large bag that was about to fall from Chelsea's arms.

"Thanks, Emma. I went into the grocery store looking for roasted red peppers and came out with four shopping bags. How exactly does that happen?"

"Happens all the time," Emma answered.

"Back to your situation. Not to worry. Maggie expected your time at the inn to end when your lease was up. Don't worry one bit about it."

"Yes, I know, but no one expected Michael to get shot, or for Maggie to go to Boston. The timing is terrible. If you really need me, I guess I can call my work and…"

"Stop. What did I just say to you? Do not worry about this.

Did you say that you're going back to work? At the National Geographic?"

Emma smiled and nodded. "Yes. I know you and I haven't had much deep conversation about what I've been going through, but…"

"I know about your struggles trying to decide to become a nun. Is that what you're referring to? I didn't know it was a secret. Maggie mentioned it to me and I haven't said anything to anyone."

Emma shook her head. "No. It's not a secret. Staying at the cottage these three months has given me the time I needed to make my decision. I've got a little over a week on the lease but my sister Jillian is here on vacation so she'll stay in the cottage while I go visit my parents. I promised to see them before I head overseas."

"I'm glad you feel at peace with your decision," Chelsea said.

"I am and I have Sarah, Maggie and this island to thank for helping me."

"And Gareth? Or would you rather tell me to mind my own business?"

Laughing, Emma took the butter out of the grocery bag and put it in the refrigerator.

"I'm calling Gareth and I a 'work in progress'. I'm not sure where our relationship is headed, but we have talked about collaborating on a book."

"Really? Isn't he a mystery author? You'd help him with that?"

"No. Not that kind of a book. He wants to help me put together a coffee table book of my photos. He said that his publishing company is interested. I've no connections in that industry, but Gareth has all kinds of people he wants to intro-duce me to. Who knows what will come of it, but I'm excited."

"Emma, that's wonderful. You'll have to let us know when you get published. In the meantime, tell me where you're going overseas?"

"Sardinia. I've never been there before so I'm excited about that. Gareth is going there as well. We're going to need more time together to see if it makes sense to pursue a relationship."

"You have doubts?" Chelsea asked.

Emma nodded. "I think relationships that begin when the parties involved are already in transition, usually fail. I'm convinced that Gareth and I met when we were supposed to, but whether that's a healthy basis to continue, I'm not so sure."

"Wise girl. As long as you keep that in mind, I think the two of you will find your way."

Emma hugged Chelsea. "Thank you for everything. I'm headed to Naples to visit my parents today. I'll be back to see Sarah and Maggie before I leave. What's the word on Michael?"

"He's out of the coma and is on the mend. They removed his spleen. I don't know much more about his injuries but he's got a long road to recovery. The important thing is that he's going to heal."

"When will Maggie be back?"

"I expect any day now, Sarah too. It will be good to get back to normal around here. The Key Lime Garden Inn just isn't the same without Maggie and Paolo running it."

—————

Maggie's eyes widened as she entered Michael's hospital room. He was sitting by the window eating breakfast.

"Michael! You're up."

"Yeah, look at me! I'm up and about, enjoying a meal like a regular person."

She laughed at his attempt at humor.

"Glad to see you're in a good mood."

Maggie kissed his cheek and then stepped back, taking in the sight of her son and the indomitable spirit that had carried him through the darkest of days.

Michael looked at her, his eyes sparkling with a newfound vitality that had been absent only the day before. His once pale complexion now held a hint of healthy color, and the lines of pain that had etched his face were gradually fading away.

Maggie did her best not to cry but it was no use, Michael had seen her blubber over far less many times in his life.

"There's the mother I know so well. Why are you crying this time?"

"Oh, stop, you. Can I help it if I'm overwhelmed with happiness not to mention relief?"

Michael shook his head and smiled. "No. I guess I can give you that. We've got lots to be grateful for. Speaking of being grateful. My lovely family just left. Brea brought the kids in to see me…finally."

Maggie sat on the edge of the bed. "Oh? How did that go?"

"As expected. They kept asking when I was coming home. Well, that was after they wanted to see my stitches. Jackson didn't care about any of that. He wanted to push all the buttons on the machines. Brea has had her hands full while I've been in here."

"That's your family, Michael. They love you."

His smile gone, his face looked sad.

"What is it, honey?"

Michael shrugged. "I don't know. One minute I'm upbeat and hopeful and the next I feel like I'm falling into a dark hole."

"Oh, sweetie, if I could take away whatever it is you're going through, I would. Something tells me that whatever you're feeling, you have to feel it. You've been through so much. You have to give yourself time to heal, both physically and emotionally."

Tears filled Michael's eyes. "I killed a man, Mom."

Maggie didn't know what to say. She'd already prepared herself that Michael would have to come to terms with the reality of what he'd done sooner rather than later.

"Listen, I'm not stupid. I'm a cop for heaven's sake. I signed up for this very thing, knowing full well that this day might come. But…"

"But it's harder than you imagined?"

Michael nodded. "Yes."

Maggie pulled a chair up next to Michael and leaned close to him.

"Honey, I don't how much you remember of what happened, but make no mistake, you saved lives that day. That woman and her two little children were in serious risk of being killed by that man."

Michael put his fork down on top of his plate. Maggie could see that he'd lost his appetite. There was more to be said, but for now, all she could do was stay close to her son and listen as he shared his pain with her.

Looking down at his lap, Michael shook his head.

"How can a husband and father want to kill his family? It's an unimaginable thing. If I ever lost Brea and the kids I don't think I could go on."

"I know, baby. I know. Something happened to that man. Somewhere in his life he lost his way. The public doesn't have all the details, but I'm sure as they investigate that day, more will come out."

Michael nodded. "My buddy and partner came to see me yesterday. He said there will be an investigation into my actions. They're going to want to talk to me as soon as I'm able. The fact that I'm doing as well as I am tells me they'll be in this hospital room any day now."

"Does that worry you?" Maggie asked.

"No. Not at all. That's protocol. I just wish I could be certain of everything I remember. The doctor said my memory shouldn't be compromised, but I do wonder if what I recollect is what happened."

Maggie realized that Michael was pretending. She could tell it worried him more than he let on. Frustrated, she couldn't wait for Michael and his family to put that awful day behind them and move forward with a focus on healing. Until then, she'd do what she could to lighten the mood.

"Hey, what do you think about both Beth and Chris getting engaged?"

"It's something all right. I can't imagine how the wedding planning will go."

"The only thing they've all agreed on is that it should take place in December before Christmas. Becca has work and school conflicts and Beth apparently has always wanted a Christmas wedding, which was news to me."

Michael laughed. "The next six months ought to be fun."

Maggie smiled. "Fun? Let's hope it isn't a disaster. In the meantime, there is something else that I wanted to talk to you about. Paolo and I are thinking of flying home tomorrow. I've been putting this off waiting to see if you need me. Tell me that you need me."

"Mom, I always need you. What is this really about?"

Maggie didn't know how to explain her fears but there were two and she needed to tell someone.

"Well, my concern of course has always been you. If there is something you need me to do, you know that I'll stay here as long as you need me. You might have heard about my little breakdown."

"You mean thinking about selling the inn? Yeah, I heard about that. Sarah told me that you came to your senses and changed your mind. You did change your mind, right? Because, if not, I'd have to remind you what a huge mistake that would be."

Maggie shook her head. "You don't have to remind me. What can I say? I panicked. It's understandable when your child gets shot. By the way, try not to do this again."

Michael laughed. "I think I'm going to be sitting behind a desk for quite a while. So, what else is bothering you?"

Maggie got up from her chair and went to the door. She

looked up and down the hall, making sure that no family members were around to interrupt them. When the coast was clear, she came back into the room, leaned against the bed and faced Michael.

"I don't know why I feel this way after having chemo, but I'm scared to have the radiation…well, correction, not really scared of it. It's just that after chemo, I got my head into a place of being cancer-free. I know that's not the correct term these days. I think I'm supposed to say that there's no evidence of disease."

"Mom, I don't think it matters how you say it. It matters where your head is at. If you want to say that you're cancer-free, then say it."

Maggie shook her head. "No, you don't understand. I don't feel like a cancer patient anymore. Now, going back to the hospital for appointments and seeing doctors again, I hate it. I just hate it all. It makes me feel like a patient, and I don't feel strong when I see myself that way."

"Mom, you're talking to a guy in a hospital gown. If anyone knows what it feels like to be a patient, it's me."

Maggie laughed, "Yea, I must admit, this isn't your best look."

It wasn't lost on Maggie that she was allowing herself the vulnerability of being the child and her son, the parent. She didn't care. Her eldest son always possessed a quiet wisdom that she'd depended upon over the years. Even when he was a child, Michael instinctively knew when his mother needed a hug or a kiss or just quiet time alone with him. He'd sit with her as she knitted or read a book and seemed content to be in her presence without asking anything for himself.

Michael reached for Maggie's hand.

"Mom, you're amazing. You've been the best mother. I can think of a million words to describe you but not one of them has anything to do with cancer. You're kicking cancer's butt and soon, after this radiation is over, you'll be looking at it in the rearview mirror. It will be gone and all the doctor's appointments and treatments will be nothing more than a distant memory. Through it all, you'll still be my mother, and the most formidable woman I've ever known. I hope Olivia and Lilly grow up to be just like you."

Maggie fell into Michael's arms as the tears welled in her eyes.

"Ouch!" Michael yelped.

"Oh, sorry. Did I hurt you?" Maggie asked.

Michael smiled. "Nah. 'Tis but a scratch."

They both laughed and continued to laugh until the nurse came in to take Michael's food away.

Because their laughter was so contagious, the nurse laughed right along with them even though she had no idea what was so funny.

CHAPTER 10

*L*uke Powell gave the customer his receipt with change as his father secured the lock on the golf cart's key box.

"Thank you. Have a nice night," Crawford said, closing the door and locking it.

Joshua threw a volleyball at Finn who caught it in mid-air.

Looking at his brothers, Luke said, "Thanks a lot for helping Dad and me close the store."

"Oh yeah? Where were you when we were bringing the jet skis in?" Joshua asked, as he and Finn continued to throw the ball back and forth.

"What are you boys doing tonight?"

Pointing at Joshua, he said, "I'm going to assume that you have a date."

"This will come as a shock to you all, but I don't, at least not tonight. We're going to hang out over at The Mucky Duck so don't bother making us dinner. Care to join us?" Joshua asked.

Luke caught the panicked look on Finn's face. The plan was to get Joshua alone and talk about Luke's vision for the family business. They couldn't do that with their father present.

"No. Thanks. This is Ciara's and my date night. She's making me her famous lasagna. I've only heard about it and my mouth has been salivating for the last few hours just thinking about it. I'm headed for the shower. You boys have a nice night and I'll see you all tomorrow."

Relieved, Finn started for the garage. "I'm heading over right now. You guys coming?"

"I'll be there in a minute. I've got to call Bellamy. I'll meet you over there."

"Poor Luke," Joshua said. "That woman has you on a short leash."

"Stop it," Finn said. "He's happy. She's happy. Leave them alone."

Joshua laughed. "Hey, as long as it's him and not me. I don't care. You won't catch me glued to one woman, at least not for long. Give me a couple of minutes. I've got to run out to the beach. There's a girl I met this afternoon and I want to give her my number. I'll meet you over there. Get us a good table away from the live music."

Finn nodded and continued the path down Andy Rosse Lane toward The Mucky Duck. There were several families still leaving the beach and some arriving to see the sunset.

With his mind firmly on his plans to convince Joshua to join Luke in expanding the business and taking on more responsibility, Finn wouldn't allow for any distractions. Yet, he couldn't help noticing couples kissing and snuggling under blankets they'd wrapped around themselves to secure their intimacy.

Without realizing it, Finn's thoughts turned to the woman he'd met only a few days ago. He knew her first name was Jillian and that she had no interest in going out with him. Beyond that, he knew nothing about the woman.

Once, years ago, he'd fallen hard for a woman who visited the island from California. Even though she lived miles away, they didn't give up trying to make their relationship work. She even traveled back to Captiva a few times after their initial meeting.

It had been a connection that spanned distances, a romance woven through letters and cherished moments shared during her brief visits to Captiva. Finn had considered moving to be with her, but she ended their romance when she'd fallen for someone else. As sad as he was to end things, Finn realized how ridiculous the situation was from the start and promised never to fall for anyone who lived in another state.

The ache of past wounds did not extinguish Finn's yearning for connection. If anything, it fueled a flame within him and he was jealous of the closeness that Luke and Bellamy had. There were even times when he envied Joshua's love life. At least the potential to meet "the one" was ever present.

"Where's Joshua?" Luke asked as he sat across from Finn.

"Where do you think?"

Pointing to the beach, Finn answered, "He's out there talking to some woman he met. He said he'd be here in a bit. If he doesn't get over here soon, we'll have to go get him."

Luke frowned. "Do you see what I mean? This isn't going to work. The guy takes nothing seriously."

"Give him a break. He doesn't know what we're going to talk about. All he knows is that we're getting together for a beer. Speaking of which, are you buying or am I?"

Luke got up from the bench. "I'll get it. If Casanova shows up, tell him I'm getting his beer."

Joshua finished talking to the woman and joined Finn at the table. "What are we drinking?" he asked.

"Luke is getting three beers," Finn answered.

Laughing, Joshua asked, "Yeah, but what are you guys drinking?"

"Funny," Finn said.

When Luke returned, the three of them lifted their bottles and Finn said, "To the future."

They drank to the unknown and Finn wasted no time getting the conversation started.

"Josh, Luke and I wanted to get together with you tonight because we have some ideas for the business and wanted to run them by you."

"What? You guys know I don't care what you do. I'm not going anywhere. Do whatever you want with the place. I'm in whatever it is."

"You don't understand, Josh," Luke said. "There might be more work involved. More work for you, for all of us."

"What are you talking about?" Joshua asked.

"What I'm talking about is that you can't keep doing things the way you've been doing them," Luke answered.

Confused, Joshua asked, "Has dad complained about my work?"

Finn tried to explain. "No. Listen, before this gets out of hand you need to know that I want to leave Powell Water Sports. I want to be a commercial airline pilot and that means leaving Captiva and going to school on the east coast. I've put off doing anything about this because of Dad. It was never my plan to stay working in the family business forever. When I talked to Luke about it, he told me that he didn't want me to leave because he has all kinds of plans for expansion. Unfortunately he can't do it alone, and I'm not going to be here. So little brother, it looks like you're going to have to step up."

"Step up? What does that mean? I like what I'm doing. Dad doesn't complain. This is what I want to do."

His voice rising, Luke was losing patience. "You mean to sit on the beach all day and flirt with women?"

"Keep your voice down. We don't need the whole world listening." Finn said.

Finn tried to explain. "Listen to me, Josh. You've always said you wanted to keep working in the family business forever. That's great. All we're saying is that if I'm not here, and Dad either gets married or retires or wants a different life, he's going to pass the store down to us anyway. We just think that you need to be more involved with the business if it's going to grow. Whatever happens, we all need to be prepared that things will change in time. We're not kids anymore. We have to plan for the future."

Joshua looked at his brothers and shrugged. "I like what I'm doing now."

"There's a difference between having a job and having a career," Luke said. "If you want to stay working in the family business, you're just going to have to do more. That's just reality. There's no getting around it. There might be travel involved, it certainly means business meetings, and it also might mean not taking a salary for a while."

At the mention of money Joshua was undone.

"You guys have been bossing me around my whole life . You've told me what I should do, when I should do it, who I could see and where I could go. This has been going on for years. Does Dad know about your plans Luke? Is he involved with this whole idea of expansion? Because I've got to tell you that he is still a young man. He's nowhere near getting ready to retire and as far as I can tell, he's still in charge. So whatever the two of you are cooking up, you can keep me out of it. I plan to work in the family business for as long as Dad wants me."

"You mean until a better offer comes along?" Luke said.

"A better offer?" Joshua asked.

"Yeah, you know, a woman with money, a family with money, someone with luxury yachts and summer homes and all the money you can spend to keep their daughter happy. You can parlay this lifestyle of yours into a career by marrying into the right situation. You won't need Powell Water Sports at all because you'll be living a playboy's life," Luke said.

"Joshua, tell me that Luke is wrong," Finn said.

Luke's jaw set with determination, "He knows I'm right. The life he wants isn't sustainable without money."

Finn's anger matched Luke's. He didn't know what to do. Frustrated by his brother's reaction, Finn gave up trying to work things out. He was determined to be a pilot, and he refused to be at the mercy of Joshua's whims.

Looking at Luke and Joshua, he got up from the table and slammed his hand against it.

"The two of you can do what you want. I'm out of here."

He didn't bother finishing his beer, instead, leaving his brothers to do as they pleased, just as he planned to do.

Frustrated and simmering with emotion, Finn kicked the sand beneath his feet and then walked along the edge of the water. He'd done his best to work with Luke on a plan going forward, but now realized that he'd wasted his time. Nothing would ever change in their family.

He was suddenly aware that if their sister Becca was here, the problem would have been resolved within minutes. Becca would probably have dragged him to their father and explained why leaving the family business to become a commercial airline pilot was a wonderful idea and that the family should fully support him in fulfilling his dream.

But, Becca wasn't here, and he didn't have the courage to go to his father.

What was it about Becca? Life seemed lighter and more fun when she was around.

"I thought that job of yours was a full-time party on the beach. What happened? Someone drown?"

Finn looked up in the direction of the voice. Sitting in a wicker chair with a book on her lap, was Jillian, the woman with the dog.

His frustration momentarily forgotten, he took a deep breath and walked toward her.

"Jillian, right?" he asked.

"And you are?" she answered.

"Finn Powell. My family owns Powell Water Sports up on Andy Rosse Lane. Do you live here?"

"No. My sister rented this cottage and I came to see her. She's visiting our parents in Naples for a couple of days and then we're both going back to work."

"What do you do for work, if you don't mind my asking?"

"I'm a veterinarian. I run a vet hospital in Naples."

Finn was impressed that a woman her age would have such an accomplishment. "Wow. You run it?"

"Actually, it's my hospital. You seem surprised."

"No. Well, um…I."

"That's agism you know."

"Huh?"

"You're surprised that I could run a business because I'm so young."

She seemed determined to make him feel uncomfortable. Moving his sandaled feet back and forth in the sand, Finn felt awkward and lacked the confidence needed to speak to her. He didn't know why he felt so uneasy, but he wanted to run the clock back a few minutes so he could start over.

"Before I continue to put my foot in my mouth, how about we start over?"

"Sure. I'm Jillian Thurston. Nice to meet you Finn Powell."

That she was so willing to excuse his lousy attempt at conversation made him feel more relaxed.

"It's nice to meet you, Jillian. I guess that man the other day picked the right person to help him find his dog."

"Do you have any pets?" she asked.

"No. I wish I did. I've wanted a dog for a long time, but my living and working situations make that difficult."

"Oh? What exactly is your living situation that would make owning a pet so dangerous?"

"Did I say dangerous? I didn't mean to imply that. It's just that I don't live alone. I'm living with my family. My mother died several years ago and so my two brothers and I have stayed living and working with our dad. It's convenient with the business being right there as well. I have a sister, Becca. She's in medical school up in Boston. She's engaged to Christopher Wheeler. Do you know the Wheelers? They own the Key Lime Garden Inn."

Suddenly, Jillian put her book down and walked to the beach to join Finn.

"Yes. I know the Wheelers. My sister's college roommate was Sarah Wheeler. My family knows the Wheelers very well."

Finn hated that Jillian didn't live on the island. Even though he didn't plan to stay himself, he didn't like that she'd be leaving Captiva soon. He didn't know what to do, but he knew that he wanted more time with her.

"It's too bad you're leaving Captiva soon. There's a lot to do here."

"So, you've lived on Captiva Island your whole life?"

Finn nodded. "That's right. I went to school off-island, but otherwise, I've been here all twenty-nine years."

Jillian nodded and turned to go back to the porch.

"Okay," she said.

Confused, Finn said, "Okay?"

Jillian nodded and turned to look at him.

"Okay, I'll go out with you. You offered food and drink the other night. Maybe you can add a tour of the island to that offer?"

Finn couldn't believe she agreed to go out with him. "That would be great. How about I pick you up tomorrow around ten in the morning? I'll show you the island and maybe a bit of Sanibel too. How does that sound?"

"Perfect. Maybe whatever it is that's troubling you might get resolved by then?"

Embarrassed that he'd almost lost the chance to see her again due to his foul mood, he nodded. "I promise you'll see a more cheerful guy tomorrow."

Waving as he headed toward home, with a mixture of relief and excitement, Finn couldn't believe that such a lousy day had turned into one of the best of his life.

CHAPTER 11

A tour of the islands of Captiva and Sanibel seemed the right way to start Finn's date with Jillian. He didn't want to appear anxious or suffocating, but he couldn't wait to kiss her. The only way to keep his emotions in check was to focus on playing tour guide.

After telling his father that he would take the day off, Finn drove his Jeep which had open doors and a more convertible feel.

He knew both islands like the back of his hand, which he hoped would impress Jillian. Without showing off, he took his role of professional tour guide seriously and tried not to look into her eyes too often.

"What are the buckets for?" Jillian asked.

"Seashells, of course. You can't come to Sanibel and Captiva without collecting some seashells."

"You do remember that I live in Florida, right? We have seashells in Naples."

Finn shook his head. "Not as many as we have down here. Bowman's Beach is covered with them."

Finn drove the Jeep down a few off-road spots to see how

Jillian handled the bumpy ride. With every bounce of the Jeep, she laughed and held on to her hat.

"It's so interesting the way Sanibel and Captiva Island are connected. Which island came first?"

Finn could tell that she was trying to test his knowledge of the islands, but he wasn't going to let any of her questions go unanswered if he could help it.

"Sanibel Island is the larger and older of the two islands. It formed naturally over thousands of years through geological processes. Captiva Island is smaller and a more recent formation. Over time, sediment and sand deposits connected the two islands, resulting in their physical connection through Blind Pass. The constant ebb and flow of the tides, combined with the power of the Gulf of Mexico, carved and molded the land, creating a complex system of barrier islands along Florida's coast. So, to answer your question, Sanibel came first and Captiva occurred later."

Jillian nodded, her smile and freckles captivating Finn. He wanted to pull the Jeep over to the side of the road and hold her in his arms, but resisted the urge, knowing full well that with his luck he'd most likely get stuck in the sand.

"Are you hungry?" Finn asked.

"I could eat. What do you suggest?"

"How about Doc Ford's? They have great crab cakes if you like that sort of thing. Their menu is pretty extensive, so I'm sure you'll find something you'll like."

"Sounds good. Let's go."

Finn drove the Jeep over Blind Pass Bridge and headed south. He turned on Tarpon Bay Road and then right again on Island Inn Road. Doc Ford's was on the right as he parked.

After the hostess seated them, they each ordered a tall glass of iced tea and looked over the menu. Finn already knew what he wanted to eat but pretended to look over the menu. Instead, whenever he could he over it to watch Jillian.

Her braided hair had flecks of gold and her skin was quite tan considering that she'd only been on the island for a few days.

"Do you get much time off from your job?" he asked.

"Not a lot. This is the first time in months, but I love what I do so I don't mind. Do you love your job?"

"Ah, sore subject," he answered.

"Seriously? I can't imagine anyone being unhappy sitting at the beach all day."

"First, I don't sit at the beach all day. I help run my family's business. I'm at the store most of the time, but occasionally I help my brother Joshua with the jet skis, which is what I was doing when I met you the other night."

Jillian didn't want to let it go. "So, what's the sore subject part? I really want to know."

She seemed so sincere and, looking in her eyes, Finn melted.

"Let's just say that it's not how I want to spend the rest of my life."

Their iced tea arrived and Jillian ordered crab cakes.

"I'll have the same thing. Thanks."

She raised her glass and waited for Finn to raise his.

"To plans, may they not laugh at us when they fall through."

She sipped her drink and Finn smiled at her.

Confused, he asked, "What?"

"You haven't heard about Plan B?"

He shook his head. "Nope."

"Well, it goes like this. The people who are the happiest and live the longest are the ones who are able to adapt. Those whose Plan A falls apart and are able to adjust and be content—not just happy—with Plan B are the wisest, most well-adjusted people on the planet."

"And, are you one of those people, Jillian Thurston?"

Sadness seemed to blanket her expression.

"Unfortunately, no. You see Finn, I have lots of wise sayings, but little wisdom. There's a difference."

He didn't know what caused her to share such profound introspection, but he was dying to know. He wanted to learn everything about Jillian, but there was little time to do that.

"When do you go home?"

"In a few days. Why?"

"Don't go. Don't leave."

He heard his words when she did. He couldn't believe he'd said them, but he knew he was serious.

"What? Finn…we just met. I mean, I like you a lot, but we don't know each other at all. I have to go back. My business is the most important thing in my life. Haven't you ever had something that meant so much that you'd give up everything to have it? That's what my vet practice means to me. It took me years to become a vet. Do you understand?"

He understood better than she could ever imagine.

"Jillian, I need to tell you something, and then I want to ask you something."

"Okay."

"I want to be a commercial airline pilot. It's what I've always wanted to do. I'll have to get to the east coast to attend the school that I want."

"That's awesome. If you want it, then you should do it. What stands in your way?"

It felt to him that the whole room was lit, making everything clear to him. "Nothing. Nothing at all."

She raised her glass again.

"Here's to you becoming a pilot and living your best life, Finn Powell."

He raised his glass and met hers. He took a sip and put his glass down. Taking her hand in his, he continued.

"I said I'd be asking you something, so here it is. Do you think you could date an airline pilot, even if he lived three hundred miles away from you…at least for the foreseeable future?"

It was hard to imagine Jillian could be even more beautiful than she appeared, but her smile made his heart skip a beat.

"Yes. I can see myself dating such a person."

Finn leaned across the table and kissed her softly on the lips. Nothing in his world would ever be the same again.

"So, when do you want to go back to California?" Beth asked Gabriel.

"You're serious? You really want to do a mock wedding for my mother?"

"Why not?" Beth answered. "I think the sooner the better because as much as I hate to admit it, my leave of absence is just about over and I'm going to have to make some decisions about my career going forward."

"Oh, that." Gabriel said.

"Oh, that? That doesn't sound like you want me to go back to work. Mitchell has been really great about the whole thing. I don't want to take advantage of his good nature."

"Beth, do you really think working in the District Attorney's office is what you were meant to do with your life? I only ask because ever since you've been on leave, you've been so much happier. I want that for you all the time. If your job gets you down, don't you think you should reconsider?"

Gabriel was right. Ever since Beth took time off from work, she felt the weight of the world lift off her shoulders. She didn't want to go back to the stresses of her job, but she needed to work and the pay was excellent.

"Gabe, I'd have to start all over again. I don't even know what I'd do for work. I'm an attorney. I went to law school because this is what I really wanted to achieve."

"Okay, so you achieved it. No one can ever take that away from you. I'm just suggesting that you rethink the type of law you want to focus on. I love you and your well-being is everything to me."

Beth loved that she could count on Gabriel being in her corner. His support meant the world to her, but the decision about returning to work was hers alone. She didn't like talking about it since there was little the discussion could do except give her more stress.

"I'll figure that all out later. Right now, we need to call your dad and see if we can put something together for your mother. I love the idea of a mock wedding just for her. Don't you?"

Gabriel nodded. "I do, and I thank you so much for the idea. It's very sweet of you. I love you."

"I love you too," she said.

They were just about to kiss when Gabriel's dog Charlie jumped up onto his sofa and tried to get in between the two of them.

"I can't believe how jealous he gets whenever we kiss or hug," Gabriel said.

"Yeah, the only thing is that I can't tell whether he doesn't want me to kiss you or you to kiss me."

"I don't care. Either way, he's a menace. Charlie, get down. Let me feed him."

Gabriel got up to feed Charlie, leaving Beth to admire her engagement ring.

"We'll have to buy our wedding rings before we go, so we can put them on each other during the ceremony. Who can we get to marry us? Do you know anyone who lives in the area who might go along with this?"

"Good question. I'll have to think of someone. I have an actor friend I could call but he lives in New York. No idea if he ever goes to Los Angeles or if he'd be willing to do so on our behalf. I can call him."

"That might work but could be costly. If he flies there just for us, we'd have to pay him. I guess he can be our last option if we can't think of anyone else. In the meantime, what day next week would work? I think the sooner we get out there the better."

Gabriel came back to the sofa.

"I talked to my dad this morning. She's doing well. Today was a good day but he said within a day she might forget who he is. It doesn't last long and she comes back but it doesn't last. You should be prepared that even if she's cognizant of her son getting married, she might get agitated and not know what's going on right in the middle of it. Are you prepared for that?"

Beth nodded and leaned her head on Gabriel's shoulder.

"I can do it if you can, honey. I know this has to be difficult for you, but I think we're doing the right thing. I know your dad loves the idea. Do you think your brother might come out for the fake wedding if you explain what we're doing?"

"Yea, why not? I think he'd love it. Maybe my sister-in-law and Willow will come too. We'll make it a family affair. Who knows, maybe having her whole family together, it might spark some recognition. I'm willing to try anything to have just a little more time with my mother. I'm well aware that a little more time might be all that we get."

CHAPTER 12

*C*hristopher glanced at his extensive "to do" list and crumpled the paper in frustration before tossing it into the trash. It seemed futile to even attempt tackling the tasks listed there. Several items demanded uninterrupted hours of solitude in his office, a luxury he simply couldn't find.

In the gym, children with prosthetic legs darted around, their laughter and occasional screams were usually a source of joy for Christopher. But today was different.

"Kids! Could you please keep the noise down? I'm trying to work here," he called out, exasperation in his voice.

Retreating into his office, Christopher closed the door, seeking some semblance of privacy. Yet, the glass walls and door failed to shield him from the mischievous faces pressed against them. Normally, their antics would amuse him, but today they only served to distract him further from his tasks at hand.

Christopher's phone rang. His brother's name appeared on the screen.

"Hey, do you have a minute?" Michael asked.

"Actually, I don't have a single second. Though, judging by

how this day is going, I can suddenly conjure up a whole day's worth of minutes. What's up?" Christopher replied.

"I was hoping you could come to the hospital. There's something I need to talk to you about," Michael explained.

"Sure thing. I can come right now if you want," Christopher offered.

"That would be great," Michael replied.

"I'll arrange for someone to cover for me this afternoon, and then I'll head over," Christopher assured him.

Just as Christopher was about to ask if everything was all right, Michael abruptly ended the call before he could ask any questions.

Christopher waved his co-worker to come into his office.

"Hey, Travis, I'm heading to the hospital to see my brother. Can you cover for me while I'm gone?"

"Sure, no problem. Let Michael know we're all rooting for him," Travis replied.

With car keys in hand, Christopher waved at the children who still sought his attention, then swiftly drove to the hospital, his mind filled with worries about what news his brother might have to share.

With their mother and sister leaving for Captiva, Christopher resolved to keep Michael's concerns to himself; there was no need to burden their mother with further worry.

When the time was right, he'd share what he could with the family.

When Christopher got to the hospital, it was bustling with activity. There was barely enough room for him on the elevator. He waved to the nurses as he passed their desk and walked to Michael's room.

"I made it in record time. Not a single cop stopped me, and I may even have exceeded the speed limit. If I'm not getting tickets because you're in the hospital, I wonder how long I can milk that excuse," Christopher joked as he entered Michael's room.

Michael reached out, and the brothers shook hands. "Hey, baby brother. Thanks for coming," Michael said.

"Yeah, no problem. What's going on? You've got me worried," Christopher replied.

"First, did Mom and everyone leave on their flight yet?" Michael asked.

"They were supposed to this morning, but Grandma needed Mom's help, so they postponed it to until tomorrow morning. Why?" Christopher inquired.

"I don't want Mom to delay her flight for me, you know how she is," Michael said with concern.

Christopher raised an eyebrow. "Are you in trouble?"

Michael shook his head. "Not really. I mean, there's an investigation following the shooting, but that's just protocol. They need to determine whether my actions were justified. I may have to write a report and answer more questions."

"I understand, but remember, you were just doing your job saving lives. Everyone knows that," Christopher reassured him.

Michael continued, explaining the details of the investigation and how Internal Affairs had requested his statement and seized his gun and bulletproof vest for analysis.

"That sounds intense. Does the rest of the family know about this?" Christopher asked.

Michael shook his head. "Not all of it. Mom might have suspected something, which is why she didn't want to leave. She knows what I'm up against."

Christopher's concern deepened. "This could become a big deal. But you're not going through it alone. We're here for you. What does Brea say?"

"She's worried of course, mixed with a bit of anger. She doesn't understand why anyone would question my actions. Then again, that's my wife we're talking about. She might be a bit biased."

"What about you? Are you sure you're not just blowing this off to make it look like you're not worried. Am I right?"

Michael looked out the window before answering. "Everything will work out. I'm not really concerned about it. And that's not even what I wanted to talk to you about. I've been having nightmares."

Christopher listened attentively, knowing his brother's struggles were far from over. He had experienced his own share of nightmares and emotional pain after losing his leg in Iraq.

"I keep reliving that day," Michael confessed, his voice filled with anguish. "From climbing the stairs to seeing those terrified kids and their mother desperately trying to protect them from her husband. I told him to put down the gun, but he..."

Christopher reached out and placed a comforting hand on his brother's shoulder. "It's okay, Mike. You're not alone in this. What you're experiencing is normal. It takes time to heal."

Michael nodded, his eyes filled with gratitude and sadness. "I know. I try to push it aside and focus on getting better, but I'm scared to sleep. It's always worse at night."

"You need to talk to someone, a professional who can help you through this," Christopher advised, recalling his own journey toward healing. "I had to seek help too. It made a significant difference. I wouldn't recommend it if I didn't believe in its power to help you."

Michael revealed that his supervisor had already referred him to a professional and mentioned the difficulty of recounting the events during the investigation.

"I'd take advantage of whatever services they make available to you," Christopher assured him.

Apologizing for disrupting Christopher's workday, Michael expressed gratitude for his brother's presence.

Christopher reassured him, "Anytime you need me, just call. I love you. I hope you know that we all love you. You're going to get through this."

Michael mustered a smile, and a hint of their usual banter returned. "I have to get better. I need to beat you at basketball. Didn't I win the last game?"

Christopher chuckled, grateful for the lighter moment. "You must have suffered memory loss because I won the last game. And by the way, your basketball needs an upgrade. I'll get you a new one. The old one matches its owner."

Their laughter filled the room, reminiscent of their carefree childhood. Christopher held onto the vision of more joyful days ahead, determined not to let the challenges overshadow the hope. He hoped that Michael would do the same.

As they shared laughter and brotherly teasing, Christopher knew that healing would be a long and uncertain journey for Michael. Yet, he vowed to be there every step of the way, offering support and reminding him that he was never alone no matter the struggle.

Christopher stayed with Michael for several hours, as they reminisced about their childhood as well as the Red Sox current standings. It was a much needed time together for both of them. With a lot of patience and prayer, Christopher planned many more days just like this one and vowed to walk this journey alongside for as long as it took to fight Michael's demons.

"It doesn't feel the same without Michael here," Sarah complained.

Everyone gathered around the table as Grandma Sarah and Maggie placed platters of chicken piccata and broccoli cheese casserole on the table.

"I think we all feel that way, honey," Maggie said. "We'll all be together soon enough. After all, we've got two weddings to plan. Keep thinking about that."

"He's going through so much. I wish I could split myself in

two. Half of me wants to be on the island and the other wants to stay here and be with him," Sarah lamented.

"I know what you mean. I feel the same way," Maggie said.

Christopher called out from the front foyer.

"Something smells fantastic, which is good because I'm starving."

Maggie laughed and remembered back to the times when Christopher came home from soccer practice. Dirty, with his body covered in grass stains, he'd announce how hungry he was every time. Maggie would insist he go upstairs and get clean before sitting at the table.

"Some things never change," Beth said winking to Maggie.

Maggie's heart swelled at the realization that her daughter understood what she was thinking.

"Only this time I don't have to tell him to go upstairs and take a shower before joining us at the table."

"I wouldn't assume anything, Mom. Come over here and let me smell you," Beth teased.

"Funny. You all are hilarious," he said as he pulled out a chair. "Pass the chicken please."

"So, Chris, how was work today? Maggie asked.

"Glad you asked. I didn't get much done. It was one of those days. I just tell myself that tomorrow is another day."

"So, Becca and Beth, let's talk weddings. I have an idea I want to run by you."

With his mouth full, Christopher said, "Oooh, I think I know where this is headed."

"Really, Chris? Can you please swallow your food before you talk? None of us needs to see inside your mouth. It's gross," Beth insisted.

Out of nowhere, Maggie's mother joined in. "When I was a young girl, I didn't get to say anything at the dinner table. Children were not to be heard from. Only my mother and father talked. We just kept our heads down and ate our food. We were so glad to have something to eat and of course we never knew whether it would be our last meal. That was always a real possibility."

Although pleased to have her mother at the table, Maggie shook her head and said nothing. Most of what her mother shared with the family had little to do with the conversation. Everyone smiled at her and then went back to their food.

Not to be deterred, Maggie continued.

"I was thinking that you all should come down to Captiva this Christmas and we'll have the double wedding there. This way everyone gets a vacation. You all can enjoy the beach and the island and attend the wedding."

She looked at Becca and Beth and smiled. "What do you think?"

"Mom, I don't know. It sounds lovely, but the truth is that Florida at Christmastime doesn't feel Christmassy at all."

"Christmassy, is that even a word?" Christopher asked.

Beth took a bread roll from the basket and threw it at her brother.

Laughing, Christopher responded, "Hey, it's a legit question."

Beth continued. "You know what I mean. My dream wedding at Christmas involves snow and jingle bells."

"And Santa?" Christopher asked.

Beth gave Christopher a dirty look and then looked at Becca. "How do you feel about the wedding taking place on Captiva?"

"Well, I like the idea but that's because I never cared about my wedding taking place at Christmas time. My family is on the island and I've grown up there. I always thought that my wedding would take place in Florida. Snow never factored into my thinking, but I understand how you feel, Beth. Maybe a double wedding isn't such a good idea after all."

Maggie's heart sank. This conversation was going in the wrong direction.

Paolo rubbed Maggie's back, indicating that he understood

her disappointment. Maggie's face must have shown her sadness as Lauren tried to soothe her hurt feelings.

"We can all still come down for the holidays though. The kids will be out of school and we'd love to visit you then."

Maggie smiled and nodded. "That would be nice."

The room was silent as everyone focused on their food. Maggie wasn't giving up.

She'd be back on Captiva Island this time tomorrow, but her heart would still be in Massachusetts planning a double wedding at the Key Lime Garden Inn.

Maggie didn't have a clue how she would pull it off, but she wasn't one to take no for an answer. Ideas were already running around in her head. She was certain she could make it happen. Besides, with Chelsea's help Maggie knew they could come up with something to get these two brides to Captiva Island this Christmas. She'd already used the family's Code Red method once before, so that wouldn't work.

There must be something I can do to convince Becca and Beth that the wedding must take place at the inn.

Everyone at the table had moved on from the wedding discussion and there were several conversations going on at the same time.

She looked over at Sarah who was shaking her head and mouthing the word "No." Surprised that her daughter knew what she was plotting, Maggie ignored her and smiled at Lauren.

"This chicken came out perfect, don't you think?" she said.

Although she did care how the chicken came out, it was Maggie's way of sending Sarah a message, and that message was, "I'll do exactly what I want and you can't stop me." Whether Sarah got the message or not, Maggie couldn't tell, but it didn't matter, because Maggie was used to getting her way, and this time would be no different.

CHAPTER 13

$\mathcal{C}$ helsea dropped Paolo off at Sanibellia before heading to the Key Lime Garden Inn.

"I'll pick you up at four o'clock," Maggie said as she waved to her husband.

Chelsea turned to look at Maggie as she pulled the car out onto the street.

"You and I need to have a nice, long talk," Chelsea said.

"Can I at least get home before you hit me with stuff that will give me headaches?"

"No headaches. The inn is doing fine. It's just that I need my bestie to sit and gossip with me. I've missed you, and I'm so happy that Michael is doing better. Tell me everything."

"I'm glad Trevor picked up Sarah and the baby. This way you and I can talk privately," Chelsea said.

"Well, if you had a car seat in this vehicle, Trevor wouldn't have had to come get her. I thought I told you to take my car? I have a car seat."

"I would have except Ciara took it to the market this morning. I forgot to tell her that I needed it for the airport. I'm so sorry to mess things up last minute."

"I'm sorry. I didn't mean to sound grumpy. I think I'm just tired. The whole trip took more out of me than I thought it would. I'm glad I was there for Michael though. He's been through a difficult time but I'm hopeful things will start turning around for him now."

"I have no doubt he'll be good as new in time," Chelsea said.

Maggie didn't want to correct her friend, but she knew that Michael was forever changed because of this ordeal. Good as new was not how Maggie saw Michael's future. He'd mend in time but she didn't deceive herself to believe it would be easy.

"There's a lot of good news too. Beth and Gabriel are engaged," Maggie shared with a bright smile.

Chelsea's eyes widened in excitement. "No way! That's wonderful news. Hold on, aren't Becca and Chris engaged as well?"

Maggie nodded, her enthusiasm growing. "Yes, they are! I have two weddings to plan now. Well, Crawford will take care of the costs for Becca but I have an idea that I hope he'll help me implement."

"Oh? I'm intrigued," Chelsea said.

"Yes. I have an idea that I think would be amazing. A double wedding right here on Captiva during Christmas. Turns out, my daughter has always dreamt of a Christmas wedding with snow and jingle bells."

Chelsea's eyebrows shot up in surprise. "Snow? How are you going to make that happen?"

Maggie chuckled, her eyes sparkling with determination. "That's the million-dollar question. I have no idea yet, but I'm really hoping to make it work. Becca is all in on my idea since her family lives on Captiva, but Beth is a bit hesitant."

Curiosity filled Chelsea's voice as she asked, "So, how did you leave it with them?"

Maggie shrugged, a mischievous grin on her face. "No double

wedding with Beth insisting on having her ceremony in a winter wonderland, complete with a foot of snow."

Both women burst into laughter at Maggie's exaggeration.

Chelsea chuckled, shaking her head. "Surely not."

Maggie's eyes twinkled with excitement. "Well, we'll see. I left Boston without a solid agreement between the girls or a plan for the snowy wedding down here. I'm determined to figure it out. You'll help me with my plan?"

"Honey, you know that I'm always your ride or die friend, but I'm not a miracle worker. I've yet to control Mother Nature."

"I know, but I'm sure we can get the girls down here. Not to mention the rest of the family. How hard is it to get snow in Florida in December?"

"Speaking of Florida in December, I assume your crazy idea about selling the inn is no longer on your mind?"

"It's not. You and the rest of the family talked me off the ledge. I panicked, but I'm all right now. Thanks by the way."

"No problem. Just don't think about leaving Captiva ever again, okay? I don't think my heart can take it. So, are you ready to hear all the Captiva gossip?"

"Bring it on. I'm ready."

"The first thing should come as no surprise to you. Emma quit." Chelsea said.

"Yeah, I expected that. I thought I'd be here when she left however, but I understand her situation. I take it she's decided not be become a nun?"

Chelsea nodded. "Correct. She hasn't left Captiva just yet, so you'll get to see her before she goes."

"Please tell me that she's fallen for that author. I thought the two of them made a lovely couple."

"I don't actually think her decision is based on a man at all. Although I do believe they've got plans to see each other. I think it was more of an understanding of how she wants to spend her life. I know she wants to help people in some way, but for now she seems content with using her platform as a photographer to that end. She did mention that she and Gareth are planning to meet up in Sardinia."

"Oh, how romantic," Maggie said.

"Anyway, her sister, Jillian came to the island to visit her. It's possible she had an influence on Emma as well."

"Somehow I'd forgotten that Emma had a sister."

Chelsea nodded. "She's staying in the cottage while Emma goes to visit her parents in Naples."

"Finally!" Maggie said. "I've been telling her that she needs to talk to them about her situation."

"I don't think she's going to bring the nun thing up. I think she's just going to visit before she heads overseas again. I should tell you, however, that I think there is a bit of romance blossoming somewhere else."

"Oh?"

"Yes, between Jacqui Hutchins and Finn Powell."

"What? How did that happen?"

"Well, Finn stopped into the inn looking for Ciara when Jacqui was there. She's home for the summer. She'll be going back to school at the end of August. The way she acted when Finn came into the room, I swear it was love at first sight, on her end, that is."

"That is exciting news. I wonder if Ciara knows more. We'll have to see what she knows of this. I'm sure we can convince her to spill the details."

"There's more," Chelsea answered. "I've been getting invitations to various events on the island that have been planned by Sebastian to introduce his new wife Isabella to people. I've declined every one."

"Chelsea, you know you can do that for only so long. Eventually, you are going to have to meet the woman."

"I already did. She came to my house the other day."

"Oh my, alone or was Sebastian with her?" Maggie asked.

"He wasn't there. She came alone. I was shocked…well, more than shocked. I was hungover."

Maggie laughed. "Ha. Why does this not surprise me?"

"It's your fault. You had me make those Key Lime-tinis when we did that Zoom thing."

"Chelsea, people don't get drunk on one Zoom meeting drink. How many did you have?"

Trying to muster an innocent look, she answered, "A few."

Maggie couldn't help but giggle over the image of her hungover friend meeting her nemesis.

"A few? If you were hungover, you had more than a few. So tell me, how did it go? What's she like?"

"Honestly, Maggie, she's really nice. I hate to say it, but I can see us hanging out with her. She's the type of woman who has gone through a lot in her life and came out stronger for it. You know, like us."

The two women laughed at Chelsea's observations. It was true, both Chelsea and Maggie had persevered through the most difficult of times. To find a kindred spirit in Isabella was a wonderful thing.

"I can't wait to meet her," Maggie said.

Chelsea pulled into the driveway of the Key Lime Garden Inn.

"Oh, by the way, if you don't have any objection, I'm going to ask Jacqui to help out with the room cleaning. I don't want her spending the whole summer down here batting her eyelashes at Finn Powell. I've no doubt that she'll be hanging around Captiva this summer. I bet you anything that she'll jump at the opportunity to be here instead of Cape Coral with her parents."

"Wow, opportunistic much?" Maggie said laughing.

"Why not? It's not that easy to get someone out here to clean rooms at minimum wage. If you have someone who has a reason to be on the island, why not take advantage?"

Maggie nodded. "Sounds like a plan. I've met Jacqui. I wouldn't say she's the type to take her work seriously though.

Any way you can emphasize to her that this really is a job…you know, like she has to work?"

"I hear you. I know how to deal with Jacqui. You let me worry about her. In the meantime, I'll let you know what she says after I talk to her."

"Sounds good," Maggie said as she got out of the car. "So, now that you've told me everything, do we still need a late night girl's night to gossip? There can't be anything left to talk about."

Chelsea didn't realize that she'd shared everything on the drive from Sanibellia to the inn.

"Huh, I guess you're right. Well, you know what that means? I'll be here bright and early for my coffee and scones. You are making scones tomorrow aren't you?"

Maggie laughed. "Yes, Chelsea. I'll have scone ready for you first thing. Right now, I've got to go inside and call my doctor. I just got an email from his office. Looks like I can't avoid the next phase of this awful cancer."

"You'll do just as well with the radiation as you did with the chemo, Maggie. Don't worry about it. You've just got to get these appointments done and it will finally be over," Chelsea responded.

"From your lips to God's ears my friend," Maggie said.

Maggie left Paolo's luggage at the bottom of the carriage house and carried her overnight bag up the stairs to their apartment.

She looked at the email from her doctor. He had made her first radiation appointment for three days from now and wanted her to call the office to confirm.

She dialed his number and waited for his assistant to come to the phone. Instead, it was her doctor on the other end of the line.

"Hi Maggie. How are you doing? I heard about your son."

"I'm fine, Doctor, thank you. Michael is doing much better.

They removed his spleen and he has some other injuries that aren't life threatening thank heaven, but he'll be okay."

"Good. I'm glad to hear it. I just wanted to let you know that I'm thinking of you all. So, are you ready to do this next phase in your treatment?"

Maggie sighed. "Ready as I'll ever be."

"You'll do fine. I have no doubt. You're all set for your first appointment. I've sent you instructions to help prepare you for your first visit with the radiation oncology department. There isn't much you have to do to prepare, I just wanted you to know what that appointment looks like."

"Yes, I've looked it over. Basically, it's marking my body up with markers and making some sort of mold behind my arms and back? Do I have that right?" she asked.

"Pretty much. Nothing is painful. You won't feel anything in particular but you might hear the noise of the scan. Your first appointment will be longer than the others but not too long. You can expect to be there about an hour. I want you to have someone drive you to and from the appointment though. I tell all my patients to do that. It's just a precaution in case you feel weak or tired, that's all. I've got patients of all ages so it's a good idea to put into practice."

Maggie couldn't imagine that she needed anyone to drive her but rather than take any chances, she'd ask Paolo or Chelsea to take her to her appointments.

"I understand," she answered.

"Fine. As I said, I expect that you'll do well. I'll stay in touch to see how you're doing and of course the radiologist will make sure I get all results of your visits. We'll talk soon."

"Thank you, Doctor."

She ended the call and sat on the bed. She wasn't a drinker but felt the need for something to calm her nerves. She opened the refrigerator and grabbed a bottle of Pinot Grigio and poured a glass.

Why am I so unnerved by a simple phone call?

There was far more possibility of reaction from chemo-therapy than from radiation, but she was stressed about the appointments, nonetheless. She took a few sips of her wine and sat in the overstuffed corner chair.

You're going to get through this, Maggie Moretti. Stop being such a baby. You got through chemo, you'll get through this.

Careful not to drink and drive, Maggie decided to take a nap so that by the time she had to get Paolo she'd have nothing in her system that might alter her focus.

The trip to Boston and back had been a long journey of sorts. It wasn't the distance between Boston and Captiva that felt beyond reach but rather the distance between fear and surrender.

Before leaving Captiva to be with Michael, Maggie pushed aside thoughts of cancer as being something she conquered and banished from her body.

Now, she'd come to a different place of acceptance. An acceptance that she might have to coexist with the illness, or at least that she was a cancer patient, soon to be a cancer survivor.

She'd ride the wave of whatever came but would firmly remember that what defined her was what she willingly saw as her mission in life…to be, to struggle, to combat and finally to overcome.

Maggie saw herself as a warrior, one who was about to do battle with an unrelenting opponent. Soon, the battle would be over. There would be no war, instead, only peace. She lived for that day.

CHAPTER 14

"*W*hat do you think? Are you in?" Chelsea looked at Jacqui who was twirling to show off her new skirt.

"Seriously? Maggie agreed to this? Does she know that I've never worked a day in my life cleaning anything, much less several rooms?"

"Trust me, Maggie knows. This obviously is only for the summer, just until you go back to school."

"Sure, I'd love to do it. You know how much I enjoy being on Captiva Island. A job like that will mean that I'm not working a 9 to 5 sort of thing. I like that there will be plenty of time during the day to enjoy my summer. It's crazy to go back and forth to Cape Coral though. I think I should tell my parents that I'm going to stay on the island while working here. Any chance I can stay with you?"

Chelsea expected Jacqui to ask to live with her, and already thought it was a good idea. Jacqui's past invited drama and although she seemed to have matured, Chelsea wasn't so sure.

"I was going to suggest it if you didn't."

Jacqui threw her arms around Chelsea's neck.

"You're the best. Thank you so much. Well, I better get out of this skirt and get over to the inn. I'm sure Maggie will want to explain what my duties are. I'll drive to my parents' place later and pick up my things. This is so exciting."

"Whoa, slow down. It can wait until tomorrow. Give the woman a chance to get caught up. I'll see Maggie in the morning and will tell her that you'll stop by sometime in the afternoon. How does that sound?"

"Oh, of course, you're right. I'm just anxious to get started. Since I've got nothing to do, maybe you can tell me what's been going on around here. Since I left for school, I haven't really talked to anyone except my brother, Trevor, and he's no help. All he talks about is his family. I mean, Noah, Sophia and little Maggie are adorable, but I want a bit of gossip and he's useless in that department."

"Oh, and you think I'm any better? What makes you think that I have any knowledge of things you'd be interested in?"

"I don't know. Why don't you update me and we'll see? For instance, I know about Maggie and her cancer. I hope she's doing better."

Chelsea didn't feel it right to share Maggie's personal struggles with her treatments.

"Maggie is great. I'm sure she appreciates you asking about her."

"Paolo and his sister seem well. What's going on with Ciara? I think I heard something about some guy coming over from Italy to see her."

Chelsea laughed. "That didn't work out. He wasn't the right guy for her. I'm so happy that she's seeing Crawford Powell now. They make a lovely couple."

"Crawford Powell? Isn't he the owner of Powell Water Sports?"

Chelsea knew exactly where this conversation was headed. If

she wasn't so amused by the whole thing, she'd move on to another subject, but instead, she decided to play along.

"Yes, that's right. It's just down the street. I'm sure you know the place."

"Oh, yes. I do remember seeing it. Wasn't that his son that I met the other day? What was his name? Finn, I think?"

"Yup. Finn and his brothers, Joshua and Luke, also work at the store. Ciara's been helping out as well. They have a sister too but she's up in Boston going to medical school. She's engaged to Maggie's son, Christopher."

"Oh, that's exciting. I love weddings. They're so romantic, especially ones on the beach. Don't you think?"

Chelsea tried her best to keep from laughing out loud. She continued to let Jacqui talk while she secured a new canvas on her easel. She planned to get in some painting the next day.

"You're not working with watercolor anymore?" Jacqui asked.

"Not lately. I've been working with oils. Maybe this summer you can join me and we can paint together like the old days."

Jacqui nodded. "I'd love that, Chelsea, thank you. Anyway, I guess I'll watch something on tv. Thanks again for recommending me for the job at the inn. I'm so excited, I can hardly stand it."

In Chelsea's opinion, cleaning rooms at the inn couldn't be described as exciting. There was only one reason for Jacqui's reaction, and that reason was Finn Powell.

As Jacqui moved into the living room to watch a reality show on tv, Chelsea wondered how long it would be before Jacqui admitted her interest in Finn Powell.

However long it took, Chelsea would go along until it was necessary to get involved. Jacqui wasn't known for making the best choices and although she didn't know Finn very well, something in her gut told her a train wreck was about to happen right before her eyes. She knew enough about Jacqui to know that manufactured drama was surely right around the corner.

Isabella Barlowe needed more than Chelsea's approval, she needed female friends. She had several close friendships in France, but on Captiva Island she knew no one. Get togethers with Sebastian's friends in the last few weeks was a start, but she needed something of her own.

She searched online for book clubs, women's groups, and Captiva events but there was little on the island that interested her. She'd have to travel off-island if she was going to find "her people".

Frustrated, she closed her laptop and sighed. Designed for tourists and part-time residents, there was little to do past ten o'clock at night on Captiva island. The quiet was unsettling. She'd been used to staying up late and socializing until the early morning hours.

"How was your day, my love?" Sebastian asked.

"Sans incidents," she answered.

"English Isabella. You need to practice more and perfect the inflection."

"Ah, oui, yes. English is such a difficult language to understand. There are so many contradictions, I don't know why everyone isn't confused all the time."

Sebastian laughed, and Isabella shrugged.

"So, for today, I had nothing on my calendar. I was thinking of going for a walk but I did that early this morning and then I was immediately bored."

"Bored? How can that be? Captiva is a beautiful island, don't you agree?"

"Yes, of course. It is beautiful, but unless I want to go swimming in the ocean or spend the day collecting seashells, there is nothing to do. In Paris, I slept until noon and then in the afternoon I would meet friends in the café and then at night we would be out again enjoying music and dancing. Here, everyone goes inside their home and won't come out again until morning. What kind of life is this?"

Isabella didn't want to hurt Sebastian's feelings but she needed to find a way to live in his world while they were in Florida. Soon enough they would return to Paris, but until then, searching for like-minded women friends was crucial.

Sebastian leaned on one of his crutches to lower himself into his wheelchair. He put his hand on Isabella's face and kissed her.

"I have work to do. I'll be in the study. Take the car and go for a ride. You know how to get on and off the island. You've seen Captiva and Sanibel, maybe it's time you look around off-island. There is always live music somewhere nearby."

Isabella nodded. "Au revoir, mon amour."

She watched Sebastian wheel himself across the white marbled floor and into his office. She thought about his suggestion to drive off the island but didn't want to do that alone.

Isabella wondered if Chelsea might join her. Their first meeting seemed to break the ice between them. There was something about the woman that made Isabella believe they had more in common than having loved the same man.

She grabbed the car keys and threw them into her purse. It was time to find out more about Chelsea Marsden and, if she could, help Sebastian's ex to find new adventures beyond Captiva Island.

Chelsea opened the door and found Isabella Barlowe standing in front of her with two bottles of wine…one in each hand.

"Bonsoir, Chelsea. You see, I have come with gifts."

Chelsea smiled. "I see that. Won't you come inside?"

Isabella shook her head. "No. You must come outside…with me."

Chelsea turned to look at Jacqui who was sound asleep on the sofa.

"It's rather late," she whispered.

"No. It is not. You only think that it is. In truth, it is early."

Confused and not wanting to insult Isabella, she tried again. "Isabella, thank you so much for coming by, but maybe tomorrow or the next day we could…"

Isabella wouldn't let her finish her sentence.

"Chelsea Marsden, am I to understand that you are refusing your new friend? I didn't think you would be so rude. Now, come. Get your things and let's go."

"Go? Where?"

"I have a place I have found that is perfect. Trust me. Get your things."

Unable to dissuade Isabella, Chelsea agreed.

"All right. Wait here and I'll be right back."

She reached for her cell phone and ran upstairs to change into a pair of jeans and throw a pashmina scarf over her t-shirt. Then, she dialed Maggie's cell phone.

"Hey, what are you doing calling me at ten o'clock at night? Is everything all right?"

Whispering, Chelsea pleaded with Maggie. "Isabella is here. She's out on the porch with two bottles of wine and she wants me to go with her someplace. I have no idea where she's taking me, but I'm not going alone. You have to come with me."

"What? Are you crazy? I'm not going out at this hour," Maggie insisted.

"Hey, remember me? Your ride or die friend? I need you, so

get yourself together because we're coming over in about five minutes."

Chelsea hung up the phone and looked in the mirror. She put on her favorite sterling silver drop earrings and tousled her wavy hair. She rubbed on a dab of lip gloss on her lips and then grabbed her cross-body handbag. She returned to the first floor and wrote a note for Jacqui before meeting Isabella on the porch.

"Can I ask where we're headed?" Chelsea asked.

"One of the most important aspects of friendship is trust. I want you to trust me, otherwise what's the point?"

Chelsea certainly agreed with the concept, but where Isabella was concerned, Chelsea wasn't sure what she believed.

"Turn here," Chelsea insisted. "If you want friends, then you have to include my best friend, Maggie. If she doesn't go then neither do I."

Isabella turned into the Key Lime Garden Inn driveway and watched Chelsea get out of the car.

"Where the heck is she? I told her to be ready in five minutes."

"Perhaps she doesn't want to come with us," Isabella said.

Chelsea picked up a small rock and threw it at Maggie's window.

Maggie opened the window and whispered, "What is wrong with you? I'm coming."

Chelsea turned to Isabella. "She's coming."

"I heard," Isabella responded.

When Maggie reached the driveway, she pointed a finger at Chelsea. "We're not in high school you know. You act as if we're sneaking out in the middle of the night."

Chelsea didn't say a word, instead waited for her friend to calm down. After a few seconds she turned to look at Isabella.

"This is my best friend, Maggie Moretti. Maggie, this is Isabella Barlowe, Sebastian's wife."

"My pleasure," Isabella said. "I've heard much about you."

Maggie smiled. "Oh? I hope it was all terrible, that way you

won't be surprised when you see me lose my temper at Chelsea."
She then glared at Chelsea before walking to the car. "Well,
where are we going?" Maggie asked.

"I tried that. Don't bother. She won't tell you," Chelsea
answered.

"We don't need the car," Isabella said as she opened the back
door of the vehicle, pulling three glasses and three bottles of wine
and a large blanket from the backseat."

"How did you know there'd be three of us, and where did this
third bottle come from?" Chelsea asked.

Handing Chelsea and Maggie a bottle of wine and a glass,
Isabella answered, "I didn't. I have four glasses and four bottles.
You never know who you might meet along the way."

"Oh, I like this woman," Maggie said.

"Good, I think I like you too. So, Maggie Moretti, you lead the
way to the beach. If Sebastian's accounting of the area is correct,
there should be one around here, right?"

"We're surrounded by ocean, Isabella. I'm pretty sure I can
find one for us. Follow me," Maggie instructed.

The three women walked along the path through the garden
and down to the sandy shore. So that they wouldn't disturb
guests from the inn or surrounding cottages, Maggie walked to
the left and led Isabella and Chelsea toward the tall lifeguard
chair.

They each took a corner of the blanket and laid it on the
ground. Isabella pulled a corkscrew from her bag and opened a
bottle.

"Let me guess, you've brought French wine?" Maggie asked.

"Of course. There is no other wine," Isabella answered.

"California has some good wine," Chelsea said.

It was as if Isabella had been handed the ultimate insult.

"Listen to me, ladies. If we are to be good friends, then you
will have to trust me on this. First, you must swirl the wine in the
glass, then smell the wine. Bring the glass to your nose and take a

deep sniff. Inhale the aromas and recognize the different scents. Then, take a small sip and allow the wine to coat your mouth. Pay attention to the initial flavors and let me know what you think."

Chelsea had no idea if there was a wrong or right answer to her response. All she knew was that the wine was delicious and said so.

"It's wonderful. I don't think I'll ever drink wine the same way again. What do you think, Maggie?"

"I agree. I can sense sweetness and the taste of apricot."

"Wonderful. You both are experiencing wine for the first time. I'm sure you'll agree with me."

Neither Chelsea nor Maggie wanted to upset Isabella by disagreeing with her. They'd both had plenty of delicious California wine, however Isabella was right about the amazing French wine. The entire wine-drinking experience matched the excitement of the night.

"Thank you, Isabella. I needed this. I was ready to turn in for the night and never would have considered going out if you and your partner in crime here didn't kidnap me."

Chelsea laughed. "Maggie's right. People who live on the island don't usually go out this time of night. It's a shame because look at that moon."

"I hope the three of us do this more often. So what if others don't go out at night? It doesn't mean that we can't."

Isabella looked up at the sky. "After all, if we didn't come here we would have missed such a night."

Chelsea gazed at Isabella, captivated by the radiance emanating from her face. Despite the late hour, Isabella's eyes shimmered, gleaming with vitality. Turning her attention to Maggie, Chelsea found a warm smile directed at her. In that moment, they shared an unspoken understanding—a serendipitous encounter with a kindred soul.

CHAPTER 15

The smell of cranberry-orange scones wafted through the kitchen of the Key Lime Garden Inn. Maggie made sure there were plenty for the guests but also for Paolo and Chelsea who just happened to join her in the kitchen.

"I'm headed out to the garden, but I need one of your scones for energy," Paolo said.

Laughing at her husband, Maggie offered two. "Here, take two, just in case you feel faint."

"I need energy too, Mags. Hand them over before the guests get some," Chelsea said.

Paolo kissed Maggie and pushed the screen door with his foot. "See you ladies later."

"How's your head this morning?" Maggie asked Chelsea.

"Surprisingly, fine. Maybe it's the difference between French wine and California wine. I have no idea, but I didn't get my usual wine headache either. How about you?"

"Same. I'm no expert on wine, but I'm feeling great this morning. I didn't get that many hours of sleep and, yet, I've got energy to spare. I wonder how many other secrets of youth Isabella has. The woman exudes joie de vivre."

"Oh, now you're speaking French?"

Maggie laughed. "You know what I mean. There's a vibrancy to her—a sort of sparkle…a bit of pizzazz."

"Oh, for heaven's sake. All right, I grant you that she sparkles all over the place, but you're starting to worry me that she'll take my place as your new best friend."

Maggie filled Chelsea's coffee cup and then her own.

"Hardly. You're not exactly the kind of friend who is easily replaced."

"I'm glad to hear it. I like Isabella but if she took you away from me, I'd have to hate her. Anyway, have you heard anything from Michael?"

Maggie nodded. "Yes, I just got off the phone with him. He's going home from the hospital today. Isn't that wonderful?"

"That's fantastic news. Being home will help him heal faster."

"Absolutely. Brea and the kids are over the moon. The girls decorated the house with all kinds of artwork and I think they got a welcome home cake too. Lauren and Jeff were going over there this afternoon and then I think the rest of the clan will stop by. It's a regular party. I'm only sorry I can't be there, but they plan to video me in."

"So, listen, I spoke with Jacqui yesterday and she plans to come by this afternoon to meet with you and go over her responsibilities. She's really excited about working here, at least for the summer."

"Excited? I would have thought a young girl like that would rather party or spend the summer at the beach with friends, not clean guest rooms."

"I told you why she's excited to spend her summer on the island."

"Oh, right. Finn Powell. Well, I'm glad to have the help, but as far as Finn goes, he doesn't come around here at all. How does she plan to run into him?"

Chelsea laughed at Maggie. "Are you kidding me? That girl

has a million sneaky ways. It's just her personality. I think of all the members of the Hutchins family, she's the one who gives them the most headaches."

Maggie shook her head. "Oh, I don't know about that. Trevor's brother Clayton has been a real problem over the years. Somehow he and Trevor found a way to work together and get along, but it took a long time. I've always felt that Jacqui uses getting into trouble as a way to get attention."

"Yeah, well I think their father, Devon, hasn't made things easy on any of them."

"Do you think I should warn Ciara? I mean, she and Crawford are probably going to get married one of these days and Finn will be her step-son."

Chelsea shook her head. "I wouldn't get involved, at least not right now. Nothing has happened yet and it's possible that nothing will. Although, where Jacqui is concerned, I may have to eat my words."

Jacqui could have waited for fate to run its course, but it wasn't her style to leave anything to chance. Instead, she decided to stop by Powell Water Sports before heading to the Key Lime Garden Inn.

The store was crowded and she didn't see Finn anywhere. She pretended to look at the diving equipment in the hope that he'd show up eventually.

"Hey, can I help you?" a young man asked.

Disappointed to see that the sales clerk was someone other than Finn Powell, Jillian shook her head barely acknowledging him.

"No, thanks. I'm just looking. I meant to shop for stuff before I came to the island, but then I saw your store."

"Oh, you're looking for something for yourself?" Joshua Powell asked, his smile almost a smirk.

"Yes, that's right," she answered.

"Well, then, you'll want to be on the other side of the store because these are dry suits for men."

Embarrassed that she'd been caught lying, she tried to cover her mistake.

"I know that. I was also looking for my boyfriend."

"Uh-huh," he responded. "How long are you visiting Captiva?"

His arrogance annoying her, she answered, "Why do you want to know?"

"Because maybe you and I could dive together. That is, if your boyfriend isn't here or wouldn't mind."

Jillian looked at him. "What makes you think my boyfriend isn't here?"

Joshua shrugged. "Just a hunch. Hey, I'm sorry, I should have introduced myself. I'm Joshua Powell."

"As in Powell Water Sports."

"One and the same. And, you are?"

"Leaving," she answered and turned to walk out of the store. Just then, Finn walked to the register.

Jillian smiled his way, "Oh, hello. It's Finn, right?"

Finn looked at Jacqui but didn't seem to recognize her at first.

"We met the other day at the Key Lime Garden Inn? I'm Jacqui Hutchins, Trevor's sister."

"Oh, right. Yeah. Hi. Nice to see you again. Did Joshua help you find what you were looking for?"

Jacqui didn't acknowledge Joshua. "I'm all set. I've got to get to the inn. I'm working there now, so I'll probably see you around this summer."

"I'm sure. It's a small island," Finn answered, smiling at her. "Have a great day and say hello to Mrs. Moretti."

"I will."

Finn walked to the back of the store, and Joshua took his opportunity to tease her once more.

"Yes, Jacqui. Have a nice day."

———

Maggie sat on the back porch swing sipping a glass of iced tea when Jacqui came up the steps to the porch.

"Hello, Mrs. Moretti. I don't know if you remember me, but…"

"Yes, of course, Jacqui. Come on over here and sit for a spell. Chelsea tells me that you're here for the summer and want to work at the inn."

"I do. That is, if you'll hire me," she answered.

"Consider yourself hired. We can go inside in a minute and go over what I need you to do, but first why don't you tell me more about you and how school has been. Would you like a glass of iced tea?"

"No, thank you," she answered as she joined Maggie on the porch swing.

"School's been great. I'm learning a lot but of course, I'm enjoying the social aspect of it as well. Doesn't every student go through that?"

Maggie nodded. "All my kids did, I can tell you that. I think Freshman students, particularly, think of partying as one of their required courses. Although my kids went to college right after high school which speaks to some immaturity. Not that I'm implying that you're immature."

Jacqui laughed. "Oh, I don't claim to be mature. I think just because I went to college a bit later than my friends doesn't necessarily mean I missed my partying days. Let's just say, I'm participating in the entire college experience."

Maggie smiled at Jacqui's words. "I was surprised that you wouldn't want to spend the summer having fun instead of working. Do you mind me asking what made you want to work here at the inn?"

Maggie knew full well what motivated Jacqui, but she wanted to see how the young woman would spin the reason for her choice.

"I'll be honest with you, Mrs. Moretti…"

"Call me, Maggie, please."

Jacqui nodded. "Okay, I'll be honest with you, Maggie. It's because of a guy."

Maggie didn't expect such a truthful response.

"A guy? Explain that one to me."

"His name is Finn Powell. I think you know him."

"I do, indeed. How did the two of you meet?"

"I just met him the other day, right here at the inn. I understand that his father is dating Ciara Moretti."

"That's right. Tell me, does Finn know about your feelings for him? I mean, the two of you just met."

"I know. Crazy, right? No, he has no idea. I just figured that if I'm working and living on the island for the summer, he and I might get a chance to get to know each other."

Maggie nodded. "That makes sense, although I have to tell you that there is little here on the island for nightlife. If the two of you are working every day, I'm not sure how the two of you will get together."

"Oh, no worries. I can make that happen, no sweat."

Remembering Chelsea's words and now listening to Jacqui, Maggie had no doubt that by the end of the summer, Finn Powell and Jacqui Hutchins would be a couple.

"Well, I never question my employees' motivation for working here. I'm just glad to have the help. We've been especially busy this season and I don't see it slowing down anytime soon. How about we go inside and I can get all your information and we can go over your responsibilities?"

Jacqui jumped up from the swing. "Sounds good. Lead on."

Maggie smiled to herself thinking of the drama this young girl would bring to the island. She was certain that whatever Jacqui Hutchins set her mind to, she'd make it happen. Her only concern was Finn Powell. She didn't know much about the young man except to hear Ciara speak of Crawford's boys.

Last Maggie heard, Joshua Powell was the island's playboy, Luke Powell was in a long-term committed relationship, and Finn Powell was a kind, hard-working young man with pensive and quite ways. He sounded like the perfect guy to date anyone other than Jacqui Hutchins.

Chelsea was right. This very well could be a train wreck of a situation.

CHAPTER 16

*B*rea's car pulled up in front of her house and she turned to look at Michael.

"We're here. How are you doing?"

Michael smiled and nodded. "I'm fine. It's going to be great."

"All right then, let's get you inside."

She came around to the passenger side of the car as Jeff ran outside to greet them.

"Let me help you," he said.

"I'm good. I've got it," Michael replied.

Neighbors came of their homes to witness the return of Officer Michael Wheeler, and clapped as he leaned on Brea and Jeff for support heading up the walkway.

Michael turned and waved, thanking them, and then continued into the house where the entire family waited for him.

"Daddy!" Olivia and Lilly yelled in unison.

They ran to Michael and wrapped their arms around his legs. Lauren brought Jackson to Michael so that the little boy could hug his father.

"Hey, kids. I've missed you."

"We missed you, too," Lilly said.

Laughing, Brea stood next to an overstuffed chair. "Michael, sit here and let everyone come to you instead of the other way around."

"Good idea," he answered. "It wouldn't do if I fell over onto the floor my first day home."

Once settled, the children ran to get gifts they had made for him.

"I wrapped it myself," Lilly said.

"You did? I can't wait to see what's inside."

Michael opened Lilly's gift first. Layers of colorful paper wedged between two thicker carboard-like sheets to look like a sandwich with the words, "You're My Hero" written on top made Michael laugh.

"This is perfect. You made me a Hero Sandwich."

Cora nodded and was happy that she'd pleased her father.

"I'm next," Olivia said.

"Did you wrap your gift too?" Michael asked.

"No. Mom did it. I wanted it to look professional."

Michael looked up at Brea and smiled. "Well, Mom did a great job. Let's see what's inside. It's really heavy."

A box filled with black rocks painted white on top with colorful words written on each one. The box too, was black with white letters on the front that read, My Dad Is... Michael read the words on the rocks. "Hero, Brave, Smart, Loving..." He looked at Olivia. "Thank you sweetie, this is really lovely."

"It's really from me and Jackson. Jackson's too young to write so I told him the present can be from both of us."

"That was very kind of you to include your brother. Come here all three of you and let me give you a big hug."

Lauren bent down to give Jackson a chance to be included in the group hug.

"They couldn't wait for you to get home and see your presents," Brea said.

"Michael, what can I get you? Would you like a beer?" Jeff asked.

"Actually, no. Do we have anything non-alcoholic? How about a ginger ale?"

"One ginger ale coming up."

Michael was glad to be home, and happy to see his family, but he was tired and wondered how long he'd be able to stay sitting up.

"Dad, we got pizza. Your favorite," Olivia said.

"Oh boy. Would you get me a slice?"

Olivia seemed excited to play waitress to her father. She and her sister didn't leave Michael's side.

Beth sat in the chair across from Michael. "It's so great to have you home. How does it feel?" she asked.

"Surreal. A few weeks ago I was going off to work without a care in the world. I had no idea what the day would bring. I'm just glad I survived. We're very blessed that my partner didn't get shot. So, now, here I am."

He took a sip of his ginger ale. Gabriel sat on the arm of Beth's chair.

"You know, I'm not sure I formally congratulated the two of you. I'm thrilled to hear that you guys are getting married."

"Thanks, Michael," Beth said. "We're getting ready to go back to California to see Gabriel's parents. We're going to do a mock wedding so his mother can see us get married. She doesn't need to know that it isn't real. It just needs to be real for her."

Michael looked at Gabriel whose face seemed troubled. "I'm sorry, that your mother is struggling."

"I think it's harder on everyone around her. The tough part for me is learning to meet her where she is. No one tells you about this. In the beginning you want everything to be as it was. Eventually, you understand that can't happen. If she looks outside on a sunny day and says it's raining, then we nod and agree with her. That's a small thing, but you get what I'm saying."

Michael nodded. "I do get it. I've heard others talk about family members who have Alzheimer's disease, and they say the same thing. Try to adjust to the new normal."

Christopher and Becca joined them.

"Are you getting tired of people asking you how it feels to be home?"

"Well, I've only had one person ask so far."

"Good. I'll be the second. How does it feel?"

Michael laughed at his brother. Christopher loved to tease everyone in the family and Michael normally had the energy to give it right back, but not this morning.

"The truth? I don't think I'll be able to stay at the party too long. I already feel wiped out."

Brea overheard Michael. "Do you want to rest in the bedroom for a while? We're going to call Mom and Sarah at noon."

"Oh, man. I'll never make it until noon. Yeah, why don't you all enjoy the party while I take a nap? Wake me up when you're ready to call them."

Michael hated the concerned look on Brea's face. It bothered him that he felt compelled to keep his complaints to a minimum. Looks of pity and sympathy were everywhere, and he felt certain that people were staring and judging him. These thoughts kept his heart racing and a permanent sweat on his brow.

"It's awfully loud in here, isn't it?" he asked.

"We'll keep the noise down, honey. Don't worry. You'll be able to rest. Let's go."

Brea let Michael steady himself. He realized that she was trying not to hover, but he accepted there was no way he could walk to the bedroom without her.

She unlaced his sneakers and removed them, placing his slippers beside the bed in their place.

Once in bed, he watched Brea close the door. He didn't need to hear the exact words spoken in the living room. The muffled voices reached his ears and his mind went into overdrive.

They're talking about poor Michael. What a shame to see him so vulnerable. What's going to happen to him? He'll never be the same.

The voices played over in his head. He placed his hands over his ears to mute the sounds. He wanted to cry, to scream and so he did, only no one could hear him because no sound came from his throat.

When it was close to noon, Brea decided that it was time to get Michael out of bed.

"I should have given him his pain meds before he took his nap," Brea said, handing Christopher a beer. "I'm so worried about him."

"You and me both. I haven't said a word to anyone, but the other day he called me when I was at work and asked me to come to the hospital. He'd been having nightmares and needed to talk."

"What? Chris!" Beth said. "Why didn't you say anything?"

"I was going to tell you all. I didn't want to say anything at the time because Mom and Sarah were still here. You know if Mom knew what he was going through, there's no way she would have flown home to Captiva."

"What exactly did he say to you?" Brea asked.

Christopher shrugged. "We just talked about how difficult it was for him and how he was afraid to go to sleep at night because of the nightmares. He wanted to talk to me because of what I went through in Iraq."

"What did you tell him?" Lauren asked joining the conversation.

"I told him that he needed to talk to someone, you know, a professional. I gave him my experience and we talked extensively about that, but I explained that the best thing I could ever have done was to seek help."

"Did he agree to see a therapist?" Brea asked.

"He seemed to think it was a good idea. He said that his supervisor gave him the name of someone to talk to. I don't know who that is but you should ask him."

Brea plopped down on the sofa. "Great. Exactly how am I going to do that? I can't tell him that I know the two of you talked. I'm assuming he wanted that kept private, which I want to respect."

"Maybe I can help," Gabriel said.

Everyone turned to look at him. "You?" Beth asked. "Why do you think you can help Michael?"

"Because I'm seeing a therapist," he answered.

The shocked look on Beth's face indicated that she knew nothing of this news.

"You are? Why didn't you tell me?" she asked.

Gabriel shrugged. "I don't know. I guess I would have eventually, but I felt like keeping it to myself for a while. There's nothing wrong with that, is there?"

Everyone shook their heads as Beth tried to lighten the awkward moment.

"No. Not at all. I think it's great that you're seeing someone. Maybe you *can* help Michael."

"Well, right now what we have to do is get him out of bed and into the dining room. Becca has set up the iMac on the table so Maggie and Sarah can see us all," Brea said.

"Chelsea is joining them. Maggie just sent me a text," Becca said.

Brea opened the door to the bedroom and tiptoed toward the bed. Michael was fast asleep and she hated to wake him, but it was time.

"Michael, honey, it's time for the video. Do you need help getting up?"

He stirred under the covers and lowered his legs to the side of the bed.

"If you can grab my arms and pull me up, that would help."

Brea did as Michael asked and waited for him to feel ready to stand.

"It's always hard the first moments getting from a lying down position to a sitting one. Then, it takes a few minutes to go from sitting to standing. I miss the days when I hopped out of bed. I want those days back."

"You'll see them again. Rehab is hard, but you'll get there," Brea said.

He slid into his slippers and then let Brea help him stand. They walked out of the bedroom and into the dining room where a seat was ready for him.

"Hey guys, sorry to be such a wet blanket. I hope you all didn't eat all the food, especially the cake. I'm starving."

"First you have to say hello to me, young man." Maggie's voice came from the monitor on the table.

"Hey, Mom. I'm finally home."

"I see that. Congratulations, sweetie. You'll get better faster now. No one ever gets enough rest in a hospital. Chelsea and Sarah are here, Trevor and the kids too."

Maggie moved her laptop to the left so that he could see the others.

"Hey, Trevor. Long time no see," Michael said.

"Hey, Michael. I'm glad to see you're up and about. I'll get up to Massachusetts one of these days. Better yet, you get well enough to fly on a plane and come down here. If you want to heal, there no better place than sitting by the ocean and eating fresh-caught fish every day."

"Yeah, not to mention, Mom would spoil you rotten," Sarah added.

"Hey, I might take you up on that offer. I could use a vacation under the Florida sun," Michael answered. "It's good to see you again, Chelsea. I take it you're keeping out of trouble?"

"Are you kidding me? No way. Trouble is where the fun's at," Chelsea responded.

Everyone enjoyed the light banter and spent the next thirty minutes talking about everything under the sun. The children shared what was new in their world and after the video call, the rest of his family enjoyed time together until two o'clock.

Michael did his best to remain engaged and happy but he was glad when the party ended and everyone went to their respective homes.

He knew there would be plenty more days like this. His family refused to be absent during major events or difficulties in each other's lives, but it was that very nature of closeness that was suffocating him. He didn't know how to tell them to back off and leave him to find his way on his own.

Eventually, he'd find a way because if he didn't, he might say or do something that would cause tremendous pain, not just to himself but to those he loved most in the world.

What was most evident was that his world looked different to him. He anticipated the uphill struggle that was before him and was acutely aware that he lacked the will to fight.

He couldn't explain his feelings to anyone. Intense fear gripped his body and except for the fact that he had a family who depended upon his recovery, the urge to crawl back in bed and stay there was overpowering.

With tears in his eyes, Michael looked at Brea and believed that she deserved better than him. How long before his wife came to the same conclusion weighed on his heart. He prayed for an end to this pain one way or the other.

CHAPTER 17

*L*auren sat at her kitchen table looking at the clock. It was nine-thirty in the morning in both Massachusetts and Florida. Grateful to be in the same time zone, she dialed her mother's cell phone.

"Hey, honey. It's so nice to hear your voice. Is everything all right?"

"You know, Mom, until I had children, I always wondered why you asked that question whenever I called your cell phone."

"Well, let's not forget that you kids seem to have forgotten how to talk on the phone. It's always texts with you guys. You're not as bad as my other children though. So, I'll ask again. Is everything all right?"

"Yes, we're all fine. It was good to have everyone together for Michael's return. I had to drive Grandma home before the party ended though. She had to run over to see Mr. Peabody. I know the man has dementia, but I still think there's a little romance in Grandma's mind."

"Whatever makes her happy," Maggie responded.

"Mom, I wanted to call you this morning to say good luck at your first radiation appointment today. I realize no one said a word about it yesterday as they were all focused on Michael, but I didn't want you to think that we aren't thinking of you and what you're about to go through."

"Oh, honey, that's very sweet of you. I appreciate it. I appreciate all of my kids. You know what I plan to do today? I'm going to think of how lucky I am to have such great kids and an amazing husband. That will get me through."

"Do you know what they'll do today? Is it more preparation or is it the actual radiation?"

"No radiation today. They call it a simulation appointment. The way the doctor explained it to me, they'll give me some tattoos."

"What? What do you mean tattoos?"

Maggie laughed. "That's what I'm calling it. They write on my body with this marker and then I think he said something about making a form of my upper body behind my head and back so that when I go for the radiation I won't move around. Sounds like I'll be all snug as a bug in a rug."

Lauren knew her mother was trying to make light of the situation.

"How fun. Sounds like everyone should get radiation," Lauren said sarcastically.

"Well, maybe it won't be all fun and games, but I'm not worried. I won't feel anything. I am a little worried about neuropathy in my hands or feet when all this is over, but maybe I'll get lucky and not have any side effects."

"I'm sure everything will go well. Promise me that you'll call me after your appointment? I want to hear how it went."

"I promise, honey. I have to go now, though. Paolo and I have an hour's drive to get there. Thank you for calling me. I Love you."

"Love you, too, Mom."

Lauren was proud of her mother, who had consistently demonstrated her ability to rise to any challenge.

Reflecting on Maggie's journey, Lauren couldn't help but wonder if she would possess the same resilience and fortitude if faced with the same burdens her mother had endured.

She vowed to learn from her mother's example so that she might share the same spirit, determination, and inspiration with her daughters, Quinn and Cora.

"Do you have everything?" Paolo asked Maggie.

"Yup. I'm ready to go."

The walked down to the car as Sarah pulled her truck into the driveway. Taking care not to block Paolo's car, Sarah parked the truck next to it and got out.

"Oh, I'm so glad I caught you before you left. I just wanted to give you a hug and say good luck with your first appointment."

"How sweet. Isn't that sweet, Paolo?"

Paolo smiled and nodded. "It's sweet all right."

He got into his car and waited for Maggie and Sarah to finish their conversation.

"Honey, we really have to go. Thank you for the support though."

She hugged Sarah and got into the car. Sarah put up her hand to stop them from leaving. Maggie rolled down the window. "What is it?"

"Don't forget to call me when you get home. I want to hear everything about your treatment," Sarah said.

"Okay. I will." Maggie rolled the window back up and put the air conditioning on. They were barely out of the driveway when Beth called.

"Hey, Beth. How's my girl?"

"I'm great, thanks. I just wanted to call and wish you good luck today. I know it's a big day. Is Paolo driving you?"

"Yes, honey. We're in the car right now on our way."

"Oh, I won't keep you. Give me a call when you get back. I want to hear how it went. Say hello to Paolo. I'll talk to you later. Bye."

Maggie ended the call and looked at Paolo.

"Have you ever in your life seen such behavior? These girls barely got in touch when I started chemo. What the heck is going on?"

Paolo shook his head. "No idea. Maybe Michael getting shot really scared them that any one of us could be gone in a heart-beat. I don't know, but if I were you, I wouldn't complain about it. Most parents aren't as lucky as we are."

Maggie settled into the leather seat and closed her eyes. She knew exactly how blessed she was to have such a loving family to support her. She smiled thinking how silly she was to bemoan her good fortune and tried to relax and focus on her breathing.

Meditation was fast becoming Maggie's new favorite self-love quiet time practice. Since chemotherapy, she'd learned several new ways of relaxing and planned to study more.

She hadn't mentioned anything to Chelsea, but taking Zumba dance classes was next on her list, followed by pickleball, and she wanted her friend to join her. Knowing Chelsea, she'd probably complain about the exercise and refuse several times before finally agreeing.

When they arrived at the hospital, Maggie kissed Paolo. "It's going to probably be almost two hours before I'm done. You really should get lunch or go for a walk. Get some fresh air."

"Sweetheart, I get fresh air all day, every day. I think I'll sit right here and read a book. I never have time to do that. If I'm hungry, I know where the cafeteria is. I'll be fine," he answered.

Maggie nodded.

"Maggie Moretti?"

A cheerful nurse looked at her.

"Yes, that's me."

She squeezed Paolo's hand and then followed the nurse down the hall remembering her deep breathing and visualizations. She would get through the next two hours with images of the sand between her toes and the warm breezes of her Captiva Island.

———

"Are you all packed?" Gabriel asked Beth.

"Almost done. I'm glad you decided to stay here tonight instead of your place. Traffic to Logan airport in the morning can be brutal from your place."

"You should have seen me say goodbye to Charlie. He acted as though he was never going to see me again. I think our last trip to California traumatized him. Now, he has separation anxiety. I feel guilty for leaving my dog again."

"You know what that tells me? That you don't travel enough," Beth said.

"You're probably right. I'm sure you plan to change all that?"

"Yup. I love traveling and there's so many places I want to see," she said.

"I'd love to pack up and go around the world with you my love, but there's a little thing called money that we have to earn. Makes it hard to travel without it."

Christopher and Becca arrived home from brunch in Boston.

"I see you guys are ready for California," Christopher said.

"How was brunch, where did you go?" Beth asked.

"So good. We went to Cafe Landwer in Brookline. We had Halloumi Shakshouka," Becca said.

"You had what? I don't think I can even pronounce that," Gabriel said.

"It's basically poached eggs capped with crispy halloumi cheese and spinach, smothered with tomato sauce and tahini. You've got to try it."

Gabriel's face scrunched up and shook his head. "I don't think I can wrap my head around tomato sauce and tahini together."

Becca looked at Christopher and then at Beth and Gabriel. "And then…"

Christopher finished Becca's sentence. "And then we went to a couple of Open Houses."

Beth's mouth dropped open. "No way. You guys are looking to buy a house?"

Becca nodded. "Yup. We've been talking about it for a while but hadn't settled on when exactly to start looking. I think it makes sense. You and Gabriel will be getting married and will want your privacy and we do as well."

"What? Wait, you guys. I'm moving north to live at Gabriel's place in the fall. It's never fun to move in the winter, so…"

"You're kidding me," Christopher said. "Why didn't you say anything before?"

Beth shrugged. "I don't know. It just never came up. We've all been dealing with so much lately, it got put on the backburner. It makes sense though. Gabriel's entire woodworking business is there as well as the house. Acres of land and a huge barn where he does his furniture making is not exactly something you can move, so I'm going there. You guys should stay here."

"It does make sense, Chris. I don't know why we didn't consider it. What do you think?" Becca asked.

"We'll have to talk to Mom. I don't know what she wants to do with the house."

"The house is mortgage-free, Mom owns it free and clear," Beth said. "If you and Becca want to live here, then you'll have to ask her about it. My guess is that she won't expect you to buy it.

Knowing Mom, she'll tell you to live here for as long as you want."

"I'm going to have a rather large student loan to pay when I get out, Chris. It does make good financial sense if your mother will agree."

Christopher shrugged. "I guess it all depends on whether she needs the money. I honestly don't know. She's not the type to share her financial situation with her children, but in this case, I think we better have that conversation."

"I agree," Beth said. "In the meantime, who wants pizza for dinner tonight, because there is no way I'm cooking anything. We leave pretty early for the airport tomorrow."

"Don't talk to me about food right now. I'm still full from the Halloumi Shakshouka," Christopher said.

"By the way," Beth announced. "I'm waiting to hear from Mom. She should be calling soon. She had her first radiation appointment today."

"Oh, that's right. She shouldn't have had a difficult time of it though. The first appointment is just a simulation. She won't have had any radiation today."

Beth's phone buzzed.

"It's Mom," she said. "Hey, how did it go?"

"Everything was exactly as the doctor said. No treatment today. I go back in four days for radiation. Do me a favor, Beth. Will you please call Lauren and Sarah and tell them what I've told you? They made me promise to call them after my appointment and give them a blow-by-blow but truthfully, I'm exhausted and need a nap."

"Of course. Are you sure you're okay?"

"Yes, I'm fine. Just do me that favor, please. I love you all, but I can't recite the same thing over and over. Not when I'm craving a nice late lunch and nap."

"Will do. Gabe and I are headed out early tomorrow morning for California, so I'll say my goodbyes for now. I'll be in touch."

"Thank you, honey. Give my love to Gabriel and you have a safe trip. I love you."

"Love you, too, Mom. Take care."

Beth ended the call and then looked at Becca. "Everything went just as you said. Only a simulation. She wants me to call Sarah and Lauren to tell them as well. I might as well call Brea and let them know too. You know, sometimes this family is high maintenance."

Christopher looked at Gabriel.

"She's just realizing this now?"

CHAPTER 18

*E*mma's visit with her parents was a complete full circle that represented the culmination of a year-long journey. Now back on Captiva Island, she was ready to close the cottage and return the key to the owner.

She had one more day on the rental lease which gave her the time to say goodbye to her friends at the Key Lime Garden Inn and have lunch with her best friend, Sarah Hutchins.

Emma made Jillian pull her blouse down off her shoulder. "I can't believe how tan you are. Looks like you've enjoyed your vacation."

"It's been great. How are Mom and Dad?"

"They seem really relaxed these days. I can tell that Dad's retirement has had a positive impact on both of them. I'm glad for his sake because of his health. He doesn't need another heart attack."

"Did you talk to them about what you've been going through?"

Emma shook her head. "No. What's the point? I needed time to figure things out on my own, and I did that. I wanted the visit to be about other things. We played cards and Mom made her special sweet tea. I couldn't stop them from their annual nagging me about getting married and having babies. Other than that, it was a lovely visit."

"That's great. I'm glad you got to see them before you head to Sardinia. So, what's on your schedule for today?"

"I've got to get over to the inn to say goodbye to Maggie and thank her for her friendship and support these last three months, and then Sarah and I are having lunch. What about you?"

"I might as well tell you that I met someone while you were gone. I want to say goodbye to him so I've sent him a text to see if we can get together for lunch. He has to work today, so we'll only have an hour to talk."

Emma could see the sadness on Jillian's face. "You're upset to leave the island because of this guy?"

"Does it show?" Jillian asked.

"Pretty much. Where does he live?"

"Here, on Captiva. His family runs Powell Water Sports. His name is Finn Powell. Do you know him?"

"I do, that is, I know the family. I'm not sure which one of the sons is Finn though, but I've seen them here and there. Ciara Moretti is dating their father. Did you know that?"

"Ciara is Maggie's sister-in-law, right?"

Emma nodded. "You see what a small place this island is? If you're not a tourist, you're probably related to other islanders."

Jillian pulled her suitcase down from the closet shelf.

"I might as well start packing. I was thinking of getting on the road tonight. I would have left in the morning if Finn was free tonight, but…"

Emma grabbed Jillian's arm and pulled her away from her luggage. "Hey, you're really upset about this."

Jillian sat on the bed. "I know it's stupid since I just met the guy, but I know how this is going to go. We'll stay in touch for a while. We'll text and email and maybe even visit each other a few times, but in the end, it won't last."

"Wow, does Finn know his fate? Why so glum? It's not like he lives on the other side of the country. At best, in traffic it's probably only a couple of hours."

"Finn is leaving Captiva and going to school near Fort Lauderdale."

"So what? That's still only about a three-hour drive. That's hardly enough of an obstacle, that is, unless you're already looking for a way out."

Jillian looked up at Emma. "That's just it, I'm not. I think what's worrying me is that for the first time, I met a guy that I worry might actually dump me first."

"Geez, Jilly. What a depressing way to start a relationship. Give the guy a chance. He might surprise you."

"Right, because somewhere along the way, he's going to think I'm not worth all the effort."

Emma sat on the bed next to Jillian. "Listen to me. You are very worth it, and if he lets a few miles come between the two of you, then he's not the one, plain and simple. Try to remember that every time you get down about him and stop imagining things that haven't happened."

Jillian smiled and hugged Emma. "I'm glad you and I got to spend a little time together, Em. What would I do without my big sister?"

Teasing, Emma responded, "You're right. You'd be a mess. Good thing I'm here to help you."

Jillian reached for a pillow and hit Emma in the face with it. They fell back onto the bed and laughed. Emma didn't want to admit it, but she needed her little sister just as much as Jillian needed her.

Maggie was in the garden with Paolo when Emma arrived at the Key Lime Garden Inn. Maggie waved and pointed to the porch.

"I'll be right there," Maggie yelled.

She grabbed a tomato from Paolo's basket and bit into it.

"Nothing in the world tastes as good as a fresh tomato off the vine."

She kissed Paolo and took another tomato for Emma.

"I'll see you later."

When she got to the porch, she handed the tomato to Emma, and took another bite of hers.

"Thanks," Emma said. "I love vegetables from the garden. My parents have a garden too. Jillian and I were really lucky growing up and eating fresh, organic fruits and vegetables."

"Back home in Massachusetts, I had a vegetable garden, but not as big as my flower one. I used to dream of living in a small English cottage with the most beautiful flowers. Pretty funny considering that I ended up on an island in Florida."

Emma laughed. "I guess life doesn't always turn out the way we plan."

Maggie sensed a bit of longing in Emma's voice. "Then again, Emma, sometimes life turns out better than we plan, at least it did for me."

"I'm going to miss you and the island," Emma said.

Maggie put her arm around Emma. "We're going to miss you too, but I know you've got wonderful adventures in your future. I'm glad you went to visit your parents. Did they know that you had been thinking about becoming a nun?"

Emma shook her head. "No. I never told them about that. The truth is that there was so much more attached to that struggle. I haven't been sure how to articulate it. I'm still processing it. I think I'm finding my way on how best to share what I have to give while helping others who might not be able to help themselves or ask others for help."

Emma looked down at the floor and smiled. "I'm sure I'll tell my parents about it one day."

Maggie was impressed with Emma's understanding of herself.

"You know, Emma, you should be very proud of yourself. You didn't run off and join a convent without first taking the time to decide if it was truly a calling. I'm proud of you, and I know that Sarah is as well."

"Thank you, Maggie. That means a lot."

Figuring that she might never get another chance to talk to Emma privately, Maggie asked, "Care to share how things went between you and Gareth Graham?"

Emma giggled. "Oh, now that's a work in progress."

"Oh?" Maggie pressed her for more. "Perhaps there is a future there?"

Emma hugged Maggie. "Tell you what, as soon as I know the answer to that, you and Sarah will be the first people I call."

Maggie laughed at Emma's delightful response. "I hope you'll stay in touch and send us lots of pictures."

"Sarah would kill me if I didn't," Emma answered.

Maggie nodded. "Yes, you don't want to get on my daughter's bad side. Make sure to come back now and then and see us, okay?"

"I will," Emma answered.

Maggie watched Emma walk through the garden and down the path to the beach.

Lauren, Sarah and Beth kept Maggie on her toes most of the time, but there was enough room in her heart for the young woman who had become a fourth daughter and loving member of the Wheeler family.

Carrying her sandals, Jillian strolled barefoot along the water's edge. The rhythmic lapping of the waves provided a soothing soundtrack to her thoughts.

As she walked toward the Cantina Captiva restaurant, she thought back to her last few days getting to know Finn Powell. Spending most of their time nestled away from his brothers' prying eyes, the cottage was their private oasis and the best opportunity for privacy.

There was still so much to learn about Finn. She hoped that Finn wanted to see her after she returned to Naples. His plan to become a commercial airline pilot would involve months of schooling on the east coast of Florida which, to her, wasn't a problem.

In fact, Jillian liked the idea that they would get to know each other slowly. She loved her independence and the last thing she wanted was to be in a relationship with a clingy guy. Her work, Finn's school and three-hundred miles was a perfect situation as far as she was concerned.

She promised Finn that she'd meet him at a table in the Cantina Captiva restaurant instead of the overpopulated spots near the beach. With more intimate surroundings, they'd be able to say goodbye without too much fanfare.

He was already waiting in front of the building by the time she reached the restaurant.

"I forgot to ask you if you like Mexican food," Finn said.

"No problem. As it happens, I love it."

They went inside and marveled at the walls which were covered with dollar bills and writing. Even the ceiling had money stapled to it.

"I hope they never have a fire," she joked.

Finn asked for a table in the corner and followed the waiter there.

"Is this good?" he asked.

"Yes, fine."

They ordered margaritas and salsa and chips and then looked over the menu.

"I think I'll get the fish tacos, how about you?" she asked.

"That sounds good to me. I'll get the same."

The waiter took their order and quickly delivered the drinks and appetizers.

Finn raised his glass, and Jillian did the same.

"Cheers!"

They sipped their drinks and each waited for the other to speak. Not once in their time together did they struggle for things to say, but suddenly, an awkward silence, like a heavy fog hung in the air between them.

"Have you talked to your father about your plans?" she asked, breaking the silence.

"No. Not yet. I'm going to talk to him tonight."

She nodded. "I'm glad. I've worried that you were putting it off."

Finn smiled. "Yeah, well, you're not that far off. I haven't been putting it off, but I also haven't been looking forward to it. I've done everything I can to prepare myself and to seek support from my brothers, but now, it's time to deal with it. I'm just worried that I'll hurt my dad."

"How can you be so sure that he'll be hurt? Don't you think that he must have thought you and your brothers might have a life beyond the family business? I mean, it's only natural to want to find your place in the world. Otherwise, all your choices will be made for you. I can't imagine your father would want that for his children."

Jillian didn't want to push the subject, but if things worked out between the two of them, she had a stake in how things played out between Finn and his father.

Finn nodded. "I understand, and I agree. It's time he and I had this conversation."

"Do you know when the next flight class begins?"

"Yeah, in September. I'd have to leave the island in August if I want to find an apartment near school. I've been saving my money for years for this very moment. I'm ready."

The awkward silence was back, and Jillian knew why. Neither of them wanted to put pressure on the other to make promises they couldn't keep.

"Jillian, along with planning school and a place to live, I want to keep seeing you after you leave tomorrow. For the next few weeks, I can drive to Naples or you can come here for a weekend or two; beyond that, I won't know much until I'm firmly settled on the east coast."

Finn's suggestion was commitment enough for Jillian.

"Why don't we take it one day at a time? Is that all right with you?" she asked.

"How about one week at a time?" Finn teased. "We may not want to be too possessive here, but I think I can commit to a week at a time."

Jillian laughed and raised her glass. "To one week at a time."

Finn clinked his glass against hers as the waiter brought their fish tacos.

If Finn Powell had flaws to complain about, Jillian hadn't found them yet. Nonetheless, she focused on the operative word "yet".

With her sister and mother's words on her dating life swimming in her head, Jillian chose to remember only one comment. That when the right guy came along, she'd love everything about him…even the flaws.

CHAPTER 19

Sarah, covered in spaghetti sauce, answered the door.
"Hey, come on in" she said as she raced back to
Sophia who was in her high chair, playing with her lunch.

Emma laughed at the sight. "Wow, has Chelsea seen this? I think Sophia has a future in abstract painting."

"You see Picasso? That's funny. When I look at this mess all I see is a mop and a pail."

"Come on, Sophia. Let's show Aunt Emma what a big girl you are. Here comes another spoonful of your favorite food."

The spaghetti, already cut into small pieces, made its way into Sophia's smiling mouth, but that didn't stop her from spitting it right back out when she saw Emma laugh.

"Don't do that," Sarah said.

"Are you talking to me or Sophia?"

"You. If you laugh you only encourage her."

Emma took the spoon out of Sarah's hand and pushed her out of her chair. "Go wash up and let me finish feeding Sophia."

Sarah took her apron off and threw it on the chair. Sophia stopped laughing and wondered what was happening. Her serious look, complete with wide brown eyes, stared at Emma who was having a stern conversation with the child.

"Ok, here is how this is going to go. I'm going to put this spoonful of food into your mouth and you're going to chew it and swallow. Do you understand?"

Sophia had no idea why Emma was speaking in that tone, but however she interpreted Emma's meaning, Sophia did as she was told.

"Good girl. Let's do it again."

Emma had never babysat or changed a diaper in her life. She had no idea how to take care of a toddler, but somehow that didn't matter. Sophia continued to behave well, and Sarah came into the kitchen stunned at the change in her child.

"All this time we thought you didn't know a thing about children. I beg to differ. You're a natural."

Laughing, Emma responded, "Oh, I don't know about that. I just talked to her like an adult. Maybe that's the key. More likely, she's confused, and can't understand why I'm feeding her instead of you."

Sarah sat at the kitchen table and watched her friend and daughter continue their albeit one-sided conversation.

"So, are you all packed and ready to go?" she asked.

"I am. Jillian too. She's having lunch with Finn Powell right now."

"Finn? What in the world? How did that happen?"

"Apparently while I was visiting my parents in Naples, she was spending time with him."

"Oh, I'll have to get all the gossip from Ciara if I ever see her again."

"What does that mean?"

Sarah pointed to Sophia and the rest of the house.

"I've taken a leave of absence from the Outreach Center because I can't juggle everything. Trevor is busy at work. We have a nanny, but I hate leaving the kids and missing out on seeing them grow. I do miss work, but I love being with the kids."

"I think that's wonderful, Sarah. I can't believe my college roommate, who swore she'd never get married or have children, is living that very life and is blissfully happy."

Laughing, Sarah said, "Did I say I was blissful? I don't know, maybe I am. What about you? I've gotten used to you being on the island. I'm going to miss you like crazy."

Emma got up from her chair and walked to Sarah.

They hugged and Sarah said, "I love you, woman. You come back soon, okay?"

"I will, just as soon as I can. Don't make me cry. I love you, too."

They both turned and laughed at Sophia who was making kissing sounds with spaghetti sauce covering her lips. When Sophia saw she had made them laugh, she giggled, which only made them laugh even louder.

"I could never live here," Beth said. "Seriously, how can people drive these highways?"

"It is strange what people will tolerate," Gabriel answered. "Landing in LAX is busy enough, but then, it takes another two hours to get to my parents' place."

"I'm still glad we're doing this anyway," she said. "I think it will make your mother happy."

Gabriel shrugged. "Yeah, as long as she understands what's happening and who we are. I don't know about you, but when we left her last month I felt like I was saying goodbye forever."

Beth held Gabriel's hand and squeezed it. She felt awful that he was dealing with the loss of his mother even though she was still alive. She couldn't imagine what it would feel like for her mother or siblings to forget who she was.

Gabriel's father's ringtone rang as they got off the highway. "Hey, Dad, we're about twenty minutes away. Do you want us to pick up anything before we get there?"

"No. I don't need anything. I'm calling just to let you and Beth know that I'm admitting your mother into a memory care facility in Temecula."

"What? When?"

"Today. I'm going to bring her over in a couple of hours."

Gabriel's father, Thomas Benjamin Walker, was not one to cry in public. In fact, he wasn't the kind of man who wore his emotions on his sleeve. Early in their relationship, Gabriel explained to Beth that his father was a strong, conservative man with a kind heart, but it was rare that he'd allow his two sons to see his vulnerable side.

Now, on the phone, Beth was certain she could hear Thomas's voice cracking under the stress and emotion of losing his wife to Alzheimer's disease.

"I'm sorry, Gabriel. I didn't want to do this, but your mother… well, it's what she wants. I couldn't tell you this when we last talked."

"Dad, we're almost at the house. Let's talk about this when we get there, all right?"

"Okay. I'll see you soon," Thomas answered.

Gabriel ended the call and threw his phone down on the side of the door.

Beth put her hand on Gabriel's arm.

"Babe, this was coming. I think we all knew that."

"Yeah, I get that, but what does he mean this is what my mother wants? She's in no way able to make such decisions. He's just assuming it's what she wants. I don't understand."

Beth understood all too well. The man she loved more than

life, was unable to accept that his mother was gone. She felt Gabriel's pain and hated that there was little she could do to help him.

They sat in silence until they reached his parents' home. "Leave the luggage in the trunk. I want to get inside."

Beth nodded and followed Gabriel into the house.

"Hi son. Hello, Beth."

"Hey, Thomas." They all hugged each other and then Thomas handed Gabriel a piece of paper.

"I found this in the nightstand next to your mother's side of the bed. Look at the date."

"November 19th…eight months ago."

Thomas nodded. "She must have written it when she got the diagnosis."

My sweet Thomas,

I'm writing this note to you so that when the time comes, you'll fulfill my wishes.

There is a lovely memory care facility in Temecula that I've researched. It's a very nice home where I want to live when it becomes obvious that you can't take care of me any longer.

If you're reading this, then you and I both know that time has come. I know that you've been struggling with my illness and what it means for our future.

My love, you have been the most wonderful husband and father to James and Gabriel. I have always trusted you to make decisions for our family and you've never failed to make the right ones.

And now, it's time to make another one.

You will always be my husband and I will always be your wife. It's just that this is the next phase of our marriage. It's going to look different for a while, and then, when it's my time, I'll go home. We'll see each other again when it's your time, and we'll pick up where we left off.

Take care of Gabriel and especially James who will, in time, struggle with his own experience with this awful disease. He'll need the same love and patience that you've given me.

I'm choosing to believe that even with all evidence pointing to my not recognizing my family, that you, Gabriel and James will reside in my heart...forever.

Please do this last thing for me.
All my love,
Veronica

Overcome with emotion, Gabriel sobbed in his father's arms. Beth's tears fell and she joined their embrace when Thomas reached for her.

There was nothing left to do but take Veronica to her new home and the people who knew best how to help her.

———

They were welcomed by the staff at Serene Horizons Memory Care Facility. After introductions, a woman wearing a lavender-colored suit gave them a tour of the residents' living space, common areas, dining rooms, and outdoor spaces.

Beth watched Veronica, who had little interest in anything the woman had to say. She obediently followed along the halls and firmly held on to Thomas as they walked.

There was an orientation to the various services and amenities and they explained the dining options, activity programs, therapy services, medication management, housekeeping, laundry, and other support services.

Gabriel seemed pleased with what he saw and started to relax. The Director of nursing, caregivers, activity coordinators, and social workers reassured Thomas that his wife would get the best care.

They were all surprised when a nurse along with another resident enticed Veronica to the piano. With little effort, she released her grip on Thomas and followed them to the instrument.

Beth joined them.

"Do you know how to play the piano, Veronica?" Beth asked.

Veronica nodded her head and sat on the bench. Without sheet music, she began to play a medley of songs from the Beatles. When she finished playing Hey Jude, a woman came up to the piano and smiled at Beth and Veronica.

The woman had tears in her eyes.

"Oh, thank you so much. My mother hasn't spoken in months. She really hasn't said one word to any of us since Christmas, but when she heard this woman play the piano, she began to sing. It was the first time in months that I heard her voice. I can't thank you enough. Would you please play that song again?" she asked Veronica.

Confused, Veronica began playing the same Beatles songs in the same order that she first played them. When she got to Hey Jude, the woman's mother sang along.

"Music sometimes reaches a person where nothing else will," the nurse explained.

Gabriel smiled as his mother continued to play without sheet music. The longer they stayed at Serene Horizons Memory Care Facility, the more comfortable with the place Veronica became.

While she played the same songs on the piano over and over again, it gave the staff an opportunity to go over the facility's Policies and Procedures. They shared information on safety protocols, visiting hours, resident rights, emergency procedures and any rules or guidelines that residents are expected to follow.

The next few hours were spent not only learning more about the facility, but getting Veronica acclimated to her new surroundings, and her new room, which was painted and decorated in soft pastel colors.

Gabriel looked at Beth and took her hand in his.

"I think she's going to be fine, don't you?"

Beth nodded. "I do. We'll come visit her as often as you like."

"What do you think about the mock wedding?" he asked her.

Thomas overheard and interrupted. "Maybe another time. Why don't we let your mother get settled. You'll come out again before Christmas won't you?"

"Absolutely," Beth answered.

"Where are you having the real wedding?"

Gabriel looked at Beth and they both smiled and shrugged. "It depends who you ask. Asking us, we'll tell you that we're not sure, we just want it to be a Christmas-themed wedding. If you ask my mother, it will be on Captiva Island."

Rubbing his beard, Thomas said, "Oh, I see."

"Yeah, it's a bit up in the air at the moment. Not only that, but it's also a double wedding. My brother Christopher is getting married as well. We all thought we'd join forces and have a big party. I have another motive for wanting the double wedding."

"Oh, this ought to be good," Gabriel said.

"Good? I think it's brilliant. If we do a double wedding then all the focus won't be on me and I won't be the only one who has to deal with my mother. See, brilliant, right?"

"Uh-huh, we'll see how brilliant it is the closer to the wedding we get."

"Well, wherever it is, I promise, I'll be there," Thomas said.

"You will? That would be wonderful," Beth responded.

Turning their attention back to Veronica, the nurse announced it was time to say goodbye. Beth watched as Thomas walked away from his wife. She never looked up from the piano to see him leave.

CHAPTER 20

How can people be so sloppy? Jacqui wondered as she picked up the towels from the bathroom floor. Coming from a wealthy family, she wasn't used to cleaning bathrooms or making beds. Her family had housekeepers for that. Even away at school, Jacqui hired someone to clean her large apartment.

It wasn't something she asked for, but her parents insisted she focus on school and not worry about such mundane things.

Jacqui thought back to last year when Chelsea explained to her that Devon and Eliza Hutchins didn't do Jacqui any favors paving the way in life with red carpets and opulent surroundings.

Maybe Chelsea was right. I sure could have used some instruction on how to clean and do laundry.

Disgust etched across her face, Jacqui carried the towels to the laundry room. She dropped them on top of the others and looked at the washing machine with angst.

She never told Maggie that she'd never done laundry before, nor was she acquainted with the workings of a washing machine. Even if she had mentioned it, she doubted that Maggie would have believed her.

Who doesn't know how to use a washing machine? Jacqui pondered.

"How are you doing?" Riley asked, stopping by the laundry room to get a bunch of linen napkins.

"Great," Jacqui lied. "I'm learning as I go."

Riley smiled. "You'll get the hang of it. It's not that hard. You're lucky, Maggie only needs you for a few hours here and there. You'll still be able to enjoy the beach if you plan things right."

"Yeah, as soon as I get this laundry done, I might do that very thing."

Risky though it was, Jacqui had no choice but to ask Riley for help.

"This machine is a lot different than the one I'm used to. Can you give me some pointers?"

"Sure. I'll show you." Pointing to the large drum she said, "First, put all the towels in there and then shut the door. Make sure you hear a click. That way you know it's really locked."

Jacqui filled the washing machine with the towels and closed the door.

Riley grabbed the detergent. "You open this lever and fill it with this. Don't overfill it though or you'll never get all the soap out. Fill it to the line. Then close it up and hit the silver button."

"That's it?"

"That's all there is. Not too hard. What kind of washing machine do you have?" Riley asked.

Pretending to forget, Jacqui continued lying, "Oh, you know, I'm not sure. It was already there when I moved into my apartment."

"Really? You're lucky. Most people who rent have to share a washer and dryer. You must have a really nice landlord."

Laughing, Jacqui answered, "Yeah, I guess. He's my father."

"Ah, that explains that. Well, I better get the dining room set up. I'll see you later," Riley said.

"Thanks for your help," Jacqui said.

"No problem. Stop by the kitchen any time if you need a snack or an iced tea. Maggie lets all the employees eat here."

"Great. I'll do that."

Glad to have the towels in the wash, Jacqui looked over at the buttons on the dryer and rolled her eyes. She didn't dare ask for help twice in one day.

Maggie rocked the porch swing and enjoyed her iced tea. She waved to Paolo who was working in the garden. Ciara's car came up the driveway. She parked it in front of the carriage house, got out, looked toward the garden, and then at Maggie.

"I see he's at it first thing this morning," Ciara said.

"Yup. As long as he's had his breakfast and coffee, he heads out there before going to Sanibellia. I have a very important job as supervisor. I sit on the porch swing and observe."

Ciara laughed. "And a very important job, that is, my friend. How are things with everyone? Is Michael doing okay?"

Maggie nodded. "No news is good news these days. Honestly, Ciara when my cell phone rings my heart does a hundred flip flops if it's one of my kids. I love them all, but they do give me stress now and then."

Ciara shrugged. "Yes, but you really are lucky to have them all. Even at my age I find myself wishing I had children of my own."

"Oh, Ciara, I didn't mean to be so insensitive," Maggie said.

Shaking her head, Ciara tried to relieve Maggie's concern. "No, please, I'm fine with how things turned out. There was a time when I couldn't walk near where the children's clothes are displayed in stores, but I'm past all that now."

Maggie reassured her. "What do you mean? You are not that old, Ciara. There is still time for you. You could still have a child, that is if you want one."

"I don't know about that. I mean, I'm in love with Crawford and we have a wonderful relationship. It's just…"

"You're not certain that you want to marry him?" Maggie asked, finishing Ciara's thought.

"Oh, no, nothing like that. If he asked me tomorrow, I'd say yes. I'm just not sure he's going to ask."

"Oh, I see," Maggie said, suddenly sorry she brought up the possibility of children.

"Crawford already has four grown children, then there'll be grandchildren. It's hard for me to imagine that he's going to want to get married and start another family."

"Have you thought about talking to him about this?"

Ciara shook her head. "Oh, no. I couldn't do that."

Maggie reached for Ciara's hand. "Of course you can; as a matter of fact, I think you must. This is a conversation that the two of you need to have. If you want to be married and have children with him, then you must let him know."

"I'm scared, Maggie. What if his answer is that he doesn't want either of those things? Just like you said earlier about having children…how stressful it can be. His sons are giving him problems lately and it's possible that this might not be the right time to bring it up."

"First, I guess you'll need to decide how important marriage and children are to you. As far as having children goes, the joy far outweighs any stress. I'm sure Crawford feels that way about his boys. What's the problem anyway? Is it Joshua? I only ask because of the three boys, he's the wild one."

Ciara shook her head, "No. Actually, I don't think it is. He's told me that it's all three of them. He's worried that his boys are moving away from one another. He doesn't think they are as close as they were when their sister lived on the island. I know

Becca is alive and well, but it's almost like her leaving to go to medical school in Boston was like a death. First they lose their mother to cancer, then their Gran dies and then Becca leaves, they all seem to have scattered somehow."

Just then, Jacqui came out onto the porch. Maggie couldn't be certain, but she thought it possible that Jacqui was listening from around the corner.

"I'm finished with everything, Maggie. Do you need me to stay and do anything else? Oh, hello, Ms. Moretti."

"Hello, Jacqui. I understand that you're working here now."

"Yeah, for the summer. I'll head back to school at the end of August."

"If the rooms are cleaned and ready for our next guests, then I'd say you're finished for the day. I won't need you tomorrow, but the next day I will. Does that work for you?"

"Yes, that's perfect. I'm going to enjoy a day at the beach tomorrow. Since I've been back on Captiva, I haven't done that yet."

"Sounds like a fun day. Enjoy your day off."

"Thanks. Bye, Ms. Moretti."

"Bye, Jacqui," Ciara said.

After Jacqui left, Ciara looked at Maggie and asked, "Is it my imagination, or was she wearing a bathing suit under her shorts?"

Maggie laughed. "I think you're right. Something tells me that she's not going to wait until tomorrow to head to the beach. I'd bet money that she's on her way to swim in the ocean directly in front of the jet skis."

Confused, Ciara asked, "What? Why there?"

"Because that is where Finn Powell is sitting right about now."

Ciara's eyes widened. "Oh no. Are you saying that she's interested in Finn?"

Maggie nodded. "More than interested."

"That might not be a wise move for her," Ciara said. "Finn hasn't confided in me, and I'm not sure his brothers or Crawford know this, but I saw him with someone else just the other day. They seemed very close."

"Where was this?" Maggie asked.

"Cantina Captiva. They were in the corner, but I stopped to get take-out and saw them."

"Oh dear, this isn't good. Should I say something to Jacqui?"

Ciara shook her head. "I wouldn't get involved. You know how these summer flings have a way of working themselves out. The last thing you want is to start trouble for Jacqui. She's the type who'll pack her bags and leave you without a housekeeper."

"Good point. She's staying with Chelsea. I'll at least have to let her know. If anyone can get through to Jacqui Hutchins, it's Chelsea."

———

"Speak of the devil," Maggie said to Ciara.

"Which explains my ears itching," Chelsea said.

"You mean ringing. Itching means you're coming into money. Besides, it's your hand that's supposed to itch and your ears are supposed to ring when someone is talking about you."

Chelsea seemed out of breath when she climbed the stairs to the porch.

"Maggie, my dear, I don't care who's talking about me and I don't expect any money to fall out of the sky and into my hands. So, whether it's itching, ringing or buzzing or chirping, my body only hears and feels one thing, thirst. I've just gone for a walk on the beach. I don't remember the last time I sweated like this, but I don't like it."

"It's called exercise, Chelsea. Have you never heard of it?"

"Hearing about exercise is not the same thing as experiencing exercise. I didn't mind hearing about it. Hearing about it didn't make me sweat."

Turning to Ciara, Chelsea smiled. "Good morning, Ciara."

"Good morning, Chelsea. Let me get you some iced tea."

Ciara left them and went into the kitchen.

"I'm glad we're having this conversation. I've been thinking that you and I should join a Zumba class," Maggie said.

Chelsea fell into a wicker chair and stared at Maggie.

"Why are you looking at me like that?" Maggie asked.

"Because, clearly you haven't paid attention to one word I've said. Exercise and I do not go together."

"Oh, that. Don't be ridiculous. It's just that you're out of shape, that's all."

Ciara returned with a tall glass of iced tea and handed it to Chelsea.

"Thank you, Ciara. You're an angel." Chelsea took a long gulp of the tea and leaned back against the floral cushion.

"I'm not really sure what my shape is supposed to be. I know that my arteries aren't in shape, I can tell you that."

Ignoring Chelsea's complaints, Maggie continued. "I think Zumba would be great, but I'm also thinking about Pickleball. We'd need to get two other people to play with us though."

"Can we please talk about something that won't raise my resting heart rate?"

Maggie shrugged. "Okay, How about this? Jacqui is crazy about Finn Powell and Finn is crazy about someone else. How's that for relaxing talk?"

"Maggie!" Ciara burst out, unable to contain her laughter. "I entrusted you with that secret, not as fodder for gossip. What will Chelsea think?"

Chelsea put her iced tea down on the table and leaned forward. Answering as if she were speaking of someone else other than herself, "Chelsea will want details. Come on ladies, tell me everything."

CHAPTER 21

*G*abriel sat on the edge of the pool and let his feet dangle in the water. Beth joined him and swirled the water with her legs.

"Penny for your thoughts," she said.

He shook his head. "I can't believe how she went downhill so quickly. I mean, is that normal?"

Beth shrugged. "Honey, when it comes to Alzheimer's and dementia, I don't know what's normal. I don't think the way she is this morning will necessarily be how she is this afternoon. I think that's the nature of the illness."

"This is what my brother James will go through when he's her age…and then Willow. This is insane."

"All we can do is pray that they'll find a cure or something to slow the progression by that point," she said.

Thomas joined them carrying a tray with lemonade. "Who wants my delicious homemade lemonade?" he asked.

Beth jumped up and nodded. "Me, that's who. Gabe, honey, do you want one?"

Gabriel shook his head. "No. Thanks."

Beth and Thomas looked at each other. Beth knew they were

both thinking the same thing. Something had to be done to get Gabriel out of this funk. The entire situation was awful, but being miserable about it wasn't helping. In fact, Beth felt bad that they couldn't lighten the mood for Thomas.

"You know what I think?" she said. "I think we should have that mock wedding anyway."

Gabriel turned and looked at Beth. "What exactly is the point of that? She might not have a clue who we are or what it's all about."

Beth was losing patience with Gabriel. "What if she does know who we are and what's going on? You have to consider both possibilities, Babe. Either way, we'll have made a memory for us if not for her. We'll get married and your mother will be there. We'll take pictures and then frame them. We can even hang them in her room for those moments when she is aware."

She looked at Thomas who was smiling from ear to ear.

"What do you think?" she asked him.

"I love it. Let's do it," he said.

Beth went to Gabriel and pulled him up from the side of the pool.

"It's time to get you dressed into your suit. I'm not marrying you looking like this," she said.

Beth had packed a short, lacy white dress and Thomas picked flowers from his garden for a bouquet. He made a second bouquet for Veronica just in case she was able to participate in any way. If not, he'd ask someone to put the flowers in a vase for her room.

Thomas called ahead to let the staff know what they had planned for the afternoon, and they promised to get Veronica dressed up for the occasion. However, when they got there, she'd pulled the necklace off from around her neck and started to unzip her dress.

When the nurse tried to put the dress back on, Veronica got mad, and began to cry. Rather than create a fuss, they let

Veronica pick out what she wanted to wear and went with that. The vase filled with the new flowers made her smile and that was enough for Thomas.

Thomas walked Beth down the makeshift aisle and she smiled as she reached the front of the room. When the director was done pronouncing Beth and Gabriel husband and wife, an elderly man yelled out, "Kiss her!"

On cue, Gabriel leaned down and Beth wrapped her arms around him. They kissed and everyone clapped, including his mother who had just witnessed two young people getting married.

There was a large bowl with a strawberry punch and cupcakes that remained from an event held in another, less restricted part of the facility. Most of the people in attendance were residents but also several staff members stood nearby watching the ceremony and a few even had tears in their eyes.

The ceremony went off without any problems, and Gabriel tried not to laugh when his mother turned to the man next to her and said, "This was a lovely wedding. I'm so glad you invited me."

Beth knew that Gabriel's mother had no idea who he was, but it didn't change the fact that they'd made his mother smile even if it was only for a few fleeting minutes.

As if a light switch had been turned off, Veronica tired and seemed to get upset again. The nurse, recognizing the change in mood, quickly reached for her.

"Would you like to go to your room now?" she asked.

The nurse steadied her frail body, as Veronica shuffled past Gabriel, Thomas and Beth. The nurse smiled at them as she and Veronica walked down the hall.

"I took lots of pictures, son. I'll make sure they hang in her room."

Gabriel couldn't say anything so he just nodded.

Beth hugged him tight as he wiped the tears from his eyes.

———

Later that evening, when Thomas and Gabriel were asleep, Beth got up from her bed and walked downstairs to the kitchen. She had a lot on her mind which was making it impossible to sleep.

Gabriel wanted to stay in California longer in case Thomas didn't want to be alone, but his father insisted that they get back to their lives on the east coast.

For Beth, there was much to think about. The next six months of her life would change in so many ways. Soon, she'd be moving into Gabriel's home…their home.

The thought of moving wasn't the only thing keeping her mind swirling. The wedding location had been a bone of contention between her and her mother and she purposefully left things undecided to allow some space and time to think things over.

It made sense that Becca was already committed to having the wedding on Captiva Island since her family lived there, but for Beth, she wasn't as excited about a double wedding on the island.

She sat by the window and watched a sliver of moonlight casting a glow across the room. She traced the lines of her engagement ring with her finger and thought about Veronica and Thomas. Many years ago they were starting their life together just as she and Gabriel were doing now.

Beth knew what lay ahead for Thomas in the coming days and weeks. He'd hold onto a glimmer of hope, treasuring those rare and precious moments when the fog of Alzheimer's temporarily lifted and Veronica's eyes would lock with his in a flicker of recognition. As time ebbed on, those cherished instances would gradually slip through their fingers, becoming increasingly scarce.

What pained Beth more than anything else was that what Thomas and Veronica were dealing with could happen to anyone at any time. The full moon, its brilliance flooding the room, seemed to whisper secrets of wisdom and revelation.

Thomas' love for Veronica, Michael's devotion to his job and commitment to protecting his fellow citizens as well as her mother's dedication to family over the years reminded Beth that some things were worth sacrificing.

She finally understood that it didn't matter the setting, the extravagance, or the perfect timing of her wedding or the impossible dream of a stressless job as Assistant District Attorney.

What mattered was the people who gathered, the families who would be cared for and protected, the bonds that would be strengthened, and the memories that would forever be woven into their shared tapestry.

Michael's valiant act had not only saved lives but had also ignited a fire within her. Beth had the sudden urge to call him. She looked at the clock…It was three-thirty in the morning but six-thirty in Massachusetts.

She found her cell phone and walked outside near the pool. Sitting on a lounge chair, she dialed Michael's cell phone. It rang only once before he picked it up.

"Hey, aren't you in California?"

"Hey, yourself. Yes I am. It's three-thirty here. I just needed to call you. I've figured out a couple of things and needed to tell you," she whispered.

Michael laughed. "Well, I'm flattered that you'd wake up at this hour just to talk to me."

"Hey, I'm being serious. I needed to tell you how incredibly proud I am of you. You risked everything to protect that family. You're my hero, but not just because you were so brave that day. You've helped me to see a few things that I couldn't before.

Remember how I needed time off from work? I was in a dark place and the job was taking an emotional toll on me."

"Yes, I remember and I totally get that," he answered.

"I couldn't bear it any longer. But seeing you, seeing what you were willing to endure to protect others, it reminded me of why I became a prosecutor in the first place."

Beth closed her eyes, her words flowing from a place deep within. "I've made my decision, I'm going back to my job. It's what I was born to do."

"I'm glad, Beth. I really am. I don't think I can take credit for it though. Maybe you did, but I never doubted your strength. I'd put you up against any of the tough guys I deal with on a daily basis. Do me a favor?"

"Yeah, anything," she said,

"Promise me that if you ever get to that dark place again, you reach out and talk to me?" he asked.

"I will, if you will," she answered.

"You've got a deal. By the way, you said you figured out a couple of things. What was the other thing?"

Beth laughed and wiped her wet cheeks.

"Oh, that? I'm going to get married at Christmas on Captiva Island, in a double wedding with Chris and Becca. Imagine that. Mom is finally getting what she wanted."

"Oh man. Did you call Mom to tell her yet?"

"Are you kidding me? If I called her this early in the morning, she'd be on the next plane to California."

"Good point," he said.

"Well, I guess I better get back in bed. Gabriel will wonder where I am. Hang in there okay? I'll come by to see you when we get back."

"I'll be here. I love you, sis, and thank you for calling me. You have no idea how much I needed to hear your voice. It means more than you know."

"I love you, too."

She hung up the phone and waited a minute before going back inside. As the moon continued its journey across the night sky, she took a deep breath and felt at peace for the first time in months. A glimmer of hope for both her and Michael, that their shared resolve would light the path towards justice and healing.

Beth was in the kitchen as soon as the sun came up. There was no point in going back to sleep. Adrenaline pumped through her veins from the excitement of her earlier phone call with Michael.

After breakfast, Gabriel put their luggage inside the trunk of the car and then went back inside to say goodbye to Thomas.

"Are you sure there isn't anything more Beth and I can do for you before we leave? Do you need help with anything inside or outside? I don't have my tools, but I'm sure we can…"

"Stop," Thomas said. "I don't need anything and I'm going to be fine. You need to stop worrying about me. As long as your mother is nearby, I need to be here for her."

"You promise you'll be at the wedding in December, right?" Beth asked.

"I'll be there. Not to pressure you two, but I wouldn't mind a trip to Captiva for your wedding. I've never been there before."

Beth smiled, "I think you're going to get your wish."

Gabriel looked at her. "Are you sure?"

She nodded. "I'm sure."

"Oh, by the way, Gabriel, who is your Best Man?" Thomas asked.

"James, of course, and Beth wants Willow to be a flower girl."

"Oh, fine. She'll love that. Come on. Let's get the two of you out of here or you'll miss your plane."

The three of them walked out to the car. Beth hugged Thomas. "You take care of yourself. I realize that you're independent but that doesn't mean you can't call us if you need us."

"Beth's right, Dad. Please get in touch if you need anything."

Thomas nodded. "I will. Now get going."

Beth felt like she was going to cry all over again watching the two men hold each other in a loving embrace. Gabriel got into the car and as he pulled away, Beth leaned out the window and waved.

CHAPTER 22

*F*inn spent the morning looking over the flight school PDF. There were several steps to get through before becoming a commercial airline pilot, and he wanted to be prepared before he spoke with his father. He could already hear the negative comments about dreaming his life away.

He was prepared to explain to his father that with the steady rate of commercial airline pilots retiring, there was a desperate need for pilots. In Finn's opinion, he couldn't have picked a better time to apply.

Frustrated that Luke and Joshua didn't come together to figure out how best to talk to their father, Finn didn't have more to explain than his desire for this new career, and that would never be enough to sway Crawford Powell. Crawford needed facts, numbers, and return on investment details, none of which spoke to the most important thing from Finn's perspective…his heart.

"Dad, can I talk to you for a minute?"

"Sure, what is it?"

Luke and Joshua were closing the store. Finn wasn't sure

whether it would help if his brothers were in the room or if it might make things worse.

Crawford seemed distracted, and Finn waited until he could get his father's attention.

"Well? What is it?" Crawford asked.

"It's important. I really need you to focus on what I have to say."

Crawford looked up from his paperwork and then put his pencil down.

"I've been thinking about this for a long time. I wanted to come to you before but I always put it off. Dad, I want to go to flight school on the East Coast. I want to be a commercial airline pilot. It takes time, it takes studying and flight hours and…"

"This isn't a good time, Finn. It means that you'd be leaving Captiva, and that's not an option."

Finn nodded. "Yeah, of course I'd be leaving the island. Dad, I'm talking about a career in something other than the family business."

Just then he noticed Luke and Joshua walking towards them.

"I've explained to you that this isn't a good time, Finn. It's the busiest time of the year for us. You can see how we are barely able to manage with all the help we've got. I can't spare you for you to go off and…"

"And what? Fulfill my dream? Live my life on my terms? What exactly are you saying?" Finn's voice was raising.

Crawford got up from his desk and walked toward the front of the store. Finn and his brothers followed behind.

"Dad, listen to him. This is something he needs to do and I think you need to give him your blessing," Joshua said.

"Joshua's right, Dad. You need to let Finn do this." Luke added.

Luke looked at Finn. "We all have to support him in this."

Stunned that his brothers were on his side, Finn smiled.

Crawford remained unmoved by the gesture.

"You boys have no idea what it took for me to build this business into the success that it is today. Your mother and I did without so we could put all our money back into the store. It's always been run by the family and that's the way it will remain."

"No one is talking about the store being run by someone other than family. You have Luke and Joshua to help you." Finn insisted.

Luke took that as his cue to mention his ideas.

"Yeah, Dad. I've been thinking about expanding our business to online retail. It's called e-Commerce. I think we can make a lot of money and…"

"So that's it. The three of you are in this together? How long have you all been plotting this mutiny?"

Joshua laughed. "Seriously? Aren't you being a bit dramatic? We haven't been plotting anything. Finn came to us to tell us what he wants to do. Luke and I weren't very supportive at first."

Joshua looked at Finn. "I'm sorry about that, Finn. Luke and I talked and feel that you're brave for doing this. It takes a lot of courage to move out of your comfort zone."

Crawford moved closer to his sons. "Listen to me, all of you. Finn isn't brave. He's running away, and if you think that makes him brave, then you haven't a clue what his leaving will mean for all of us. You boys have it made here on Captiva. I promise you when you step off this island, no one will care about you more than family. This is a mistake."

He stormed out of the store leaving Finn, Luke and Joshua to discuss next steps.

"What can we do? This is a mess. I wasn't sure how Dad would take this news, but I didn't expect him to be so angry," Finn said.

"You definitely struck a nerve. I think there's more to this than we know. As a matter of fact, Finn, I don't think this has anything to do with you."

"What do you mean? Of course it has to do with me. I'm the one who upset him," Finn responded.

Luke shook his head. "No, you're just the first one to say out loud what all of us have thought at least once. Dad isn't stupid. He's had to know that as soon as we were old enough to question things, that sooner or later at least one of us might want something different for our lives…something more than this store."

"I've got to talk to Becca. She's the only one who can get through to Dad," Finn said.

"That's a great idea," Joshua said. "Becca will change Dad's mind. She's always been able to get him to listen."

"I agree. When will you call her?" Luke asked.

Finn shrugged. "I don't know. She's been so busy lately. I'll send her a text and ask her when the best time is to FaceTime or Zoom. If Becca can't get through to Dad, then I don't know what I'll do."

"I do," Joshua said. "You'll leave and go to flight school. You're not a prisoner, none of us are. You have as much right to live your life the way you want as anybody."

Finn couldn't believe his brothers came through for him when he needed them most. Now, with a phone call to his sister, he might make his father see how unreasonable he was.

Regardless of the outcome, and because of his brothers' support, Finn felt a weight off his shoulders for the first time in months. Whatever happened now would only strengthen his resolve.

The thought of Finn hurting Jacqui, albeit unintentionally, worried Ciara. She wasn't sure who to talk to about it. There was her dear friend and co-worker, Sarah Hutchins, who would want her sister-in-law safe from heartbreak, but Ciara worried that Finn might get mixed up in something he would never choose for himself.

In the end, Ciara decided that a stop at Sarah and Trevor's house was in order.

"Knock, knock. Can I come in?" Ciara laughed when she saw Sarah on the floor with several blankets piled on top of her.

"Are you under there?"

"I am." Sarah's muffled voice came from under the pile. "Sophia thought it would be fun to bury me. If I come out now, she'll be upset."

Ciara sat on the sofa and tickled Sophia's stomach. Sophia giggled and piled on another blanket.

"Sarah, I don't think I can talk to you while you're under there. I'm afraid Sophia will just have to accept that you have a visitor who likes to look at you when she talks."

The blankets fell away as Sarah sat up, her hair sticking up in the air from the static electricity. Her red face, buried in Sophia's tummy, made the little girl giggle even louder than before.

Sarah stood and grabbed Sophia and swept her up in her arms.

"I'm glad you stopped by. I wanted to ask you how things were going at Powell Water Sports. I understand Crawford has been really busy."

"It's been crazy, that's for sure. I need to get over to the Outreach Center though. I promised them I'd be there for the Food Pantry deliveries."

"Well, that is your primary job, after all. I'm sure Crawford understands. What else is new?"

Ciara hesitated, trying to find the right words to explain her concern.

"I'm a little worried about your sister-in-law and I thought I should let you and Trevor know."

"Should we be alarmed?" Sarah asked. "Jacqui has been known to get herself into situations that she claims are innocent misunderstandings."

"No. It's nothing super serious. It's only me being cautious.

Jacqui has set her sights on Finn Powell but what she doesn't know is that Finn is in a relationship with someone else. At least I think he is. I've seen him with her and from the look in his eyes, I'd say he's fallen in love."

"And Jacqui doesn't know anything about this other woman?"

Ciara shook her head. "No. Not that I can tell. She's been flirting with Finn, although I don't think he's even aware of what's going on. He's pretty clueless about it. I might add that the 'other woman' is Emma's sister, Jillian Thurston."

"Jillian? Well, maybe this isn't the disaster you think it is. Jillian and Emma have just left Captiva. I doubt Finn and Jillian will keep seeing each other now that she's left the island. Emma would have mentioned it to me if they were serious."

"I don't know, Sarah. Maybe you're right. To add to the mix is Finn's brother Joshua who seems to have a sense of what's happening. I've watched him whenever Jacqui is around. I'd be lying if I said that Joshua was a one-woman-man, but I wonder if he's interested in Jacqui. Either that, or he's having fun at his brother's expense."

"Oh, Ciara, that's an awful thing to say about Crawford's son. Don't you like Joshua?"

Ciara laughed. "Don't get me wrong. I love that kid. He's funny and likes to show off like he's some kind of playboy. I don't believe he's the heartless type. I think there's more to him that he'd like us to know. Anyway, I'm probably making a big deal out of nothing. You know how summer romances on the island end up."

"I do, indeed. Most of them never get past September. I'll talk to Trevor about it just in case. If Jacqui does get her heart broken, Trevor will probably be the first person she runs to for sympathy."

Ciara shook her head. "I wouldn't be too sure about that. If I had to guess, she'd first run to Chelsea. That woman has more wisdom in her pinky finger than the rest of us do in our entire bodies."

That evening, at dinner, Sarah decided to mention Jacqui's potential heartbreak.

"Have you talked to your sister lately?" Sarah asked Trevor.

"Which one? I have two, you know."

Sarah rolled her eyes. "The one that's always in need of help."

"Ah, Jacqui. No. I haven't. Why do you ask?"

Sarah explained Ciara's earlier visit.

"Seriously, Sarah? Do you really think it's wise for any of us to get involved with Jacqui's romance of the week? My sister's legal name should have been Jacqueline Drama Hutchins. Honestly, this is kid's stuff. I'm surprised at Ciara. She's not usually one to get involved with such shenanigans."

"I think she's worried about Crawford's kids. She's pretty invested in her relationship with him. Having no children of her own, I think she's starting to feel protective of them."

"They're not kids. They're grown men. I'm sure they can take care of themselves. Besides, I doubt any one of them would be happy to know that Ciara is getting involved in their personal lives. Can you imagine if Finn knew we were sitting here now talking about him this way?"

"I guess you're right. Just don't be surprised if Jacqui comes crying to her big brother for advice, and a shoulder to cry on."

CHAPTER 23

*B*ecca and Beth finished cleaning up after dinner and Gabriel and Christopher went into the living room to watch the Red Sox game.

"Why is it that the women immediately go into the kitchen to clean up and the men head directly to sit in front of the tv?" Beth asked.

Christopher yelled from the living room, "Don't mess with the natural order of things."

"Enjoy tonight because tomorrow night we're switching off. Becca and I will go do something fun and leave the cleaning to the men."

Gabriel laughed. "Works for me. I won't be here tomorrow night."

Beth looked at Becca and rolled her eyes. "Oh, right. He's going back to his place in the morning."

Beth yelled to them once again. "That's all right. We'll get you next time."

Becca laughed. "So, have you called Maggie yet to tell her you've agreed to the wedding being on Captiva Island?"

"I'm going to call her after we finish cleaning up," Beth answered.

"She's going to be really excited. I bet I hear her scream through the phone. Are you really certain this is what you want?"

Beth nodded. "I am. Honestly, I'm excited about it. The only problem is that I've never even seen a double wedding. How do you suppose we'll pull it off without either of us losing our minds?"

"Oh, I don't think we can guarantee there won't be chaos. One wedding can stir up drama, I can't imagine what two weddings will do. Why don't we plan to sit down later this week and go over ideas?" Becca suggested.

"Sounds good. I'll make a list of what we need to coordinate. There's a lot that we need to agree on, like the music, food, flowers, and photography. When I talk to Mom tonight, I'll let her know that we're getting together to figure this stuff out and then we'll get back to her with our thoughts. It's best to tell her that right up front before she starts running away with a million ideas that she'd probably implement without checking with us first."

"Is that your cell phone ringing?" Beth asked Becca.

"Oh, right. I left it in the dining room. Hang on, I'll be back to help you finish cleaning."

Becca reached her cell phone just before it stopped ringing.

"Hey, Finn. How are you doing?"

"Things could be better. Do you have a minute to talk?"

"Hang on. I'll be right back."

Becca ran back into the kitchen. "Beth, it's my brother, Finn. I think this might take a while."

"No worries. I'll finish up here. Say hello to Finn from us."

Becca nodded and went back to her phone. "Everyone here says hello. So, tell me what's got you so upset. I can hear it in your voice. Where are you anyway?"

"I decided to walk down toward the beach. I know it sounds like I'm at a party, but it's The Mucky Duck crowd. Now that the sunset has passed, everyone is ready to drink and listen to music. I'm walking over toward the marina. It will be quiet there."

"Finn, what's going on? Is Dad all right?"

"Yeah, he's fine. I mean, he's mad at me, but other than that, he's fine."

"Mad at you? Why?"

"That's why I'm calling you. I'd Facetime but it's getting dark and the marina isn't really lit up this time of night."

"That's fine. Talk to me. Tell me what happened."

Finn explained the conversation with their father and how badly he wanted to be a pilot.

"Finn, this is so exciting. I'm thrilled to hear that you want to do something more with your life than work at Powell Water Sports. I mean, come on, it's fine for Dad and maybe even Joshua, but there's nothing wrong with wanting something else…something more. Dad will come around."

"No, Becca, you're not hearing me. He's adamant. He will not support my leaving to do this. Make no mistake, I've made my decision, and I will leave. It would be so much easier on all of us if I left with his blessing."

Becca understood Finn's feelings. Their father had a heart of gold but he could be stubborn. She had the same stubborn streak that her father had - they were so alike. She thought back to the time when she was fifteen and called her father ignorant to his face. It was the first time her father had ever hit her. She'd put her hand to her red cheek and ran out of the room. Furious that he'd been physical with her, she vowed never to speak to him again.

After two days of silence, her mother insisted that Becca go to her father and apologize. The sting of pain that she felt from his slap was nothing compared to the humiliation she felt at having to apologize to him for her actions. Her mother explained that nothing would change between them unless Becca humbled herself before her father.

While Crawford worked on a car in the garage, Becca walked gingerly, toward him. She cleared her throat so that he knew she was near. Her voice barely a whisper, she mustered the courage to apologize. She was shocked when Crawford turned to her and, with tears in his eyes, apologized to her as well.

For years, Becca thought about that day and remembered her mother's words, that sometimes you need to give a little to get a lot. However, she never doubted that even if she didn't apologize first, given time, her father would have.

"Dad loves you, Finn. He loves all of us and wants us to be happy. I think I know why he's acting this way. It's not your fault. It's more about losing Mom and then me and now you. Let me talk to him. There is a big difference between losing Mom to cancer and you and I going out on our own and away from the island."

"I was hoping you'd say that. Luke and Joshua have been great but I don't think Dad is listening to them any more than he's listening to me."

"Don't worry. It's a little late now. Let me pick a time when I know he'll be available and we won't be interrupted. I'll let you know how it goes."

"Thanks, Becca. I really appreciate this."

"How much?" she asked.

"Uh-oh, what's this going to cost me?"

"I haven't figured that out just yet, but with the wedding coming up in December, I'm sure I'll need you for something."

"The wedding is in December? That's awesome. Give me details."

"I'd love to, but right now all I can say is when it is and that it's on the island. Oh, and Chris's sister Beth and her fiancé Gabriel are getting married at the same time."

"A double wedding?"

"Yes, but don't say anything to anyone about it. I want to tell Dad when I talk to him."

"No problem. Talking about weddings is not really my thing. I'll let you go. Thanks again, Sis. Love you."

"Love you too, little brother."

Becca ended her call and went to join the others.

"Where's Beth?" she asked Gabriel.

"She's in the bedroom, talking to her mother about the weddings."

Becca's face lit up with a smile. It was shaping up to be an evening filled with family dramas from both sides. Despite living fifteen hundred miles away from Finn and Maggie, Becca and Beth couldn't escape getting entangled in the whirlwind of events and drama on Captiva Island.

———

Jacqui walked down the stairs of Chelsea's house and up Andy Rosse Lane toward the live music. Outdoor restaurants in the area always boasted live performances, each vying to attract customers with their musicians.

As it was already nine o'clock, Jacqui took pleasure in pausing at different venues, fully immersing herself in the melodies of various musicians.

The sound of a violin wafting from the beach path added to the ambiance, even though it intensified the competition between the establishments.

Aware that everything would close down within the next hour, Jacqui refrained from dwelling on the situation and instead embraced the limited yet enjoyable nightlife the island had to offer during the quiet hours of the evening.

Joshua Powell smiled at Jacqui as he walked toward her carrying two Pina Coladas in his hands.

He offered one to Jacqui. "For you, mademoiselle."

She smiled, thinking it was possible Joshua was trying to make up with her, so she took the drink.

"Thank you. How did you know Pina Coladas are my favorite?"

"Because, everyone loves them when you're on island time. It's a tropical drink and we're in a tropical place."

"More likely a good guess," she said.

"That too," he responded.

They both laughed and Jacqui had to admit the mood between them was much lighter than the last time they saw each other.

"So, whatever happened to that boyfriend of yours?"

"Huh? What boyfriend?" she asked.

"You know, the one you were buying a dry suit for."

Jacqui's annoyance with Joshua building once again, she had no choice but to make fun of the whole thing.

"I think you and I both know there is no boyfriend. It was just my way of getting you to leave me alone."

"I wasn't bothering you. Come on, let's get this out on the table. You were there to see my brother Finn. Isn't that right?"

"What if I was? It's a free country. I'm single and fully capable of making my own decision about who I want to go out with."

Joshua nodded. "Of course you are, but did it ever occur to you to find out if the person that you're pursuing is also single?"

Jacqui's head turned to look at Joshua. "I haven't seen Finn with anyone since I've been on the island. Does he have a girlfriend or are you just trying to annoy me?"

"I have eyes. All I can tell you is that I know he's been seeing someone. Whether he still is, that I can't say. He hasn't confided in anyone about it."

"So, you are trying to annoy me. The truth is that you have no idea whether your brother is single or not. Where is your big proof? I was seeing someone too, but I'm not now. Brilliant detective work there, Joshua."

"Here's your chance to do your own detective work. Finn's coming from the marina right now. Good luck."

Jacqui handed her drink to Joshua and gave him a dirty look. "I don't need luck," she said.

Finn approached his brother and Jacqui. "Hey, what are you guys up to?" he asked.

"Who? Joshua and me? Oh no, we're not together. I came out to get a drink and listen to live music. It's a beautiful night. I see you had the same idea. It's a nice night for a walk."

"Oh, sorry about that, bro. Although, if you ask me, you've missed an opportunity to be with this lovely woman." Finn teased.

Thrilled to hear Finn compliment her, she smiled at Joshua.

"Well, I'm headed back inside. I'm meeting a few friends here. You two have a good night. I'll see you in the morning, Finn."

Joshua bowed in front of Jacqui and then went inside the restaurant.

"Would you mind walking me to Chelsea's house, Finn?"

"No, not at all," he answered. "How are you liking working at the inn? You just started, right?"

"Yes, it's great. I'm working only part-time so I've got plenty of time off to enjoy the island. I'm here until I go back to school at the end of August."

"Ah, that's right. Where do you go to school?"

"New York Academy of Art. I'm in their graduate program."

"Impressive. You must be a very good artist to be accepted into that program."

Taking a chance that boasting wouldn't turn him off, she said, "I'm not bad. How about you? Are you planning on working at your family's store forever or do you have other plans?"

"As it happens, I'd like to be a commercial airline pilot. I'm looking into their flight school now. I hope to start in the fall."

"A pilot? That's amazing. Think of all the traveling you'll do. I'd love to see as much of the world as possible. I love to travel."

When they reached Chelsea's house, Jacqui searched for how to see if Joshua was right about Finn not being single.

"Thanks for walking me home, Finn."

"My pleasure. I'm sure we'll run into each other again since we're both here for the summer. Have a good night."

He turned to walk away when she stopped him.

"Finn! Maybe we can get a bite to eat or hang out at the beach one day before I leave to go back to school."

He nodded. "Absolutely. Take care."

Jacqui's heart leapt in her chest.

Joshua was wrong. Finn wasn't seeing anyone and they still had several weeks left of summer. Anything could happen.

CHAPTER 24

*B*eth dialed her mother's cell phone and waited for the inevitable question.

"What's wrong?" Maggie asked.

"Why do you always ask me that when I call you?"

"I'm not sure. Maybe you don't call me enough."

"I should have been prepared for that response. Mom, I call you every week. How is that not enough?"

"Oh, you know me. I'm always worrying."

"Well, I do have news. Maybe you should sit down for this one."

"Oh dear, I don't like the sound of that," Maggie said.

"I've decided to have my wedding on Captiva at Christmas after all."

Beth held the phone away from her ear so that Becca could hear her mother scream.

"This isn't a joke, is it?" Maggie asked.

"No, Mom. No joke. Becca and I are going to sit down this week and talk about the things we both want at our wedding, so don't run off and start hiring people."

Beth held the phone away from her mouth once again.

"She must be talking to Paolo because she's not listening to me."

"Mom! Did you hear what I just said? No hiring anyone just yet. Becca and I aren't ready for that."

"Oh, that's fine. It's still December 14th though, right?"

"Yes, that's the date at this point. If we go any closer to Christmas, we might have problems finding Event Planners."

"What Event Planners? You've got me and Chelsea, and Ciara. We've got the best chefs on the island, and…"

"Stop! Let's not talk about this right now. Becca and I haven't even talked about the details yet."

"Okay, okay. You don't have to repeat yourself. You call me just as soon as you and Becca are ready. Six months isn't much time to plan a double wedding, at least not one as elegant as yours is going to be. I'm so excited. I've got to go. I've got to call Chelsea. I'll talk to you later, honey."

"Bye, Mom…Mom? I can't believe it. She hung up on me. She said she was so excited and she wanted to call Chelsea and then she hung up. I hope she listened to me when I told her not to hire anyone."

Becca laughed and joined Beth at the table.

"That woman drives me crazy," Beth said.

"You're lucky to have her," Becca said, a hint of sadness in her voice.

"Oh, Becca, I'm so sorry. I wasn't thinking. I know how difficult it must be to not have your mother with you on your wedding day. I know she's watching from Heaven. She'll be with us on that day. We'll make sure there's a seat right up front for her. What was her favorite flower?"

"She loved roses. If you look behind our house, you can see several different rose bushes of all different colors. Pink was her favorite color."

"Oh my goodness, that's *my* mother's favorite color as well.

We'll make sure we have pink roses on her chair in remembrance of her."

Becca reached for Beth's hand. "Thank you so much for thinking of her. I think you and I are going to get along fine when we work on the wedding planning."

Beth smiled and said a silent prayer that Becca was right. There was already far too much drama surrounding them to add more to the mix.

Michael sat outside the office of Dr. Elizabeth Wells. Brea wanted to wait with him, but Michael asked her to drop him off at the door. He didn't know why, but since the shooting he had difficulty being physically close with anyone. Brea's care for him felt more like hovering and a constant feeling of suffocation enveloped him daily.

"Please come in, Officer Wheeler."

Michael wondered if the therapist wasn't recommended by his supervisor, would she still address him as Officer Wheeler. These days, everything irritated Michael and the woman's voice he now added to that list.

He looked around the room and selected a single chair rather than the sofa. He'd never been to a therapist before, but the thought of lying down on a sofa was etched in his mind from various movies and television shows.

Her smile was pleasant enough, but he didn't like that she held a notepad in her hand.

"Are you going to write down everything I say?" he asked.

"Why? Does that bother you?" she answered.

He sighed and thought, *Here we go with the questions already.*

"No. It doesn't, I just wondered."

"It helps me organize my thoughts but I don't have to use it if it does upset you."

He was getting upset with being asked the same question twice.

"I said it doesn't bother me. Look, I guess I should get this out of the way from the start. I'm not the type of person who talks about his feelings all the time. I'm not very comfortable sitting in a cozy office with a complete stranger talking about my feelings. I just want to do my job."

Dr. Wells leaned forward slightly, her voice steady but gentle. "Officer Wheeler…"

Michael interrupted her. "Would you please just call me Michael? It would help me to not feel like I'm talking to a doctor."

"Of course. Michael, your dedication and strength are admirable. But even the strongest among us can be burdened by the weight of traumatic experiences. You stepped into a volatile situation with the intention of protecting innocent lives, and for that you should be commended. It's also natural to question if there was something more you could have done."

"Did I say that?"

"What do you mean?"

"Did I say that I've questioned if there was something more I could have done?"

"Have you?" she asked pointedly.

Michael felt hot. His body began to sweat and he felt as if he couldn't breathe. Tears welled up in his eyes as he struggled to reconcile his conflicting emotions.

Choking out his response, he answered, "I wish I could have saved all of them from that trauma, including the husband. I have children of my own. I couldn't imagine…I saw my children, my wife…they…"

Michael leaned over his legs and put his head between them. The doctor came up beside him and tried to console him.

"It's all right, Michael. You're safe here, you can say whatever you need to say."

It took some time before he was able to speak. When he felt ready, he rested his body against the back of the sofa.

"I keep having the same nightmare. I see my children and my wife, Brea, on the ground, shot. There's blood everywhere. I couldn't save them."

"Your wife and children are fine, Michael. They're safe. You keep them safe. No one is going to ever harm them. You'll never let that happen."

He nodded. "I know. You're right." He looked into the doctor's eyes. "If I could have avoided shooting him, I would have. I didn't want to kill him. He was a father and a husband. He should be here now, loving his family and taking care of them, not being a threat to their safety."

"That's right, Michael. He should have, but unfortunately that's what drugs can do to a person. It wasn't your fault. You understand that, right? It wasn't your fault."

Shocked that he'd exposed so much of his feelings in the first twenty minutes of his therapy, Michael wondered how much more would be uncovered in their subsequent appointments.

He stayed the full hour and thanked the doctor as he got up from his chair.

"Michael, I want you to understand that things might get harder as we continue to talk. It's a journey, but it will be worth the effort. Healing takes time, and progress can be gradual. But each step you take, no matter how small, brings you closer to reclaiming your sleep and finding peace within. I want you to believe that."

"I do believe it. I do. Thank you."

Michael was happy to see Brea when he walked outside. Holding a box, she offered it to him.

"What's this?"

"Your favorite. Dark chocolate truffles with cocoa powder."

Michael took the candy, but instead of eating a piece, he

pulled Brea into an embrace and held her for several minutes before letting go.

"Wow, I knew you liked these chocolates, but I had no idea how much," she said.

When he pulled back and looked at the box again, he did so through tears. Taking a bite of a truffle, he marveled at how his favorite chocolate had never before tasted so good.

"Got a minute?" Joshua asked Finn, who was folding t-shirts and putting them on the shelves.

"Sure, what's up?" Finn answered.

"I need to ask you something. It's personal, but I really need to know."

Finn stopped folding the shirts and motioned to the back of the store.

"This sounds serious. What's going on?"

"I saw you last week with a woman at the Cantina Captiva. Are you dating her?"

Confused, Finn didn't know what to say. "I'm not sure I need to divulge my dating life to you or anyone else for that matter. Why do you need to know?"

"Because Jacqui Hutchins has been trying to get you to notice her for the last two weeks and you haven't said a word about it. I think she really likes you and is trying to get you to like her. Can't you see that?"

"What are you talking about? Jacqui is just being friendly. Maybe it's you who's having issues with her. You've certainly never worried about any girl getting hurt before. What's going on?"

"Finn, I know what I'm talking about. She told me directly. I'm not making this up. She's falling for you and if you're not interested in her you better let her know soon."

"This isn't like you, Joshua. Why do you care so much who Jacqui is interested in?"

It took only a few seconds for Finn to see through his brother's motivation. "You really like her. Is that what this is about?"

Joshua shook his head. "I don't know what I feel. I haven't figured that part out. All I know is that she told me that she wants to go out with you."

Finn could see that Joshua wasn't fooling around. "You're serious?"

Joshua nodded. "She told me last night. What happened when I left? I saw the two of you walk toward The Mucky Duck."

Finn sat on a stack of boxes and ran his hand through his hair. "Oh man, she asked me to walk her home. I was just being polite. I had no idea she was interested in me that way. She got me to agree to hang out at the beach with her before she went back to school at the end of August. It seemed innocent enough, but if what you say is true, then she's going to see that as a date. What did you tell her when she said she wanted to go out with me?"

Joshua shrugged. "I told her that you weren't single."

Confused, Finn didn't understand. "Why would you tell her that?"

"Come on, man. You don't have to pretend with me. Did you really think that Luke and I wouldn't know that you were seeing someone? The last few weeks, your head hasn't been at work. You've been preoccupied. I know that you're dealing with the flight school thing, but I could tell there was something more going on."

"Oh yeah, how so?" Finn asked.

"Because, even though you were furious with me and Luke, you were still happy in a sick, vomit-worthy kind of way. I figured there had to be a girl in your story somewhere."

Finn laughed. "Well, okay, so I'm lousy at being sneaky. Now, what am I going to do about Jacqui?"

"If I were you I'd have a talk with her asap. There's no point in waiting. All that will do is give her hope. You might as well face it, she's going to be royally mad at the situation no matter when you talk to her, but you've got to pull the band-aid off in one fast move."

Joshua patted Finn on the back. "Good luck, bro. I wouldn't want to be in your sandals."

CHAPTER 25

*B*ecca thought long and hard about her conversation with Finn. Although she'd successfully found a profession that she was passionate about, her brothers had never talked about their dreams and plans for their future.

Everyone assumed her brothers would stay on Captiva and continue working in the family business. Now, hearing how Finn felt about flying, Becca was sorry she'd made such assumptions, and wondered about Luke and Joshua's ambitions as well.

She didn't need to be at school for another two hours and with everyone in the house off to work, she had the place to herself. It was early on Captiva and she knew that her father wouldn't be opening the shop for another hour.

Becca decided to Facetime with him instead of calling. She wanted her father to see her expression and the seriousness of her concern.

"Hey, pumpkin. Nice to see your pretty face first thing in the morning. How's my favorite girl?"

"Hey, Dad. I'm fine…busy. How about you?"

"It's been crazy busy here as well. You know how it can get."

Becca nodded. "I certainly do. Listen, I'm calling because I had a conversation with Finn about his wanting to go to flight school. He told me that you don't approve."

Crawford sighed. "So he asked you to intervene?"

"No. This was my idea. As a matter of fact, when he told me what you said I wanted to pick up the phone right then and there. I had to hang back a bit and calm down before I called you. What are you thinking making him feel so awful about wanting something different in his life? How could you do that?"

"Becca, listen to me. This business can't run without people working hard to make it a success. I can't spare him. It's as simple as that."

"If that were really true, then you could hire someone new for Finn to train before the summer was over. That's not what this is about and you know it."

"How can you say that, Becca? Didn't I support you when you wanted to go to medical school?"

"Yes, and that's the point. I went to medical school when Mom was still alive but then, when she got sick, I left. Years later, after she died, I went back to school but it was easier for you to let me go because Mom already approved. It was what she wanted for me because she knew how much I wanted to become a doctor. Well, Mom's not here now to tell you how she'd feel about you holding Finn back…but I'm here. Mom wouldn't want this Dad and you know it. She'd be heartbroken to see what you're doing."

Becca knew before she placed the call that she would bring up her mother's illness and subsequent death. Julia Powell loved Powell Water Sports as much as Crawford did, but she never lost sight of what was most important…her family.

"I miss your mother terribly. I'm doing everything I can to keep this family together," he said.

"Not this way, Dad. You can't keep us together by holding on so tight. Do you really think because I'm in Boston that I'm not with you every moment? It will be that way for Finn. He'll be away doing something that he loves, but he will always be with us, just like Mom is. You have to let him go."

Becca couldn't be certain, but she thought she saw a tear on her father's face.

Crawford nodded and wiped his face. "You're right. Of course, you're right. I'll talk to Finn. I'll make it right."

"Thanks, Dad. Everything will work out. You'll see."

"Hey, tell me about you and the wedding. Have you guys set a date yet?"

Becca laughed. "You bet. December 14th on Captiva Island."

"That's great, honey. I guess as the father of the bride, I've got to start planning, right? I'll have to get Ciara involved. You know us guys haven't a clue how to run a wedding."

"Well, you're in luck because you'll have lots of help. It's going to be a double wedding. Chris's sister Beth and her fiancé Gabriel are getting married on the same day. Why don't you get together with Beth's mother, Maggie? She's going to help plan the day. You and Ciara can coordinate with her. Just keep one thing in mind, Dad."

"What's that?"

"Maggie isn't very good at letting go any more than you are. She'll probably want to run the show. Don't let her. Beth and I are working out the details up here before we hand over the implementation to you all down there. I'm hoping you and Ciara might keep things on an even keel. Not to mention that Maggie's going through radiation for her cancer. I don't want her overwhelmed with planning. She'll make herself sick."

"Got it. Don't you worry about a thing. I might not know how to run a wedding, but I'm very good at organization and delegation. You keep me in the loop with whatever you girls decide. Your wedding will be the talk of the island."

Becca cringed. "Now you're starting to talk like Maggie. No fanfare. This is a private intimate wedding with family and close friends. The last thing I need to see are flyers and banners around the island advertising my wedding."

"At least it isn't the same weekend as the Christmas Fair. Can you imagine Santa Claus arriving just as you walk down the aisle?"

Becca suddenly worried that very thing might happen if Maggie wasn't reined in.

"Just keep things low-key okay?"

"Will do."

"Dad, I've got to go. Thanks for understanding about Finn. You're going to make him so happy."

"I hope so, honey. That's all I ever want is for my children to be happy. Love you, honey."

"Love you, too, Dad. Take care."

Becca ended the call and sent a text to Finn.

Becca: Talked to Dad. All systems go.
Finn: No joke?
Becca: Make sure I get discounts on my airline tickets.
Finn: Ha-ha - you got it. Thank you so much. You're the best sister.
Becca: I'm your only sister. Ciao!

The crate was the first sign that something furry was up. Brea and the kids kept smiling and looking at each other at the breakfast table.

"What's going on that you guys aren't telling me?" Michael asked.

"Oh, nothing," Olivia answered.

Giggling, "You'll find out," Lily joined in.

"Lily, you've got a big mouth," Olivia yelled.

"Yours is bigger," Lily responded.

"Girls, no need to call each other names," Brea scolded.

Michael looked at them and then at Jackson who was making a mess in his highchair. "I suppose you won't tell me anything."

Jackson smiled and then stuffed food into his mouth.

"I have a question," Michael announced. "What is a dog crate doing in the back of our SUV?"

Panic on Olivia's face meant he was on to something. Lily's eyes went wild and Brea wouldn't make eye contact with him at all.

"Brea? Do you know anything about that?"

Brea looked up from her food and was about to say something when the front doorbell rang.

Springing from her chair, she said, "I'll get that."

Olivia and Lily jumped up and followed her into the living room.

He could hear Lauren and Jeff's voices as well as Olivia and Lily squealing in excitement. He leaned back in his chair and peered around the corner.

There, on the other side of the room was his sister Lauren, holding what appeared to be a bundle of fur in burnt orange.

"Oh, my goodness, she is adorable," Brea said.

"Can I hold her?" Olivia begged.

"All right but be gentle," Lauren said as she bent down and placed the puppy in Olivia's lap.

"I'm holding her next," Lily said.

Michael threw his napkin down onto the table and went out front to join in the commotion.

"You guys got a puppy?" Michael asked.

Jeff looked at Lauren who looked at Brea.

"Yeah, we did, actually," Jeff answered. "Only not this one. We got one just like this one. I mean, it's from the same litter." Jeff went pale trying to explain.

"Oh for heaven's sake, Jeff," Lauren exclaimed. "This one is yours. She's a girl."

"Yeah, Dad, and her name is Willa," Olivia said.

Michael looked at Brea who tried to explain. "We all agreed Willa was a sweet name for a girl, don't you think?"

There was no use in disagreeing. Willa was indeed so adorable it was hard not to fall in love with her.

Everyone waited for Michael's response.

He walked to his favorite chair and looked at Lily.

"Lily, as soon as you and your sister are done holding Willa, I think you should come over here and put her in my lap. She and I have some things to talk about."

Lily took Willa from her sister's arms and carried the puppy to her father. She placed Willa in Michael's lap.

"You can take my place, Daddy. I'll hold her after you and Willa have your talk."

The lump in Michael's throat rose as he looked at his daughter. "Thank you, sweetheart. That's very kind of you."

Lily walked to the sofa and sat, waiting patiently for her turn.

Michael looked at Willa, her big brown eyes staring back at him. "You need to know that I'm in charge around here. I'm what they call the big cheese, so when I tell you to do something, you must do it."

The pup had no idea what Michael was saying but it didn't matter. Somehow in their introductions Willa decided to claim Michael as her own. She sealed the deal with a few licks of his face, and in that moment, Michael fell in love.

———

Smiling, Finn looked at photos of Jillian with a couple of her patients. As a vet, she treated every kind of animal and as soon as she got back to work, she took a few photos of the sweet fur babies to share with him. An occasional bird or reptile, Jillian's smile and her obvious love of animals was evident in each photo.

They'd sent texts back and forth for the last few days and Finn missed being with her. They'd only been together a few days, but that had little meaning for him. He already knew that it was love at first sight, but he could also tell that he'd ruin everything by rushing into a serious relationship with her.

It wasn't his heart that he feared breaking, but hers. In their time together, Finn could tell that there was a cynical side to Jillian—a cautiousness that he would do his best to respect. Whatever pace Jillian needed their relationship to go, Finn would accept.

His immediate concern was Jacqui Hutchins. After Joshua confided in him about her intentions, Finn knew he had to do something to explain his situation to her.

He started for the Key Lime Garden Inn when Crawford stopped him.

"Finn, do you have a minute?"

"Sure. What's up?"

"I want to apologize for my attitude the other day. I was a bit taken aback and I guess it threw me off balance when you told me your intentions."

Finn nodded. "I understand. Maybe I should have said something a long time ago, but…"

Crawford put his hand up to stop Finn from explaining. "No, the fault isn't yours. It's mine. Since your mother died, I've focused on keeping the family close. I've loved having my children near and it's been a wonderful thing knowing that the business will continue after I'm gone. I just assumed you boys would stay the way you are forever and that's just ridiculous. People change, times change and if you want to stay relevant, you have to change along with it."

"Dad, to be honest, I've loved working side-by-side with you.

I wouldn't want to change anything about our time together. For better or worse, I am who I am because of you."

Crawford nodded. "I have no doubt you'll make a darn good pilot, Finn. I'm proud of you, and I always will be no matter where you are or what you do. Remember that, will you?"

Finn smiled. "You know I will. Hey, you still got Luke and Joshua…well, you've still got Luke," he said, laughing.

"Oh, don't you rule Joshua out. Here's a little secret for you. If you tell anyone, I'll deny that I ever said it, but of all my children Joshua is most like I was at his age."

Shocked, Finn said, "Get out! No way."

Crawford nodded. "It's true. How do you think I got your mother to go out with me? Charm, my boy. Pure charm."

Finn hugged his father and watched him go off to help a customer. He learned a lot from his father and realized that if he was lucky enough to be even half the man Crawford Powell was, he'd be blessed beyond measure.

CHAPTER 26

Finn walked up the driveway of the Key Lime Garden Inn and saw Maggie sitting under the gazebo drinking iced tea.

"Hey, Finn. I haven't seen you in a while. How are you doing?" Maggie asked.

"I'm fine, Mrs. Moretti, thank you. I was wondering if Jacqui Hutchins was working today."

"Yes, she is. She's inside. Do you want me to call her for you?"

"Uh, no…thank you. I can come back when she gets off work. What time is that?"

"Well, it depends on how long it takes her to do her work. She doesn't work actual hours. She just comes in on the days when I have guests checking out and new ones checking in. I expect that she'll…"

"Hey, Finn," Jacqui said. "Are you looking for me?"

"Yeah, I can come back if you're not finished with your work."

"Actually, I am, that's what I came out to tell Maggie. Do you need me to do anything else, Maggie?"

"Nope. You two go on and enjoy your day. I'll see you Wednesday, Jacqui."

"Great," she said. "I guess we can go then."

"Nice to see you again, Finn. Say hello to your father for me."

"Will do," he said as he and Jacqui walked side-by-side down the driveway.

Finn's mind was spinning as he wondered how best to tell Jacqui what he'd come to say to her.

"I was surprised to see you when I came outside. I guess I should admit, happily surprised."

Afraid to respond with anything that appeared encouraging, he didn't acknowledge her words. They walked in silence for a while, until Finn finally found the courage to speak.

"Jacqui, I want to be honest with you. There's something important I need to tell you," he began, his voice gentle but resolute. "I've come to realize that there might be a misunderstanding between us. Joshua told me that you were interested in going out with me."

Jacqui's brows furrowed and she seemed angry. "He shouldn't have told you that."

"Why? Was he wrong?" he asked, pushing her to admit her feelings.

""No, but that's not the point. That information wasn't his to share. I wanted to talk to you about this myself."

"I appreciate that, and I'm truly flattered, but I don't want to lead you on or give you false hope. I hope we can be friends, but it can't be anything more than that between us."

Flustered, she didn't seem to understand what Finn was saying. "Why not? I mean we're both single. There's no reason we can't just hang out this summer. We don't know each other very well, but I sensed a connection between us. I was hoping we could spend the summer getting to know one another."

"No, you don't understand. I'm not single. Whatever connection you thought we had was all in your head. I'm seeing someone and it's serious."

Jacqui's eyes widened in surprise, her cheerful expression fading.

"So, you're telling me that I've been imagining things? You weren't flirting with me when you walked me home?"

"No. Jacqui, please, I'm sorry if I gave you that impression. You asked me to walk you home. I was trying to be polite."

She put her hand up. "Stop. Don't keep talking, you're making it worse."

Unsure of what to do next, Finn stood frozen in place. He let Jacqui make the next move.

Shaking her head, she put her hand on her hip. "I don't know what happened here, but I think you should go."

Relieved to be dismissed, Finn nodded and tried to preserve whatever gentlemanly reputation he had left.

"You're a wonderful girl. Any guy would be lucky to be with you. I'm sorry if I hurt you."

She didn't respond to that, and so he turned and walked home.

The humiliation was bad enough, but Jacqui suddenly realized that she'd left her purse back at the inn. Her face was red and the white of her eyes were soon to be the same color.

How can I go in front of Maggie and everyone right now? I can't let them see me like this. What a mess.

Taking deep breaths, Jacqui slowly walked toward the inn and tried not to cry. Hoping to run into Joshua, she wanted to give him a piece of her mind. By the time she reached the inn, reality had set in and she understood that Joshua wasn't the problem at all.

Thankfully, no one was around when she got her purse. She quickly swung the cross-body bag over her head and walked as fast as she could to Chelsea's house.

Jacqui ran up the stairs, into the house and climbed the stairs two at a time to get to her room. When she got there she slammed the door shut and threw herself on the bed.

"What in the world?" Chelsea said. "Jacqui, are you all right?"

No answer. Chelsea went to Jacqui's room and knocked. "Jacqui, are you okay?"

Jacqui didn't answer her. Chelsea feared something awful had happened. Chelsea turned the doorknob and pushed the door open. Sprawled on the bed with her face buried in the pillow, Jacqui sobbed.

Chelsea sat on the edge of the bed and placed her hand on Jacqui's back. "Honey, what's wrong? What happened?"

Jacqui shook her head. "I'm too embarrassed to say."

Chelsea smiled. Although prepared for a summer of drama from Jacqui, she didn't expect it to materialize quite this soon.

"Come on, don't you think you might be exaggerating just a bit?"

Jacqui sat up, pushed the pillow higher and leaned it back against the headboard. Falling on it like she'd just been shot, Jacqui wiped her mascara-stained cheek and explained.

"Finn Powell has zero interest in me. I don't get it, the signals were all there."

"What signals? What did he do?" Chelsea asked, skeptical that Finn Powell would ever lead anyone on.

Jacqui shrugged. "I don't know. It was just a feeling. He was so friendly to me, and he walked me home the other night. He even agreed to go to the beach with me this summer."

"Finn asked you to go to the beach with him?"

"Not exactly. I asked him if he'd spend some time with me before I went back to school next month. He said he would. But then…then I made the stupid mistake of telling Joshua that I was interested in his brother and so he went and told Finn. Next thing I know, Finn comes to the inn to tell me that he's seeing someone and basically that I misunderstood his interest in me."

Chelsea tried not to laugh, but the mess of a situation was Jacqui's own fault.

"This happened to me at school too. Jeremy Silva said the same thing to me when I asked him out." Jacqui said.

Looking at Chelsea she started to cry again. "What's wrong with me? You remember what my social life looked like before I went off to college. Everyone wanted to party with me, and the guys lined up just to ask me out."

Chelsea handed Jacqui another tissue. "Jacqui, as I remember it, you were going out with some rather sketchy people and getting into fights at the bars down on Fort Myers beach, or have you forgotten that?"

Jacqui shrugged. "Well, maybe they weren't the best for me, but I was popular."

Chelsea smiled. "No doubt. Can I make a suggestion?"

Jacqui nodded.

"How about you try not being in a relationship for a while?"

"Huh?"

"What I mean is why not focus on building friendships instead?"

"With guys? I've never been friends with a guy before."

"No, not with guys, I'm talking about female friends," Chelsea said.

"Come to think of it, I don't have any female friends either." Jacqui responded.

"Maybe it's time you do. I can promise you that the right guy will come along when you know yourself better. You've got so much to look forward to, Jacqui. The journey is where all the fun is."

"There are groups at school that I've thought about joining, but they seemed lame. Maybe I should give them a try."

"I think that's a great step in the right direction."

Chelsea patted the bed, got up from the bed and walked to the door.

"Now, fix your face and come downstairs. I'll make us some lemonade and we can do a little painting. What do you say?"

―――――

Chelsea went into the kitchen and filled two glasses of lemonade and carried them to the lanai. She put on her art smock and then arranged her paints, thinking more about Jacqui. Although she'd never asked questions about her parents, Chelsea wondered about Devon and Eliza Hutchins.

Today wasn't the first time Chelsea had to comfort Jacqui during a difficult time. She couldn't help but feel bad that Jacqui's mother never factored into the young woman's life.

"I don't feel like painting today if that's okay with you," Jacqui said. She leaned against the door leading to the lanai and looked like she couldn't decide whether to join Chelsea or run away.

"That's fine. We don't have to paint."

Chelsea handed Jacqui a glass of lemonade sat in the chair across from Jacqui.

"Can I ask you a question?" Chelsea asked.

"Shoot." Jacqui responded by acting like she didn't have a care in the world.

"I've noticed that you never really talk about your parents. Why is that?"

Feigning indifference, Jacqui shrugged. "Devon and Eliza Hutchins, the wealthy socialites of Southwest Florida are very important and busy people. They don't have time for little 'ole me."

Chelsea's knowing smile meant to convey skepticism. Jacqui wasn't fooling her one bit. She could sense a hint of bitterness masked by Jacqui's nonchalant tone. "Come on, I'm sure you're assuming things that aren't true."

Jacqui rolled her eyes, a mocking chuckle escaping her lips.

"Oh, please. They shower me with material possessions, trying to keep me happy and out of their hair. It's all just a game to them. But guess what? I'm not falling for it. I don't need their love."

"But you'll take their money?" Chelsea's point touching a nerve.

"I could live without that as well," she said.

Chelsea felt awful for bringing Jacqui's parents into their conversation. It hurt to watch the young woman mask a deeper pain that obviously colored Jacqui's perspective on the world.

"Forgetting about the money, the luxury car, and the expensive apartment, don't you crave their affection, their genuine care?"

Jacqui's smirk faltered for a split second, a flicker of vulnerability slipping through her bravado. She quickly regained her composure, though, and replied with a dismissive wave of her hand, "Nah, it's not worth the effort. I've learned to live without it. Their busy lives and high society circles are way more important to them than their youngest daughter who has a way of getting herself into trouble now and again."

There wasn't much more Chelsea could say or do to reach Jacqui's true feelings. All she could hope for is that they'd get another opportunity to talk about what was at the bottom of her sadness.

To accept that Jacqui didn't need her parents or anyone for that matter, was to miss the point entirely. Jacqui Hutchins was more needy than most women her age, and Chelsea worried that the next young man Jacqui set her sights on would bear the burden of that need.

It wasn't often that Maggie sat on the porch swing at night, but the distant sound of live music coming from the outdoor restaurants enticed her to stay up past her bedtime. She smiled thinking about the teasing she'd get from Chelsea for thinking that nine-thirty at night was late. She imagined that Isabella too, must have thought her an old lady for going to bed so early.

A gentle sound from Maggie's cell phone indicated that she had a message. She couldn't imagine that anyone would text her at this late hour.

Christopher:Hey Mom, are you still up?

Maggie:I am. Is everything ok?

Christopher:Yeah, can I call you?

Maggie: Of course.

Seconds later her cell phone rang.

"I know I get in trouble for always starting my conversations with my children this way, but please tell me no one is sick, shot or having a panic attack."

Christopher laughed. "None of those things. It's just that I've been meaning to talk to you about the house. Beth is moving in with Gabriel soon and Becca and I weren't sure what your plans were for this house. We've been to a few Open Houses in the area and thought about buying something but thought we should talk with you first."

"Are you unhappy living in our old house?" Maggie asked.

"No, not at all. It's nothing like that. It's just, well…"

"You want something of your own, right?"

"Yeah, but we love it here too."

"Chris, can you afford to buy a house right now?"

"Not really. I'm afraid that Becca is going to have a hefty school loan when she graduates. My salary isn't bad but it's not great either. I'm not sure what to do, that's why I'm calling you for advice."

Prepared to have this conversation with her children, Maggie knew what she wanted to do.

"Honey, I think every parent deals with this sort of thing eventually. If I knew how long I was going to live, I'd be better able to give my assets away accordingly, but I don't have a crystal ball."

"Oh, Mom, please don't talk like that. You're going to be around a very long time."

"We don't know that, and I'm not saying that just because I've got cancer. It's true for all of us. So, let's say I do live a long time. I'm not financially able to give the house away. The house is free and clear with no mortgage and I might need that money. I think the best thing for all of us is that you and Becca take care of the house and live there for as long as you want, rent free. Just keep the house up and I'll take care of the taxes. If I need you two to contribute, I'll let you know."

"If that's all right with you, I think Becca and I would be thrilled to stay here."

"Great. I should say that if things don't go as well as we'd like, my wishes will be legally spelled out in a trust split between you and your siblings."

"I hate when you say things like that."

Maggie laughed. "It's no use, honey. Sticking our heads in the sand won't make it any easier. We all have to face whatever comes. You should take solace in the fact that we're a close family and no matter how things play out, we'll always deal with it together."

It wasn't like Christopher to be so serious and it worried Maggie that her youngest didn't respond.

"Chris?"

"I'm here, Mom. Do me a favor will you?" he asked.

"Anything."

"Promise me that you won't ever give up? Even if it gets really hard. Promise me."

If any of her children had asked her that same thing, she would have responded with a promise to do as they asked. But, this was Chris, her baby, the child who almost lost his life to depression and the loss of his leg. If anyone knew what it meant to fight, it was her youngest.

Trying not to cry, she answered, "Never. You never gave up, and neither will I."

CHAPTER 27

*M*aggie tried not to make a fuss about her first radiation treatment, but it was impossible not to feel nervous. Almost every visit to the hospital brought the same anxiety and it always surprised her that the anticipation was worse than the actual treatment.

"Why won't you let me take you?" Paolo complained.

"You have too much to do here and at Sanibellia, Paolo. We talked about this before. Chelsea wants to take me and we should be happy that we've got a backup when you're so busy. You can take me next time. Have a good day."

She kissed him on the cheek and ran to the driveway when she heard Chelsea's car.

"You look bright and cheerful," Chelsea said.

"Looks can be deceiving. My stomach is in knots," Maggie answered.

"So is that why you didn't want Paolo to take you? Tell the truth."

"Honestly, Chelsea, I love him to bits but he's so serious. I need levity."

"Well, if it's levity you want, then I'm your girl. Other than this pesky radiation appointment, is there any trouble we can get into before I bring you back home?"

Maggie laughed. "See, this is what I need. I don't know about trouble but we should probably see how I feel after the treatment."

As Chelsea drove, Maggie looked out the window and tried to hold back tears. It wasn't fear that overwhelmed her but rather news that she'd received earlier that morning.

"What is it, Mags? Are you nervous?"

Maggie shook her head and continued to look out the window. "No, it's not that. I got a text this morning from the brother of someone I met during chemo. He told me that his sister died yesterday."

"Oh, Maggie. I'm so sorry."

Maggie wiped her eyes and smiled at Chelsea. "I never told anyone this because it sounds so silly, but one of the things about my chemo treatments was that I'd see the same people every time I went. After a while it started to feel like I was part of this club. Not that it was a club I volunteered for, mind you, but a club, nonetheless. Is it strange to say that I made friends there?"

"Not at all. I think I'd feel the same way," Chelsea said.

"It's funny how much human beings need each other. Even in a situation like getting chemo treatments, we attach ourselves to others who are going through the same thing. I wasn't searching for Megan and she wasn't searching for me, and yet, here I am absolutely devastated at her death."

Maggie knew how difficult it was to explain her feelings to anyone, even her best friend. Maybe there was value in joining a cancer survivor's support group.

Driving the rest of the way in silence, they arrived at the hospital ten minutes before Maggie's appointment. Chelsea pulled her car into the hospital parking lot, turned the engine off and turned to look at Maggie.

"Listen to me. I'm so sorry that your friend died, but that is not going to happen to you. You're not part of some club where one-by-one people leave the group and this earth permanently. You made a friend during a difficult time and the truth is that as much as she meant something to you, you meant something to her. I know how special you are to me, Maggie Moretti. I can only imagine how special you were to her."

Maggie smiled through tears and nodded. "Thank you, Chelsea. I'm so glad you came with me today."

Chelsea pulled a tissue out of her purse and wiped Maggie's eyes. "Now, let's get in there and fight this thing. And after that, let's go celebrate with something yummy."

A surge of energy mixed with defiance propelled Maggie out of the car and into the hospital. It was day one of her newest battle and she felt more than up for the fight.

———

Jacqui finished working at the inn and felt restless. Not knowing what to do or how to spend the afternoon, she decided to go for a swim. Trying to avoid both Finn and Joshua Powell, her plan was to walk in the opposite direction of the jet skis and the Powell Water Sports rental booth.

Chelsea was off-island for much of the day, and left beach towels, a bucket for collecting seashells and a chair and umbrella for her.

It was the first time since she'd been back in Florida that she chose to spend the time alone. She felt it necessary considering all that had happened in the last few days. Chelsea's advice to forget searching for a romantic relationship felt foreign but intriguing to her.

The idea that she seek female friendship also seemed beyond reach. She'd heard the advice that you must first be a friend if you want to make friends, so she considered the concept. Pushing people away was never going to work, and thus far, it had been the only way she knew how to be.

Finding a secluded spot, she spread out the beach towel and set up the chair and umbrella. She kicked off her sandals and ran to the water, laughing at what appeared to be a seagull keeping pace with her.

The bird, relying on the wind currents for flight made her think about her lack of faith in humankind. She'd fought against every current and resisted the easiest path all her life. Assuming her way was the road to the most excitement, she suddenly tired of always ending up in the same place, hurt, angry and without any friends.

Watching a wave coming at her, she dove under it and surfaced, letting the water wash over her. She did this multiple times and when the skin on her fingers wrinkled, she decided to head back to her spot.

Coming out of the water she saw a figure standing next to her chair. As she got closer, she realized that it was Joshua Powell.

Grabbing her towel, she wrapped it around her body. "What are you doing here?"

"Nice to see you, too," Joshua answered.

"Listen, I don't mean to be rude…oh wait, yeah, I do. Please go away."

"That's no way to talk to a friend."

"We're not friends."

"What? I thought we were," he teased.

"That was before you told Finn I wanted to be his girlfriend. What gave you the right to interfere in my life anyway?"

"First of all, I didn't say you wanted to be his girlfriend. I just told him what you told me. You never said it was a secret."

Jacqui couldn't believe his attitude. "Seriously? You think I should have specifically asked you not to say anything to him? What planet do you live on?"

Jacqui dried her hair and wondered how long she'd have to tolerate his presence.

Joshua sat on the sand and looked like he wasn't going anywhere any time soon.

"Exactly why are you mad at me? I helped you and Finn both from making a huge mistake."

She turned and looked directly into his eyes. "That was my decision to make, not yours. Finn and I might not have been right for each other, but that was for me to decide."

Joshua smiled. "Ah, now we're getting somewhere."

Frustrated, she exclaimed, "What?"

"You and Finn are not right for each other and I think you figured that out even if you wouldn't admit it to yourself."

"What, are you a psychiatrist or something?"

"Nope. Just perceptive. I do a lot of people watching and I can tell you that you and Finn were completely wrong for each other."

"Whatever…I suppose you know the kind of guy who is right for me?"

It was another attempt at flirting and Jacqui wanted to kick herself for the knee-jerk response. Even if some behaviors were difficult to overcome, the last thing she wanted was for Joshua Powell to think she was interested in him.

"I have an idea but I'll keep that to myself for now. In the meantime, what do you think about the two of us being friends?"

"Why exactly would I want to be your friend?"

Joshua looked to the left, then to the right, and then turned to look behind them. "Because, I don't think you have any…friends that is."

Jacqui couldn't decide whether to be angry at Joshua or comforted by the fact that he'd guessed her situation and it didn't scare him one bit.

"How would you know how many friends I have?"

"Because, I don't have any either. You see, Jacqui, people like you and me act like we don't need anyone. But, it's not true, is it?"

She didn't want to admit there was any truth in what he said, so she didn't answer.

"Here's what I propose. Since neither one of us are particularly good at friendship, we should use this summer to hone our friendship-making skills. We've got a month to work on it, and if it doesn't work out, we haven't lost anything. What do you think?"

She thought about what he said and answered, "Have you always been this good at talking circles around people? I hear what you're saying, and it sounds simple enough, and yet…"

"And yet?"

"I'm still confused."

He looked into her eyes and smiled. "I think that will clear up as the days pass…deal?" He extended his hand and waited for her to shake it.

With no faith that anything good would come of this contract, she shook his hand and for the first time noticed his ocean-blue eyes.

"Deal."

He got up and dusted the sand off his shorts.

"Great. We can start this friendship thing tomorrow night. I'll meet you at The Mucky Duck at seven. See you then, buddy."

He walked back toward the jet skis and left Jacqui sitting on her beach chair wondering what had just happened. She scratched her head trying to figure out how Joshua found her and her secluded spot on the beach. After a few minutes she smiled and found herself happy that he had.

Chelsea and Maggie walked Fort Myers Beach licking their ice cream cones. They stopped long enough to watch the silver statue street performer sweat under the hot sun.

"That can't be healthy. I mean isn't that paint he's got on? Someone should tell him it's probably toxic," Maggie said.

"Leave it to you to find the health hazard," Chelsea said. "What flavor ice cream did you get?"

"My favorite, vanilla. What about you?"

Chelsea looked at Maggie and rolled her eyes. "Really, Mags, I can't believe you forgot. I got Cherry Garcia, and I might add that you've been getting vanilla ever since I met you years ago."

Maggie shook her head. "Nope, I've been getting vanilla since I was a child."

"Honestly, where is your adventure? You should try something new."

"Why?" Maggie asked.

"Why, what?"

"Why should I try something new? I love vanilla, I've always loved vanilla. Why get something I may not like? That would be a waste."

"It wouldn't be a waste if it turned out that you loved the new flavor."

"Why take the chance?" Maggie said, shaking her head. "I have no idea why we keep having this conversation. For the last ten years every time we get ice cream, I get vanilla and you give me a hard time about it. Isn't it time we put to bed the entire vanilla ice cream conversation?"

Chelsea shrugged. "Sure, if that's what you want."

"That's what I want," Maggie insisted.

"Fine."

They walked two blocks toward Chelsea's car and didn't say one more word about the vanilla ice cream until they reached the car.

"It's just that I hate to think you're afraid to try something new."

"Chelsea!!" Maggie screamed. "Enough about the vanilla ice cream."

They drove away from the beach without saying one more word about the ice cream. When they were almost home, Maggie thought she'd lose her mind when Chelsea said she couldn't understand why Maggie always ordered lobster mac and cheese whenever it was on the menu considering there were so many more choices and things to try.

Maggie decided to ignore the comment and couldn't wait to get home and snuggle up with Paolo who didn't care one bit what kind of ice cream she loved.

CHAPTER 28

There were nights after Maggie's chemotherapy treatments when she couldn't sleep. Then, suddenly, in the middle of the day, she'd find herself struggling to keep her eyes open. On those days, she'd sit on the porch swing enjoying early morning quiet moments, drinking hot tea and listening to the birds chirp, welcoming a new day.

Now, with her first radiation treatment behind her, she felt light and excited about what was to come. She wasn't afraid but was at peace with whatever she had to endure to finally be done with cancer.

The soft twinkling of the wind chimes and the occasional sound of a tree frog welcomed Maggie as she witnessed this morning dance. Life happened all around her and in that moment she understood that she wasn't witnessing but rather participating in this early morning ritual.

She didn't know how to explain her newfound energy and excitement. Wearing a nightgown, bathrobe and slippers, she had an urge to get out into the garden and dance but decided to stay put for fear that a guest might see her and think her crazy.

When she finished her tea, she brought her cup to the sink

and quietly walked back to the carriage house to slip into a pair of shorts and cotton sleeveless blouse. Slipping her sandals on, she went back to the inn and to her favorite spot near the window in front of the butterfly bush.

With so much on her mind, she decided to write in her journal. She didn't want to forget this moment and needed to record everything.

She began writing, her words flowing effortlessly onto the page. She described her transition from fear to faith and her feelings of tranquility in the early morning hours.

Pleased with what she'd written, she decided to get organized and start thinking about the double wedding that was a little more than five months away. Organizing the office, she looked for a box of manilla folders. There were a few out of the box that were in the drawer on the left.

She pulled out a folder and noticed another under it that had papers inside. She opened the folder to find medical papers and receipts that weren't hers but rather belonged to the inn's previous owner, Rose Johnson Lane.

I thought we boxed these and put them in the attic.

She was about to put the folder aside when she noticed the words "breast cancer."

Her eye wide with surprise, Maggie looked over the documents.

Rose had breast cancer? She never said a word about it.

Maggie's heart skipped a beat when she saw the date on the summary page.

January 16, 1997...Rose had to be sixty-two...Twenty-three years before she died.

Maggie sat back in her chair and smiled. Her friend was still giving her gifts even after her death. Maggie already felt at peace with her situation, but this news gave her the priceless gift of hope.

She looked at the framed photo of Rose sitting on the top shelf of the bookcase and smiled.

"Thank you, Rose."

———

Chelsea was still in bed when her cell phone rang.

"Good morning, Chelsea. This is Isabella. What are you doing?"

Chelsea yawned and looked at the clock. It was six-thirty and she needed at least another two hours of sleep.

"I was sleeping, actually," she answered.

"Oh, I'm sorry. I didn't realize."

"You didn't realize? It's six-thirty in the morning. I thought you said you were a night owl. What are you doing up this early?"

"Oh, mon cheri, I've not gone to bed."

"You mean you've been up all night?"

"Oui. I slept late yesterday. I'm fine. The reason for my call is to ask you to come to my house for breakfast."

"When…today?"

"Of course, today. Come at nine o'clock and we'll have a delicious breakfast out near the pool."

Chelsea enjoyed being with Isabella, but so far she'd been successful at avoiding Sebastian. She knew eventually that they would see each other again, but she wasn't prepared and hadn't a clue what to say to him.

"Oh, I don't know…"

"I won't take no for an answer. I'll see you at nine o'clock."

Isabella hung up and Chelsea sat up in bed and was suddenly very awake. She didn't think she could call Maggie and ask her to go to Isabella and Sebastian's house. It wasn't her place to invite anyone else, and she wasn't certain that Isabella hadn't already called Maggie.

Why didn't I think to ask? Now, I have to go alone.

She got out of bed and tried not to wake Jacqui as she walked to the kitchen to make a pot of coffee but was surprised to find coffee already made and Jacqui sitting out on the lanai.

"Hey, you're up early," Chelsea said.

"Yeah, I couldn't sleep. I've made coffee already. I'm going to refresh my cup, do you want me to get you a cup?"

"Sure, if you don't mind. Thanks."

Chelsea stretched her arms up over her head and then ran her hands through her hair, scratching her scalp in an effort to get the blood flowing.

Jacqui came back out onto the lanai with the coffee.

"I'm surprised that you're up this early, Chelsea. I guess you couldn't sleep either?"

"Ha, nope I was sound asleep when my cell phone rang. After the conversation I just had, there was no way I could go back to sleep."

"Who called you at this hour?"

"Isabella, Sebastian's new wife."

Jacqui made a face. "Oh, awkward."

Chelsea couldn't have agreed more.

"Have you seen Sebastian since he's been back on the island?" Jacqui asked.

Chelsea took a sip of her coffee and shook her head. "No, and that's what's keeping me awake. Thanks for the coffee by the way. I might need something stronger before nine o'clock though. Isabella invited me to breakfast at their place. It's the last thing I want to do but I couldn't think of an excuse fast enough to be believable."

"Oh, wow. What are you going to do?"

Chelsea shrugged. "What can I do except go there and act like I'm fine and that it's no big deal."

"Well, it isn't a big deal really, is it?"

"If you mean do I still have feelings for him? No, not in a romantic way. I really like Isabella and I can see her, Maggie and I getting together a lot. If I'm going to be friends with Isabella I'm going to have to be Sebastian's friend too. I'm fine with that, it's just that I needed a little more time to think of what to say to him. It is, as you say, awkward."

"Well, I'm pretty good at pretending I don't care about stuff. I can give you some pointers if you want."

Chelsea laughed at that. Jacqui was the queen of acting like she hadn't a care in the world.

"Sure, this ought to be good."

Jacqui quickly got up from her chair and demonstrated the importance of body language, "First, you stand as straight as you can. Hold your head up and stick your chin out a little. Come on, get up and do what I do."

Chelsea put her coffee cup down on the table, did as she was told and stood next to Jacqui. She focused on her posture and held her head up high.

"Don't look down. Whatever you do, don't look at your feet or the floor. Keep your head up."

"What happens if he's in his wheelchair? I'll have to look down at him."

"That's okay, you can do that but when you look at him, you should keep your head up as high as possible and let your eyes look down at him. Only your eyes should move. You still keep your head up and your chin out."

Chelsea thought the entire exercise was ridiculous. As she tried to duplicate Jacqui's posture and movements, she giggled.

"I don't think I can pull this off, Jacqui. I feel like a statue. Sebastian's going to ask me if there's something wrong with my back. I'm going to look ridiculous."

"Chelsea, do you want my help or not? Trust me, I know what I'm talking about."

"Fine."

"Okay, now after you've said hello and let your eyes go lower to look at him, then you keep your words to him light and cheerful. You should let the tone of your voice raise a little."

"You want me to yell at him?"

"No, not the volume, the tone…the pitch. Like this…Hi Sebastian, nice to see you again," Jacqui said, the pitch of her voice slightly elevated.

Chelsea shook her head, and sat back in her chair, laughing. "No. I can't do that. I'll sound like a squirrel. Honey, listen to me. I'm going to be me because that's all I've got. You do you, and I'll do me."

Jacqui shrugged and picked up her coffee mug.

"Okay, if you think that will work, more power to you," Jacqui said as she walked into the house.

Chelsea couldn't help but chuckle at the absurdity of Jacqui's plan, but it did explain why the young woman had so much trouble communicating.

Her white jeans and baby blue linen shirt made Chelsea look younger than her fifty-five years. To her look, she added gold hoop earrings, a gold chain necklace and white sandals. Pleased with how she looked, she grabbed her keys and handbag and waved to Jacqui on her way out the door.

"Wish me luck," Chelsea yelled.

She couldn't be sure, but Chelsea thought she'd heard Jacqui say, "You'll need it," right before she closed the door behind her.

When she noticed her white knuckles on the steering wheel, Chelsea accepted the fact that this first meeting would be the hardest. After that, she felt confident visiting the Barlowe home now and then would be a cake walk.

She pulled her car around the circular driveway and parked to the left of the house. There was only one car in the driveway, and Chelsea knew that it wasn't Sebastian's.

Isabella greeted her at the front door.

"Chelsea! I am so glad that you agreed to join me for breakfast this morning. I know that I don't have to give you a tour of the place since you've already been here many times. I have hired an interior decorator to help me change a few things."

The awkward feeling resurfaced when Isabella reminded her of her previous visits to Sebastian's home.

"I look forward to seeing what you did to the place," Chelsea answered.

They walked out onto the patio near the pool. It was a perfect Florida morning. By afternoon, the sun would make wearing pants a terrible choice.

A table was set with a centerpiece, a gorgeous bouquet of orange and peach flowers surrounded by lush greens in a clear square vase filled with water and sliced lemons.

The fine china and crystal glasses which caught the sunlight, casting a prism of colors, was as elegant as Chelsea had ever seen. She wasn't surprised to see two waiters standing to the side waiting for instruction from Isabella.

"How lovely. I feel so special to be waited on at breakfast," Chelsea marveled.

"Oh, I didn't have this kind of attention in Paris, but Sebastian insisted."

"Is Sebastian here?" Chelsea asked, hoping the answer would be no.

Isabella shook her head. "No, but he will be back shortly. He had to run an errand. Come, let's eat."

A waiter poured a small amount of white wine in her glass and Chelsea, remembering Isabella's instruction on how best to appreciate its flavor, swirled the liquid, brought the glass to just under her nose to smell, and then took a small amount into her mouth, letting it sit with her a moment before nodding in approval.

A platter of vibrant tropical fruits, freshly squeezed orange juice, and a delicate salad consisting of crisp baby spinach leaves, plump, sun-ripened tomatoes and velvety slices of ripe avocado sat in front of Chelsea.

Toasted almonds added a crunch while a perfect amount of a light zesty citrus vinaigrette touched the leaves. The amount of dressing was perfect. Chelsea hated salads that were drenched and swimming in dressing.

When the waiter served a plate of scallops on top of a creamy risotto, Chelsea's mouth watered, and her eyes grew wide with delight.

"Honestly, Isabella, this brunch is amazing. I've never had scallops for breakfast before."

Chelsea watched Isabella take a sip of her white wine.

"I'm going to make it my business to see that you experience many new things," Isabella responded. "Now, let's get serious about why I've asked you here this morning."

"You have something specific you wish to say to me?" Chelsea asked.

"Yes. I want to know why there is no man in your life?"

Although startled by Isabella's directness, Chelsea wasn't completely surprised. She'd already decided that Isabella had no filter and was someone who spoke her mind, regardless of how it was received.

"I'm happy with my life the way it is. I don't need a man. I'm sure that's shocking to you."

"Not shocking at all. I don't need a man in my life either, but I want one. I know how to be in the world on my own. I've had to do it many times under different situations. I suppose it's important to understand the difference between a need and a want."

Chelsea felt uncomfortable and slightly angry, realizing that there was a hidden agenda to Isabella's breakfast invitation.

"Isabella, you and I are two different people. I've had my love story with my husband, Carl. I won't forget how important he was to me."

"Nor should you, but you're mistaken if you think that you can't have more than one love story. Nothing in our lives is permanent. We live through many seasons. I choose to accept each season as it comes but always remember that it won't last and that another season is right around the corner."

Chelsea suddenly felt sad with the lightness of the day slipping away from her.

"My friend, there is joy in anticipating what's to come. Don't let the season define who you are. Enjoy what comes, be open to new possibilities but don't hold on too tight to any season. Enjoy it...live it...and let the wind take you where it will. Stress and anxiety come when you try to keep something that wishes to fly away. Let it fly, and maybe if you're lucky, you get to ride along with it."

Chelsea sipped her wine and thought about what Isabella said. *"You're mistaken if you think that you can't have more than one love story."*

Whatever season Chelsea was currently experiencing, she loved the idea that it was only temporary and that she could anticipate something wonderful just around the corner. She was certain that Isabella Barlowe had much to teach her, and maybe Maggie might think so too.

CHAPTER 29

$\mathcal{M}$aggie sat at the kitchen counter enjoying a hot cup of tea. Except for a warm, sore area where the radiation targeted, Maggie felt fine after her first appointment. She didn't feel up to making scones earlier in the day, but her energy was returning and she thought she'd enjoy the beach after breakfast.

A knock at the back kitchen door interrupted her thoughts.

"Can I come in?" Crawford Powell asked.

"Crawford!" Maggie exclaimed, as she jumped off the kitchen stool. "Of course, please come in."

"I know how busy your kitchen is at this time of the morning, but as soon as I open the door to the store, I won't get another chance to come see you."

"Oh, I'm not doing much this morning, besides, Riley and Iris have everything under control. It's so nice to see you. How are things?"

"Everything is going well. I don't know if you've heard but my boy Finn will be going to flight school in the fall. He wants to become a commercial airline pilot."

Maggie nodded. "I did hear something about that. I think it's wonderful."

Crawford smiled. "I agree, although I needed some convincing from my daughter, Becca. You know how persuasive she can be."

Maggie laughed. "I know she keeps Christopher in line and we all love her for it."

"Speaking of the kids, I just wanted to stop by and talk a little about the wedding. Becca gave me very little information except when the date is and that it's a double wedding. I wanted you to know that as father of at least one of the brides, I will be paying for half of this wedding. I don't want you to foot the bill for all of it."

"Honestly, Crawford, the kids haven't told me much either. As a matter of fact, I had to promise that I wouldn't do a thing until I heard from them. So…I wait. It's good to know that I'll have you to keep me company. We can wait together. As far as the bill goes, I appreciate you coming by to tell me. I'm sure we'll have no issues taking care of what the kids want and what we can afford."

"Thanks, I knew you'd feel the same way I do. Is Paolo around? I'd like to say hello before I head back to the shop."

"Follow me," Maggie said, as she walked out onto the porch and pointed at the garden. "Do you see that man, way in the back with the hat on?"

"That's him?"

"That's Paolo. The Key Lime Garden Inn wouldn't be as successful without him."

"Well, thanks again. I'll go say hello to him. I'll be in touch, I can't imagine that you and I will be on hold for that much longer. The weddings are in five months. Take care, Maggie."

"Have a good day, Crawford."

Maggie took her tea out onto the porch and sat on the swing and watched Paolo and Crawford talking in the garden.

Chelsea showed up at the foot of the back stairs.

"You'll never guess where I've been," she said.

"I don't know but by the way you look, I'd say someplace fancy. You look amazing."

Chelsea joined Maggie on the swing. "I've been to Isabella's for brunch."

"Oh my, why do I think this was a setup?" Maggie asked.

"Uh-huh, because it was. She wanted to fix me up with some friend of Sebastian's. Can you imagine having my ex help me find a boyfriend? It's insulting."

Maggie snickered. "Who cares who does the fixing up? I didn't know you were interested in dating again."

"I'm not. I have absolutely no interest in bringing another man into my life. How is it going to look when I just gave Jacqui a speech about staying out of a romantic relationship and, instead, cultivate female friendships?"

"Oh for heaven's sake. You're not Jacqui…thankfully, and there is no reason that you can't have a companion."

"I'll get a dog. I hear they make great companions."

"Well, I think you should consider it. Who's the guy anyway?"

Chelsea shook her head. "I don't know, some big time investment guy. I think he's been written up in a few magazines because he's been so successful making money for people."

"Hmm, I don't think it would hurt to have someone like that in your world. Even if things don't work out, you could get some stock tips."

"I think that's against the law?"

"What, dating an investment guy?"

"No, silly. Getting tips on where to put your money. It's not the same as getting advice. You pay someone to watch over your money and invest it wisely for you. What I'm talking about is called insider trading. You can't do that."

Maggie thought about it for a few minutes and then said, "Well, if you can't get any stock tips, maybe you can by accident overhear his phone conversations. There's more than one way to get information from a guy."

Chelsea looked at Maggie and didn't dare ask for clarification.

"Moving on…how's the wedding planning going?"

"It's stalled. I don't have executive clearance just yet."

"What does that mean?"

"It means that I'm not allowed to make any moves, order any vendors, or generally start collecting information about running a wedding until they get in touch with me. Becca and Beth are meeting to go over stuff and they'll bring me in when they're ready and, as Beth explained, 'not a minute before'."

"I'm glad you came by this afternoon because I have to ask you for your help in the planning and implementation of the weddings."

"Of course, you know you don't have to ask. As a matter of fact, I think I'd be insulted if you didn't."

Maggie nodded. "Good, because I'm not sure if I'm going to suffer with any neuropathy side effects, but if I do, it could make my mobility difficult."

"You don't have to explain. I'm an endless source of resources. You call and I come, day or night."

"Thanks, Chelsea. Hey, what happened with Sebastian? Did you talk to him and was it awkward?"

"No, he wasn't there. It was a shame too because I practiced what I'd say to him driving over there. I was ready. Now, I have to get nervous all over again."

"You? Nervous. I find that hard to believe."

"Okay, maybe not nervous, but concerned. Anyway, I've got to get back to my house. Jacqui promised me that she'd sit down and actually spend some time painting instead of running around trying to get a beach romance going with one of the Powell boys."

"You mean she's interested in more than one?"

"I'm not really sure. There's another month left in the summer. Whatever it is today will look different tomorrow. There's no point in asking questions, it's much better to just ride the wave, and hope you don't come crashing down on your head."

After Chelsea's visit, Maggie decided to get in some time on the beach before dinner. She put on her swimsuit, grabbed a towel and beach chair and her bucket to collect a few seashells.

The beach near the inn wasn't crowded at all which thrilled Maggie, not so much because she didn't want to compete with so many in the water, but rather she had a better chance of collecting the best seashells.

She decided to search the beach for them and it wasn't long before her bucket was filled halfway with various types. She rested the bucket near her chair and was about to go into the water when her cell phone rang; it was Michael.

"Hey, honey. I'm so glad you called. How are you doing?"

"Hey, Mom. Better than I was the last time you saw me. I've been doing a bit of physical therapy and I'm seeing a psychiatrist as well. I wasn't too thrilled about seeing her at first, but I can tell that she's helping me deal with things I didn't know I was trying to handle on my own. You know us Wheelers; we like to control everything."

Maggie laughed. "Yes, I'm familiar. I'm so glad you're doing better. Any word on when you can get back to work?"

"No, I'm not sure I'll be going back for a while. Even if I did, I'm not sure what my job would be. There's issues with PTSD that might get in the way of that. It's a work in progress. What upsets me is that I feel like my hands are tied behind my back and I can't do anything about my fate. That's the worst, because you know how much I love to get out there and make a difference in the world. If I can't do that, I have no idea how I'll feel."

"Honey, I know you'll find a way. You always do. Do you remember when you were about eight years old there was this homeless guy who walked the neighborhood? It bothered you that he didn't have a place to live and you wondered how he was able to get food."

"I remember. He used to go through the garbage cans looking for something to eat."

"Yes, and do you remember what you did? You insisted that we stop at McDonald's and get a Happy Meal. I thought you wanted it for yourself, but instead, you made Dad drive near the alleyway around the corner so that you could put the Happy Meal in the trash so the homeless guy could find it."

Michael laughed. "I'd forgotten that story. That does sound like me though."

"You and Beth were my little advocates for all the injustices in the world. If you weren't helping homeless people, you were bringing home stray cats and dogs. I even think that one time you tried to get us to invite a homeless person to our family Christmas dinner. We were going to do it but for some reason it fell through."

"Yeah, I remember that. She disappeared and I never saw her again."

"Michael, I love how much you care but I also worry about you. You've always worked hard to be fair to others but life isn't always going to play fair. You'll win some and you'll lose some. The important thing is that you keep trying. You never know whose life you might change just by doing what you do."

"I hear you. Beth gave me the same kind of talk. Did she tell you that she's going back to work at the District Attorney's office?"

"I think that's great. She's another one who has to keep fighting the good fight."

"We've got another Wheeler in the house. I just sent you a picture. Go take a look."

Maggie looked at her messages and a photo of a little apricot-colored mini poodle with big brown eyes looked back at her.

"Oh my goodness, she's beautiful. What's her name?"

"Willa. Willa Bethany Wheeler. She's a handful, but she's worth every minute."

"I guess that makes me a grandmother to a fur baby now, right?"

"That's right. You'll have to come visit again so you can hold her."

"I have no doubt I'll be there before the wedding. You stay in touch, honey. Thanks for all the good news. These are the best kind of phone calls. Love you sweetie."

"Love you, too, Mom. Talk to you soon."

After she ended the call with Michael, she left her cell phone on the chair, removed her coverup and ran to the water. She slowly walked into the water and waited for her body temperature to warm up. She wondered if the radiation therapy affected her body's ability to acclimate to cold water.

She didn't swim as long as she usually did, instead opting to dry off and go back to the inn for lunch and take a hot shower. Drying off she looked below from the window and watched her husband tend to the garden.

She felt blessed to have such a loving partner in life. Even though it was more fun to take Chelsea with her to her radiation treatments, she promised Paolo he could take her next time.

She ran down to the inn's kitchen and warmed up a bowl of lentil soup. It was crazy to feel so cold when it was blazing hot outside. In time, she'd need to find out if this was normal or not.

She took her bowl out to the garden and walked over to the koi pond. The fish always gathered near whenever a human stopped by. They knew they'd get special treats if they stayed together and didn't fight.

Maggie almost always tried to feed the smaller fish, assuming they were the least aggressive. She thought it possible she was mistaken.

What if the smaller fish were the aggressive ones and the larger fish more placid?

Maggie sat on the bench eating her soup when Paolo joined her.

"I should come back here more often. The property looks gorgeous from this perspective."

"I'd love it if you did, then I'd see more of you," he teased.

"You see me plenty. Do you want a little of my soup?"

"No. You enjoy. I've got to get back to work. Iris is making something special for dinner tonight and asked me to pick lots of kale."

Paolo kissed her on the cheek and went back to his gardening.

The sound of the waterfall cascading and windchimes swaying back and forth along with a slight breeze could only be described with one word...*Paradise.*

Beth and Becca would marry at Christmas in what could almost be thought of as a secret garden. No one from the street could ever imagine the beauty that lay only a few yards beyond the building.

The inn was an oasis from the rest of the world and a special place where butterflies, hummingbirds, and exotic flowers coexisted in perfect harmony.

The Key Lime Garden Inn, with its enchanting beauty and tranquil ambiance, would become a witness to two love stories that her family would remember forever.

Maggie could visualize it all. Right in front of her was her perfect Christmas wedding.

Now, if only she knew how to make it snow.

THE END

ALSO BY ANNIE CABOT

Thank you so much for reading

CAPTIVA HEARTS

THE CAPTIVA ISLAND SERIES

Where you will meet The Wheeler Family and a cast of unforgettable characters you will fall in love with.

Book Seven in this series:

CAPTIVA EVER AFTER

Will release July 2023.

Check out the other books in this series:

Book One: KEY LIME GARDEN INN

Book Two: A CAPTIVA WEDDING

Book Three: CAPTIVA MEMORIES

Book Four: CAPTIVA CHRISTMAS

Book Five: CAPTIVA NIGHTS

For a **FREE** copy of the Prequel to the Captiva Island Series, **Captiva Sunset** - Join my newsletter HERE.

ABOUT THE AUTHOR

Annie Cabot is the author of contemporary women's fiction and family sagas. Annie writes about friendships and family relationships, that bring inspiration and hope to others.

Annie Cabot is the pen name for the writer Patricia Pauletti (Patti) who, for the last seven years, has been the co-author of several paranormal mystery books under the pen name Juliette Harper. A lover of all things happily ever after, it was only a matter of time before she began to write what was in her heart, and so, the pen name Annie Cabot was born.

When she's not writing, Annie and her husband like to travel. Winters always involve time away on Captiva Island, Florida where she continues to get inspiration for her novels.

Annie lives in Massachusetts.

For more information visit anniecabot.com

ACKNOWLEDGMENTS

With each book I continue to be grateful to the people who support my work. I couldn't do what I do without them. Thank you all so much.

Cover Design: Marianne Nowicki
Premade Ebook Cover Shop
https://www.premadeebookcovershop.com/

Editor: Lisa Lee of Lisa Lee Proofreading and Editing
https://www.facebook.com/EditorLisaLee/

Beta Readers:
John Battaglino
Nancy Burgess
Michele Connolly
Anne Marie Page Cooke

Made in the USA
Columbia, SC
01 July 2023

19799895R00137